DON'T TURN YOUR BACK III

THE FUNERAL

James E. Stodghill, Jr.

Copyright © 2023 **StodghillWorks**

All rights reserved. No part of this publication may be reproduced, distributed, or transmitted in any form or by any means, including photocopying, recording, or other electronic or mechanical methods, without the prior written permission of the publisher, except in the case of brief quotations embodied in critical reviews and certain other noncommercial uses permitted by copyright law. For permission requests, write to the publisher, addressed "Attention: Book Rights and Permission," at the address below.

Published in the United States of America

ISBN 978-1-958518-91-5 (SC)
ISBN 978-1-958518-93-9 (HC)
ISBN 978-1-958518-92-2 (Ebook)

StodghillWorks
1443 Kings Point Way SW,
Conyers, GA 30094
stodghillworks@aol.com

Order Information and Rights Permission:

Quantity sales. Special discounts might be available on quantity purchases by corporations, associations, and others. For details, contact the publisher at the address above.

For Book Rights Adaptation and other Rights Permission. Call us at 1-678-358-3565 or send us an email at stodghillworks@aol.com.

Dedication

This book is dedicated to my pastor,
Rev. Dr. Darrell D. Elligan,

Pastor of the True Light Baptist Church in Atlanta Georgia. I thank him for teaching me the importance of diligence and determination. It is because of these qualities, I was able to complete this, the third and final book of the "Don't Turn Your Back" trilogy.

Pastor Elligan has been my primary spiritual leader and a caretaker of my soul for over thirty years. The bible says in Jeremiah 3:15, "And I will give you shepherds after my own heart, who will feed you with knowledge and understanding." That is exactly what God Almighty has done. God Himself gave me Darrell Elligan as my pastor and as my friend.

Pastor Elligan is one of the greatest preachers in the world today. He studies the scriptures thoroughly, and explains them, line by line biblically, and conceptually, so that their meaning is relevant and immediately applicable.

Through Pastor Elligan's teaching, preaching, and counseling, I have grown spiritually, and I have developed a close relationship with Jesus. I have come to understand that my life is not just about me. It is not even mostly about me. My life is about surrendering my will to Jesus and allowing Him, through the Holy Spirit, to guide me. Learning to trust God is the key and that trust begins with believing His Holy Word, the bible. God's word is truth. God speaks to us through His Word. God also speaks to us audibly, through the Holy Spirit, dreams, visions, our thoughts, and through events and circumstances.

I hope that God will speak to you, my readers, through the message of this fictional book.

Again, I thank my pastor for pouring into my life.

Acknowledgments

I want to thank and acknowledge

Mia Kenyetta Hill,

my favorite niece and the editor of all three books of the "Don't Turn Your Back" trilogy.

Mia is a source of inspiration and motivation. Because of her encouragement and assistance, I was able to accomplish my goal. I love her immensely.

I also want to acknowledge my wife

Marie Erwin Stodghill,

for her steadfast love and devotion to me.

Because of her care, and by the grace of God, we have been able to remain healthy, happy, and prosperous

in our loving home.

I love her desperately.

Contents

Chapter 1	The Introduction	1
Chapter 2	The Uncovering	7
Chapter 3	Sad Memories	9
Chapter 4	I Feel You	15
Chapter 5	On the Job Straining	21
Chapter 6	Attack of the Enemy	24
Chapter 7	Family History	33
Chapter 8	Out of Restraint	37
Chapter 9	Design Protection	43
Chapter 10	Planning to Harm	46
Chapter 11	Caught in the Act	48
Chapter 12	Foiled Again	51
Chapter 13	Crime Scenery	57
Chapter 14	Scene at the Crime	60
Chapter 15	Burning Revelation	67
Chapter 16	Crystal Dreams	71
Chapter 17	The Stakeout	74
Chapter 18	Was Lost But Now Found	77
Chapter 19	Slim Chances	83
Chapter 20	In the Wrong Hands	92
Chapter 21	Questioning My Life	94
Chapter 22	Keeping the Faith	99
Chapter 23	A New Alliance	101

Chapter 24	An Empty Home	106
Chapter 25	A New Deal	108
Chapter 26	Blasts from the Past	116
Chapter 27	Double-cross the Double-cross	128
Chapter 28	A Meditative Moment	135
Chapter 29	The Last Laugh	137
Chapter 30	Blind Faith	140
Chapter 31	A Taste of Reality	144
Chapter 32	Another One Bites the Dust	149
Chapter 33	New Hope	154
Chapter 34	Destructive Thinking	157
Chapter 35	The Key Is Not in the Mind	165
Chapter 36	Search and Rescue	176
Chapter 37	Dealing with Demons	188
Chapter 38	Just A Thought	196
Chapter 39	A Good Resort	200
Chapter 40	Food and Facilities	207
Chapter 41	A Clean Break	209
Chapter 42	Funeral preparations	213
Chapter 43	The Last Night	216
Chapter 44	Morning Gory	221
Chapter 45	The Homegoing Celebration	225
Chapter 46	Closure	252
Chapter 47	Crystal Lies	257
Chapter 48	The Eulogy	263

Chapter 1
The Introduction

(Wednesday 8:15 AM)

There was a knock at the door. Rev. Zackery turned his head toward the door. Jason and Dave jumped to their feet quickly. Jason slid his hand under his jacket and grabbed the handle of his pistol. Dave and Jason looked at each other anxiously.

"I wonder who that could be this early in the morning," Rev. Zackery said as he stood and walked toward the door. He did not see Jason pull the pistol from the back of his pants, cock it quietly, and put it behind his thigh.

Dave and Jason watched as Rev. Zackery opened the door slightly and spoke with someone on the other side of the door.

Then Rev. Zackery turned and looked at Dave. "It's for you Dave. Someone named, Walt," Rev. Zackery said opening the door revealing the tall dark-haired man dressed in camouflage fatigues.

"Walt!" Dave shouted. "We thought you were," Dave stopped his sentence. "Come in. This is Reverend Zackery," he said pointing at Rev. Zackery. "He will be conducting Pam's services." Then turning toward Rev. Zackery, "Walt was a close friend of Pam, and he wants to attend the home-going celebration."

"I'm glad to meet you, Walt," Rev Zackery said smiling. "How did you know Pam?"

"We were lovers." Walt said with little expression.

"I see," Rev. Zackery said frowning.

"Walt, would you like something to drink." Dave interrupted. "We have milk, Kool-Aid, orange juice, and water."

"I would like some water, if you don't mind."

"Jason, would you take Walt in the kitchen and get him some water, please," Dave asked?

"Okay. But after that we really need to get out of here," Jason replied.

While Jason and Walt walked to the kitchen, Dave pulled Rev. Zackery close and whispered in his ear. "Rev. Zackery, I hate to leave him here with you, but we owe him. He saved our lives. He was there. I think he saw when they killed Pam. After it was all over, I went to thank him for saving our lives. He was in his car about to blow his own brains out. The only reason he didn't do it, is because he wants to say his goodbyes to Pam at her funeral. I think he still wants to kill himself. Can you help him?" Dave waited for a reply.

"Who is he?" Rev. Zackery asked. "Is he a believer?"

"No, sir. He said he wanted to kill himself. He said, 'if I can't be with her in life, I'll be with her in death.' So, I told him that Pam was saved, that she was going to heaven, and if he wanted to be with her, then he needed to be saved. Maybe you can save him, like you did me."

"I didn't save you. It was the Lord. I just told you about Jesus. Once a person hears the word, based on their hearts, the Holy Spirit moves to cause that person to believe. Jesus saved you, however, I am glad you told him to come. I'll do what I can," Rev. Zackery said.

"Thank you, Rev. Zackery." Dave shook Rev. Zackery's hand. "We have to go, but remember, the less you know about what happened the better. So, don't ask too many questions."

Jason and Walt came back into the room.

"Are you ready?" Jason asked. "This area is going to be swarming with police soon."

"Yeah, let's go."

"There won't be any police," Walt said calmly.

"Yeah right, let's go," Jason said.

"Why do you think there won't be any police?" Dave said.

"Right now, they are probably digging a big hole to bury all the bodies in a mass grave. When I went by there on my way here, they were clearing out all the cars. There's going to be a big cover-up. The police, at least those who are not in the coven, don't even know anything about it. The only people you need to worry about are the witches from the regional council. I dumped the bodies we killed in the fire. So, the way I see it, they will think it was either an accident, or an internal job. There was nobody left to say otherwise."

"The people you killed?" Rev. Zackery said.

"I don't know about you, but I'm leaving, now," Jason said as he opened the door.

"See you Reverend," Dave said. "Don't try to reach us, we'll call you. The funeral is going to be Saturday at one o'clock P.M., at your church, right?"

"Yes, one P.M., Saturday."

"I'll try to make it back," Dave said.

"I'll be back in a few days, Rev. Zackery," Jason said as he grabbed the handle of the door. "What do you mean, you'll try to make it back?" The door closed behind them.

Rev. Zackery turned to Walt. They stared into each other's eyes for almost a minute.

"I want to attend Pam's funeral services," Walt said breaking the silence. "Dave said that you would give me the time and the location."

"Well, Dave told me, that you saved his life, and when he went to thank you, you had a pistol pointed at your head and were about to kill yourself. He said you cared a lot about Pam and that you saw when the witches killed her.

He also said, you said, 'if I can't be with her in life, I'll be with her in death.' Is that right?" Rev. Zackery asked.

"Yeah, that right," Walt said with no change in his expression.

"Dave also said, he told you that if you killed yourself, you and Pam would not be together in death. The two of you would be going to different places. Because you are not saved, you would be in hell and because she was saved, she would be in heaven. Is that right, too?" Rev. Zackery asked.

"Yes."

"Walt, if you want to go to heaven when you die, there is only one way to get there. You must be saved. Would you like for me to tell you how to be saved?" Rev. Zackery asked.

"Let me ask you a question, first?"

"Okay," Rev. Zackery said.

"Is Pam in heaven, now?" Walt asked.

"I believe that Pam is asleep now, waiting for Jesus to come. When He comes, I believe she and all who have died in Christ, all who are saved, will be resurrected from the dead," Rev. Zackery explained.

"You believe that Pam is asleep." Walt moved his head from side to side to relieve the tension in his neck. "Rev. Zackery, do you just believe, or do you know that Pam is saved?"

"I have faith that she was truthful when she said that she believed in Jesus. I can't say that I know for sure," Rev. Zackery admitted.

"So, there's no guarantee that me and Pam will be together even if I become saved, is there?"

"To be perfectly honest, I wonder sometimes if I am saved. The only thing I have to depend on is what the bible says. It says, if I confess with my mouth that Jesus is my Lord, and if I believe in my heart that God raise Him from the dead, I shall be saved, but sometimes, Walt, I wonder, whether or not my heart is right. I have failed in so many ways, so many times. In just the last few days, I was arrogant. I was filled with pride. I even used someone who needed my help. Maybe, because of me, that person is now dead. I don't know. The only thing that I can do, is say I'm sorry and fall at the foot of the cross and trust that Jesus will make my heart right," Rev. Zackery said rubbing his forehead with his hand. There was a short silence, then Rev. Zackery looked up. "I was just about to fix breakfast and some coffee. Would you eat with me? I could really use some company, today."

"Yes sir," Walt said. "I would appreciate some breakfast. But more than that, I need the company, too, because I lost the only person that I have ever loved, and my heart is completely broken. I don't want to live without her. I also don't want to die hungry."

"Thank you, Walt." They walked to the kitchen. "I understand how you feel. My heart is broken, too. Pam and I had become very close. How did you meet her?"

Walt sat down at the table and smiled. "I first saw her when me and two other guys were sent by one of the head witches, to look for the book of Witchcraft in the ruble of this burned down house. Pam and the black guy that just left, showed up. She got out of the car and ordered us off her aunt's property. She was fearless. I was impressed. We left, but we only went far enough for me be able to shoot them with my long-range rifle. I was about to shoot her, but it seemed that she could see me, cause she held up the book we had been looking for in front of her. Since I could no longer see her, I shot at the black guy. He fell when I shot, so I thought I had hit him, but I guess I missed. Anyway, I had them pinned down in the ruble, so my partners went to kill them. Well, to make a long story short, she ran in the woods and the two men I was with, went after her. When I got to the woods, I heard them talking. As Walt talked, he could see in his mind the events as they had happened.

I was able to see them using the scope on my rifle. She had beat up one of the men, badly, and she was about to kill the other one, so I had to shoot her. I aimed at her head, but I could not pull the trigger. So, I shot her in the shoulder. My plan was to just wound her, but she moved when I shot. I hit her in her lung. When I reached my companions, they told me she was dying in the woods. They didn't need to tell me that. I knew being shot in her lung, she would soon die because her lungs would fill with blood, and she would suffocate. That made me sad. The image of the bullet hitting her back kept tormenting me. The image in his mind disappeared.

I found out later, somehow, she had made it. I think the black guy took her to the hospital." Walt took a breath. "That's how we met."

"You did say that you and Pam were lovers, didn't you?" Rev. Zackery asked as he began scrambling eggs.

"Yes sir," Walt said smiling. "We were lovers for one unforgettable day. However, I really believe that I fell in love with her the first time I saw her. Every time she looked at me, I would feel a strong desire to hold her, even that first time that our eyes met. It was weird, but also magical. How did you meet Pam?"

"When I met Pam, she was in elementary school. A boy at her school had been killed by a bobcat. I thought I was being called in as a grief counselor to talk with all the children. However, when I got there, I found out that the children had already received counseling. The principal wanted me to talk to Pam. He said he felt something was wrong with her because she had no grief. She was totally unmoved by the death, and she was also unmoved that the other students were fearful of her. It seemed he wanted me to get her to grieve, at least a normal amount. After speaking with her, she looked me in my eyes with assurance. She smiled warmly and told me that most of the children there were mean to her because her guardian was a black lady, so, she could care less about how they felt about her. She also said the boy who was killed had chased her into the woods, he had thrown a rock and hit her in her back, so, he got what he deserved. I asked her if she was okay. She said she was 'lovely.' I was not going to try to convince her to be sad because someone who was trying to hurt her was killed. So, I told the principal she was fine, and I left." Rev. Zackery put the food on their plates and looked at Walt. "That's how I met Pam. Let's eat."

Chapter 2
The Uncovering

(Wednesday 9:30 AM)

Almost twenty men were in an opening in the woods where a large barn had recently burned to the ground. There was a man in a bulldozer next to a large hole containing hundreds of charred bodies and body parts. The dirt from the hole was in a large pile beside the hole. Several men, wearing fireman's gear, were carrying more bodies from the smoldering debris, and throwing them in the hole. There were men in cars, pushing cars being steered by other men, onto two car haulers. There were two black vans, a black sedan, and several guards in black tactical gear with M16 rifles scattered at various locations. Finally, there were two men in black suits near the black sedan and two black vans. They seemed to be supervising.

"Hey! Over here! I got about five or ten in one pile," a man in fireman's gear shouted. All the other men in fireman's gear went to him. One by one they carried the bodies from the pile to the hole. As they reached the bottom of the pile, they found the bodies were more intact. The faces of the last three persons and the front of their clothes were unburned, however, the fronts of their clothes were covered with blood. Each of these bodies had several gunshot wounds in the chest area. They, too, were thrown in the hole. When the last bodies were removed, a trap door was revealed. There were multiple bullet holes in the door. They pulled the door open, and the sunlight revealed steps going down into darkness.

"Hey! Is anyone down there!" the same man in fireman's gear shouted. There was no answer. He took a flashlight from his belt and went down the steps. At the bottom of the steps was a small room. On the floor, were three bodies, two males in black military gear and flak jackets, and one woman in black slacks and a black sweater. There was something very interesting about the men. They were lying side by side near the bottom of the steps and they had both been shot in the back of their heads. They carried them out first. The woman was lying near the back wall. There was a pistol lying inches from her hand. When they lifted the woman, her eyes opened momentarily.

"This one is alive. What should we do, kill her?" one of the men shouted to his superior. "They said get rid of all the bodies."

"No! Wait!" a man at the top of the steps yelled back. "Let me see what Mr. Reeves wants to do? Bring her up."

The men took the woman, who was barely breathing and laid her at the feet of Mr. Reeves, who was one of the men wearing a black suit.

"We found her and two men in an underground bunker. It looked like the two men had been murdered, probably by her," the man who had found them said.

"Throw her in the hole," Mr. Reeves said coldly.

"Richard!" the woman moaned. "It's me, Sibal."

"Sibal!" he said, pushing the hair off her face. "You sound like Sibal, but you don't look anything like Sibal."

"I was burned! I had reconstructive surgery on my face!" she shouted. "Look! You can see where some of my stitches have come loose." She lifted a portion of the new skin near her ear. "I need medical attention."

"Sergio, take her to the hospital and make sure she is very well taken care of," he said to the other man dressed in a black suit. "She will be able to tell us what happened here. You'd better take some guards and a van with you."

"Yes, sir."

Moments later, the black sedan and one of the vans were speeding down the gravel road. Inside the sedan was Sibal, Sergio, one guard, and a paramedic. In the van were five heavily armed guards.

Chapter 3
Sad Memories

(Wednesday 11:00 AM)

When Walt woke up, he was surprised to find himself lying on the sofa in Rev. Zackery's living room. His shoes were off, there was a blanket over him, and there was a pillow under his head. The most surprising thing of all was how he felt. He felt rested and relaxed. He could not remember the last time he had slept without feeling he had to keep one eye open, wondering if someone was going to sneak up on him and try to kill him in his sleep. He had slept so peacefully. There was no tension, no anxiety, no fear.

'What do I have to fear?' he thought to himself. 'So, what if someone kills me. It doesn't matter. I'm planning to kill myself anyway.' Nevertheless, he felt so comfortable. It was just as it had been when he and Pam were lying in bed after making love. He closed his eyes, and it was as if he were looking down on the bed where he and Pam had been lying just one day ago.

Pam was asleep, her head resting on his arm that wrapped around her shoulder. One of her arms lay across his chest. One of her legs lay across one of his as the sheet gently covered them from the waist down. He watched as she slept peacefully. She seemed safe in his arms. As he lay there, he decided that he would always protect her, if she allowed him to. At that moment, she was more beautiful than he had ever seen her before.

"Hi," she said sweetly as her eyes opened. "That was so good."

"Yes, it was the best," he replied.

"I'm not talking about how we made love, I'm talking about sleeping in your arms. Even in my sleep, I felt so safe and so loved."

"That's interesting, because I was loving on you while you slept," he said.

"I could feel it then, and I feel it even more now." She kissed him. "Is this real? I never imagined that I could feel so good."

"Yeah, it's too bad it can't last forever."

"Yeah," she replied.

He opened his eyes, and he was looking at the ceiling of Rev. Zackery's living room. He raised his arms and stretched.

"How was your nap?" Rev. Zackery asked from the dining room table.

"Actually, it was the best nap I ever had. Thank you so much." Walt stood up, folded the blanket, and laid it on the sofa. "I guess, I'd better be going."

"Do you have somewhere to stay?"

"I was planning to get a motel room," Walt replied.

"Why don't you stay here. I have plenty of room now that everybody has gone. Plus, I was hoping that we could talk a little more."

"That's very kind of you, Rev. Zackery. Are you sure you feel comfortable with me being here?"

"Why wouldn't I, Walt? You seem like a fine young man."

"No, Rev. Zackery, I'm not. For the last few years, I have been working for those same witches that were trying to kill you and all your friends. Once, they sent me here to kill Pam. However, when I failed, they turned on me and were going to kill me, but Pam protected me, she let me be her bodyguard. Since then, I had to kill a lot of those same witches that I use to work with. I am not a fine young man. I am an assassin, a killer, and a murderer."

"Let me ask you something, Walt?"

"Yes, sir?"

"If the witches came here now, to kill me, would I be better off here with you, or without you?" Rev. Zackery asked.

"You would be much better off with me here," Walt said confidently. "However, if the witches came looking for me, you would be better off if I were not here."

"Well, Walt, I would rather for you to be here, cause if they come looking for you and you are not here, it is still going to be bad for me. So, why don't you just stay until after the funeral? I think we will both sleep better. Anyway, Jesus said, a liar is just the same as a murderer."

"Sir, it would be an honor for me to stay here with you, and I would like to hear more about Jesus and getting saved," Walt said. "If Pam was saved, I want to be saved. I want to be where she is."

"It's settled then. You can sleep in the room where Jason and Dave slept, or you can sleep in the room where Pam slept. It's your choice."

"If you don't mind, Reverend, I'd like to sleep where Pam slept."

"Down the hall, the bedroom on the left. I'll put some fresh sheets on the bed," Rev. Zackery said smiling.

"Sir, I know it may seem strange, but I'm still not ready to let Pam go. I want to lay in the bed where she slept, close my eyes, smell her sweet fragrance, and imagine she is there with me. So, if you don't mind, would you please not change the sheets yet."

"Sure, I understand Walt," Rev. Zackery said. "I was like that when my wife died."

"How did she die?"

"She had cancer. It started in her colon. Then it spread to her liver and her lungs. She was in a great deal of pain for months before she died. It was a horrible experience for her and me, too. Watching her suffer, listening to her cries of anguish, it was almost unbearable. I spent hours, praying every day.

She was my high school sweetheart. My first and only true love. We got married as soon as I got out of the seminary. Then, five years later, she got sick. A year later, the pain got severe. It got to the point where I stopped praying for her to recover and I started praying that God would end her pain. My faith in God was tested to the limit."

"How could you continue to believe in a God who could let this happen to you and your wife?" Walt asked. "Had you done something? Had she done something so bad, that God would punish her in such a terrible way?"

"It's interesting that you would ask that question, Walt, cause that's exactly what I asked God." Rev. Zackery wiped away a tear that had fallen from his right eye.

"So, what happened, Rev. Zackery. Did your God answer your question? Did your God speak to you?"

"No, God didn't speak to me. Walt, I don't think I would have believed it was God, if I had heard a voice from the sky. Instead, He let me hear a voice that touched me to my soul. It was my wife's voice. As I sat by her bedside, her moaning began to subside. Rev. Zackery could see a younger version of himself sitting in a chair beside his sick wife's bed. The IV drips and a monitor were attached to her.

Tears were flowing from his face as his wife's moaning came to a stop. Rev. Zackery wiped his face with both hands and leaned forward because she was now silent. Her eyes opened brightly, and a beautiful smile appeared on her face.

"Lee, Lee," she said reaching her hand up. He grabbed her hand in amazement because it had been weeks since she had last spoken. Her organs had already begun to shut down. Her eyes had not opened in a week.

"Yes, honey," Rev. Zackery said tenderly. "I'm here."

"I see Him," she said excitedly. "I can see Him, Lee."

"You can see who, sweetheart?"

"I see Jesus," she said louder than before, as Rev. Zackery began looking around the room. "And He is smiling at me, Lee. He is beckoning me come to Him."

"Go to Him my darling," Rev. Zackery said as tears flowed down his face. "Go to Jesus."

Then suddenly her hand went limp, and her eyes became dull.

The image in Rev. Zackery's mind disappeared. Rev. Zackery looked at Walt. "And she was gone." Rev. Zachery got a napkin from the kitchen table, blew his nose loudly, and walked back over to Walt. "You see, Walt, that was the best way for God to answer my question. My wife's sickness was not so much about me and my thoughts, it was primarily about her and Jesus. God didn't have to let me experience their encounter, but because He cares so much for me, He let me experience that wonderful event with them and at the same time He answered my question in the best possible way."

"I've never heard anything as wonderful as that, Rev. Zackery."

"I have never experience anything as wonderful as that since then. Because of that experience, I was able to continue my ministry for more than thirty years. That happened so long ago I had almost forgotten how powerful that experience was. Thank you, Walt, for helping me re-live that precious moment."

"Thank you for telling it to me. I have asked questions, maybe not to God, but to myself," Walt said standing up.

"What questions?" Rev Zackery asked.

"Why did I get put in Reform School for something I didn't do? I didn't start that fire. Why did my mother leave me on the doorstep of the orphanage when I was a baby? Why didn't she want me? Why did my life turn out this way? And most of all, why, after all these years of not having anyone to love me and not having anyone I could love, that finally when I do find someone, they are killed and taken away from me, so quickly? Why?"

"Those are all valid questions, Walt," Rev. Zackery said. "Maybe later, we can talk about those questions. However, right now, I need to lie down. I am exhausted. Make yourself at home. Mi casa, su casa."

"Are you okay?"

"Yeah, Walt. I'm just tired. I didn't get much sleep yesterday," Rev. Zackery said as he walked back toward his room.

"Give me ten minutes. I've got something in my car for you," Walt said as he rushed out the door. Ten minutes later he came back in with a large duffle bag. He reached inside and pulled out a bulletproof vest. He handed it to Rev. Zackery. "Just in case."

"I guess it wouldn't hurt," Rev. Zackery said. "We'll talk later. Whatever you want to eat, it's yours. Help yourself to anything you see. The bathroom is right next to Pam's room. You can get a shower if you like, and, thank you for staying with me. I know I'll be able rest with you here."

"Don't worry. Rest. I got your back, Rev. Zackery."

Chapter 4
I Feel You

(Wednesday 12:30 PM)

It was dark now, so dark that she could not see her hand an inch in front of her face. Only a few hours before, the fire outside the crystal ball was so bright that Pam had to ball herself up, covering her eyes with her arm. Then the heat was so unbearable that she thought she was going to burn up. Now, it was still warm but totally dark.

"Are you okay?" Pam spoke into the darkness. There was no response. "You did that to yourself. Are you hurt? Look, well you can't look, but understand, I don't want to be in here with you anymore than you want to be in here with me. I had no choice. It was either be in here with you or die." There was a long silence.

"How did you get in here?" the voice from the darkness asked.

"You're alive. That's good," Pam said happily. "I thought you had killed yourself when that force that you pushed at me bounced off the wall of the crystal and hit you. You went down hard. Then the force bounced against the crystal wall behind you and then it hit me hard, but you took the most of it. It was a good thing I ducked. You may have killed me. You were out for a long time."

"How did you get in here, and how do we get out?" the voice said impatiently.

"We can't get ourselves out. Someone on the outside has to get us out," Pam said.

"How did you get in here?" the voice asked loudly. "How did I get in here?"

"Tamera, I'll make you a deal," Pam said. "If you promise to stop trying to kill me, I'll tell you how we can get out of here." There was a long pause. "You really hate me, don't you?"

"Okay, I promise," Tamera said.

"Pinky swear."

"Are you serious?" Tamera asked indignantly.

"Yes!" Stick out your right hand," Pam said reaching out her hand until she felt Tamera's hand. She grabbed it and hooked her pinky finger onto her sister's. "Now, say I swear I won't try to kill you ever again."

"Okay, I swear I won't try to kill you ever again. Now tell me!" Tamera said impatiently, snatching her hand away.

"When I was falling toward the spikes, I took the crystal and brought it down as hard as I could on one of the spikes. I don't know how, but when you try to break the crystal, it opens up, and you fall in. Then, it closes up with you inside."

"Spikes? Why were you falling toward spikes?" Tamera asked.

"Your people tricked me. They built a trap with spikes for me to fall in at the ceremony at the big barn," Pam said.

"Why were you at one of our ceremonies?"

"I was there to kill me some witches," Pam smirked. "Me, Dave, and Jason planned to burn the barn down during the ceremony."

"I see that didn't work out for you," Tamera chuckled.

"Oh, it worked. You couldn't see the fire because you had knocked yourself out trying to kill me," Pam said. "I didn't get out, but Dave and Jason were able to accomplish the mission."

"That's a bunch of crap. You don't really expect me to believe that. Do you? "Tamera asked.

"Believe what you want to believe," Pam said.

"Okay, that's how *you* got in here. How did *I* get here?"

"Jason rubbed the crystal, and he put it in the church while you were fighting with me. Then, he thought of himself. You thought you were looking at him, but it was his image caused by the crystal. When you charged, because of your rage, you charged into the crystal image, and it closed up with you inside."

"He tricked me," Tamera shouted.

"Yep."

"So, sister dear, how do we get out of here," Tamera said sweetly.

"We have to wait and hope that someone comes looking for the crystal. Then hope, they find it. Then hope they will know how to break us out."

"If someone finds us, I will force them to get us out. I will push them, and tell them what to do?"

"You can do that from in here?" Pam asked.

"Of course, I can?" Tamera said. "I pushed Billy and made him do what I wanted. I even pushed Jason. I didn't know what he was doing at the time, but he was going to hit the crystal with a hammer to let me out, but you and that other man stopped him."

"Jason was not trying to let you out, believe me," Pam said.

"I push him to get me out." Tamera said.

"He was not trying to get you out. He was trying to get in," Pam said. "He holds you responsible for the death of his grandmother. If he gets the chance, he is going to kill you, or die trying."

"I hope he gets his chance," Tamera paused. "Why is it so dark and so quiet? Are we buried underground?" Tamera asked.

"Probably so. I didn't want to mention it, for the purpose of keeping hope alive, but while you were out, I heard the sounds of a bulldozer."

"We could be here forever," Tamera said.

"Well, at least we are not alone. We have each other."

"You better cover your ears," Tamera ordered.

"Cover my ears?" Pam asked. "What for?" Instead of an answer, Pam heard an extremely loud scream that almost caused her eardrums to explode. Pam quickly covered her ears. After ten minutes the screaming stopped. "Thanks for the warning. Do you feel better now?"

"Shush! Be quiet. I need to listen. Maybe I'll hear something. Maybe someone heard me," Tamera whispered. They listened for several minutes.

"Okay," Pam said. "That was a good idea. Tell me. Are your ears ringing?"

"Yes, they are."

"I have a good idea," Pam said angrily. "Would you please let me know when you are going to do that again."

"Sure thing. Aaaaaaaaaaaaaaaa," Tamera screamed. "Oh, I'm sorry. I forgot to warn you."

"Aaaaaaaaaaaaaaaaaaa," Pam screamed. "You're not the only one that can scream."

Pam felt a hard blow to her hand, covering her left ear. She ducked down, reached into her pocket, and pulling out a lighter, flicked it once. For a second, she could see Tamela swinging fiercely where her head had been. Quickly, Pam, while still crouched down, moved behind Tamera. Pam flicked the lighter again and sat it on the floor of the crystal. This time she let the flame burn. She reached between Tamera's legs, grabbing her ankle with one hand and the back of her robe with the other. Pam pulled her so that Tamera was almost sitting on her shoulder. Then Pam came up, lifting Tamera as high as she could. She slammed Tamera down on her head to the bottom of the crystal. She frowned as she watched Tamera as she lay there holding her neck.

"You almost broke my neck," Tamera screamed.

"I have been trying to be nice to you because you are my blood. Even though you have tried to kill me, I was still willing to try to establish some kind of caring relationship with my only sister. However, now you have reached the end of my patience." Pam was furious. "You can decide right now. Do you want to try to get along or not?" Pam raised her boot over Tamera's head.

"Look! When you screamed in my ear, it made me angry, and I just started swinging. I'm sorry. We are stuck in here together. We may be in here forever. So, we might as well try to get along."

"Okay," Pam said lowering her boot. "But if you attack me one more time, I will mark you, and then I will kill you," Pam growled. "Do you understand me?"

"Yes," Tamera said.

The sound of the lighter closing signaled the return of total darkness.

"How is your neck?" Pam asked.

"I can turn my head," Tamera answered.

"No, seriously, does it still hurt?"

"No, actually it is fine," Tamera said in almost nice tone.

It was quiet for a long time as Tamera laid at Pam's feet.

"You said that we might be in here forever."

"Just when I was about to go to sleep," Tamera huffed. "Yes, I said it. So, what!"

"You have been in here for a week. How have you been able to survive?" Pam asked.

"I focus on getting out of here. I always keep my eyes and ears open."

"But what about water?" Pam asked. "Don't you get thirsty?"

"I hadn't thought about it, but no, I haven't been thirsty, at least not until now," Tamera said surprised. "Now, I am very thirsty. Why did you ask me that?"

"Cause I have to pee," Pam snapped.

"Don't you dare pee in here!" Tamera ordered.

"You mean you haven't peed in over a week?" Pam asked.

Think about something else," Tamera begged. "Come on! Let's scream, maybe someone will hear both of us."

"Aaaaaaaaaaaaaa!," they both screamed. "Aaaaaaaaaaaaaaaaaaaaaaa."

CHAPTER 5
ON THE JOB STRAINING

(Wednesday 2:15 PM)

Dave walked through the door of his workplace, Vi-Tech Industries. During his three-hour bus ride, he had rehearsed what he would say to his boss, first about Carol's accusations of him assaulting her, then about the events of the last week. Since she was his boss's daughter, Dave was sure his boss would believe whatever Carol had told him. Yet, he had to explain his actions and find out what his boss's decisions were concerning his future at Vi-Tech Industries.

As he walked toward Mr. Thompson's office, he passed several persons who pretended not to notice him. He walked through the door to the outer office where his boss's secretary was sitting at her desk.

"Good afternoon, Dave," she said cordially.

"Hi Corliss, how are you?" Dave asked.

"Very well, and you?"

"I'm good. Would you ask Mr. Thompson if he has time to see me, now, please?"

"Wait just a minute, I'll check." Instead of calling him on her phone, she got up and walked into his office and closed the door behind her. Dave could hear voices but could not understand what was being said. After two minutes, the secretary opened the door. She walked out leaving Mr. Thompson, with arms folded, standing in the doorway.

"Come on in, Dave. Have a seat."

Dave walked around Mr. Thompson cautiously, anticipating a physical assault. Dave sat down as his boss walked in front of him and leaned back on the front of his desk.

"Dave, I'm glad you came here to see me, first, before going back to your office," his boss said with a stern look on his face.

"I wanted to explain to you face to face, sir, everything that has happened, from my perspective," Dave said.

"Dave, I think that I know you, and I think you know me. I have always tried to be rational and realistic. I have spoken with your director, J.T. and all the other managers. Everyone agreed. You brought a gun to the managers meeting and you assaulted Monroe, almost choked him to death, and threatened to kill him." Mr. Thompson stopped speaking, looked behind Dave, and raised his hand in a stop motion. Dave looked behind him and saw two, armed security officers waiting at the door with their hands on their weapons. "I also talked to my daughter, your estranged wife. She said you falsely accused her of cheating on you, you shot at the insurance man, and you brutally hit her in her face."

"The police dropped the charges against me for hitting her. They said that she had made false charges against me," Dave argued.

"I don't care what the police said," Mr. Thompson yelled.

"I assume then, you are not interested in hearing my side of the story."

"No!" Mr. Thompson snapped. "All of your personal belongings have been collected, and placed in these boxes," he said pointing to two boxes next to his desk. "I understand that you have been under extreme mental strain, recently. Therefore, taking into consideration your, till now, excellent work record, I am going to give you the opportunity to resign. You will be given a severance package. However, you must sign a non-disclosure agreement. In addition, you must agree that you will not take any legal action against my daughter for allegedly making false statements against you concerning the assault and battery charge," Mr. Thompson said handing Dave some papers from his desk and a pen.

After reading them carefully, Dave took the pen, but instead of signing it, he began to write on it.

"What are you doing?" Mr. Thompson shouted.

"If you want me to resign and go away quietly, then I am going to need these changes," Dave said. He looked at Mr. Thompson sternly and handed the papers back to him. "I have a contract that you are required to honor. Don't try to intimidate me, man. Like you said, I've been under extreme mental strain. So, if you want to fight it out in court, we can do that, or if you want to fight it out right here in your office, we can do that, too. All you got to do is jump, if you feel froggy," Dave said as he looked ominously at his boss. "Furthermore, you know I would not hit Carol. You know how mean she is. She would cut my throat while I slept." He looked back at the security guards. "Y'all know her, don't you?"

Both guards gave little smirks and shook their heads 'yes.'

"All right, I will have Corliss make these changes," Mr. Thompson said. "I'll take your ID badge and keycard now."

Dave did not move, and he did not say a word. He just sat in the chair and waited. Mr. Thompson had his secretary redo the resignation papers. Dave looked at the check made out to him, then he read and signed the papers.

Moments later he was escorted out of the building with copies of his resignation papers in his coat pocket, and two boxes in his arms.

CHAPTER 6
ATTACK OF THE ENEMY

(Wednesday 4:45 PM)

Walt was lying in the bed Pam had slept in. He had taken a hot shower and was now under the covers in his underwear tenderly holding the pillow that she had laid her head on. He closed his eyes and kissed the pillow. His warm thoughts suddenly became cold. He could see Pam when he saw her last.

It was the night before. Using his rifle scope, he is in the tree, looking at Pam through the open loft door of the barn. She was balancing herself on the edges of the open trapdoor, one boot on each side. Beneath her was a bed of sharp metal spikes. Sibal walks over to her and reaches for Pam's outstretched hand. Just as she is about to grab Pam's hand, Sibal pulls her hand back and kicks Pam's foot, Pam throws the robe up and off, then she falls head-first toward the metal spikes beneath the trapdoor. Before she hits the spikes, the barn loft door closes, and he cannot see her anymore. However, a second before the door closes completely, he sees a flash of blue light.

Walt opened his eyes and looked at the ceiling. "I tried to save you, but I failed. I failed you, and now you're gone," he said to himself. He reached under the covers and pull his Glock out, cocked it, and put it in his mouth. He closed his eyes and began to think about how Rev. Zackery would feel if he killed himself in Pam's bed. He pulled the pistol from his mouth. Then he heard something outside his door. He aimed the pistol at the door and rolled off the bed and positioned himself beside the door. There was a light knock.

"Walt, are you awake?" Rev. Zackery said.

"Yes sir. Give me a minute to put some pants on."

"Oh, no. Take your time, we can talk when you have rested," Rev. Zackery said and then walked down the hall toward the living room.

Walt put on some jeans and a sweatshirt, then he walked into the living room and saw Rev. Zackery sitting at the dining room table, with his bible in his hand.

"Walt, you said you wanted to be with Pam when you die," Rev. Zackery said.

"And you said you were not sure that she was saved, so there is no way for me to know if I am going to be with her."

"I don't think I said it like that," Rev. Zackery explained. "I think I said I believe that Pam is saved, but I can't say I know without a doubt."

"You said you did not even know if you are saved, reverend."

"The bible says we are saved by grace through faith, Walt," Rev. Zackery said.

"What does that mean, Rev. Zackery?"

"First of all, when the bible says, 'we are saved,' what is it talking about? Saved from what? It means we are saved from death, hell, and the grave. We don't have to worry about dying, our bodies won't be trapped in the grave, and our souls won't go to a burning hell."

Outside, the house a black sedan pulled off to the side of the highway near the driveway of the house where Rev. Zackery and Walt were.

"When it says, 'by grace', the grace is the act of God freely giving his own Son, Jesus, as a sacrifice, a payment, or an atonement for our sins. Jesus suffered and died for us, He died in our place.

Now the 'through faith' means this knowledge is something that cannot be proven, it is something that you just have to know."

"It's something that you just have to know. You can't prove it, you just have to know it," Walt said. "Come on Rev. Zackery. That's not much of an explanation."

Outside, four persons got out of the car, three men and one woman. They all had on flak jackets. The men were dressed in black fatigues, black helmets, and the each carried simi-automatic rifles. The woman had a simi-automatic pistol in one hand and two manila folders in the other. She threw the folders on the car seat and closed the door. There were names printed on the tabs of the folders, David Parker, and Jason Scott.

"Let me ask you this, Walt," Rev. Zackery said softly. "Did you love Pam?"

"Yes!"

"Did you prove it to her? Can you prove it?" Rev. Zackery asked. "If you killed yourself, would that prove that you love her? Well, would it?"

"I guess not."

"If you lived the rest of your life doing things, she would want you to do, would that prove that you love her?"

"I guess not. I am not even sure I know what she would want me to do."

"So, how can you prove that you love her," Rev. Zackery asked sincerely. "How do I know you really loved her?"

"I don't have to prove that I love her, I know I love her and that's all that matters. I don't care if anybody believes me, you included. I love her, now and forever," Walt said angrily.

Outside, the armed group had made their way through the trees and were now at the corner of the house. Sibal pointed to one of the men, then point to the telephone cable. She made a scissor motion with two fingers, and she watched as he cut the telephone line with his knife.

"Walt, it is through that kind of knowing, that kind of faith, that grace saves us. By knowing that God loves us so much that he would allow His own Son to die so that we could be saved, and by accepting his Son's sacrifice for our sins, that is what saves us. Can you understand it better, now?"

"Yes sir. Just like I cannot prove my love for Pam, God cannot prove His love for me," Walt said thoughtfully. "I just have to know it, and that is what faith really is, just knowing with no need for proof."

"Just like God let me experience His encounter with my wife on her deathbed, He is letting you know through your love for Pam, that His love can't be proven, you just have to know He does."

"Okay, I understand that, but why did God let her die, why did I get locked up for something I did not do, why did my mother abandon me when I was a baby?"

Outside, the woman instructed the men by pointing with her pistol. One was to go in through the kitchen, one was to guard the back, and one was to go through the front door. They synchronized their watches and split up.

"Walt, do you have any children?" Rev. Zackery asked.

"Not that I know of."

"The reason you are unsure is because there may be a woman out there who had your son and didn't tell you?" Rev. Zackery explained.

"I guess that's possible," Walt replied.

"If that happened, how do you think your son would feel about you?"

"He could hate me depending on what his mother told him," Walt said.

"That's my point. God gives us free will. We can choose to do what's right or do what's wrong. When we make wrong decisions, wrong consequences occur, and then more wrong decisions and consequences occur from those, and on and on the wrong decisions and consequences continue. Those wrong decisions are sin. That is why God hates sin. It spreads like a plague."

"So, what are you saying? God does not do anything. He just sits there and lets whatever happen, happen," Walt said. "That doesn't seem right."

Outside, each man was in position, each one looking at his watch.

"I don't understand why God does what He does. The bible says, 'For my thoughts are not your thought, neither are your ways my ways, declares the

Lord. For as the heavens are higher than the earth, so are my ways higher than your ways, and my thoughts than your thoughts.' It may seem to us that He is not doing anything, but He is. God is a God of justice. We may not be able to see it or understand it, however, I know that God is just. When a baby dies at birth, I believe that God makes it up to the baby in eternity. So, I guess the best way for me to explain it, is to say, God's justice is eternal justice. These bad, unjust things may have happened to you, but you don't have to worry, God is going to make it up to you." Rev. Zackery smiled, feeling good about his explanation. He looked at Walt expecting to see a look of understanding, instead, Walt appeared not to be paying him any attention at all. "Does that make any sense to you?"

"What?" Walt said looking toward the door.

"Did you even hear anything I said?" Rev. Zackery said disappointedly.

"Somebody is out there," Walt whispered. "Do you have a gun?"

"I have a double barrowed shotgun."

"Get it. We need to get out of here, now," Walt said as he ran into his room.

Rev. Zackery did not move. "Calm down, Walt. If there is somebody out there, I'll handle it."

Suddenly the front door and the kitchen door were knocked in, simultaneously. The men, wearing flak jackets, and carrying simi-automatic rifles came through the doors, one through each door.

"What in God's name are you doing," Rev. Zackery shouted. He froze when he saw laser beams coming toward him. He looked down and saw two red dots on his chest. He looked at both men who had come through each door. Their weapons were trained on him. Before Rev. Zackery could speak again, a woman walked in the front door. She had a pistol in her hand.

"Go," she said to the men in front of her. Immediately, they moved toward the bedrooms. Sibal walked up to Rev. Zackery.

"You're supposed to be dead," Sibal said. "I'm going to ask you once. Where are Parker and Scott?" Sibal put the gun to Rev. Zackery's head.

"They left this morning. They went home," Rev. Zackery said nervously backing away from Sibal. Three loud gunshots were heard behind the house. Sibal turned her pistol in the direction of the shots and dropped to one knee.

"Ms. Sibal," a voice from the radios of each of the intruders echoed, "Someone just jumped out of the back window. I'm almost sure I hit him, but he ran into the woods."

Just at that moment the two men came back from the other rooms of the house. "It's clear," one said.

Sibal turned toward Rev. Zackery, raised her pistol, and shot twice, hitting Rev. Zackery in the chest. He fell back, holding his chest. He hit a chair, rolled, and landed face down on the floor.

"What are you waiting for? Let's get after him," Sibal ordered as she walked over to Rev. Zackery and fired two more times into Rev. Zackery's back. Then she turned and ran out the door.

Walt was running through the woods carrying his duffle bag and his jacket when he heard the pistol shots. He stopped, dropped the bag, and looked up to the sky. "Well God, looks like Rev. Zackery is going to need some of Your eternal justice now." He opened the bag, which had a bullet hole in it. He pulled out a bulletproof vest, his scoped rifle, and an ammo belt with pistol and holster. He put them on quickly. Then he put on his hooded jacket. He looked back toward the house. He heard them talking. They were coming after him. He was glad. He saw a small creek at the bottom of a small slope and then a hill to his right. He saw a large tree next to some bushes on the hill. That would give him cover. He had to move fast to be in position before they reached where he was standing. He got a dead tree limb and propped his duffle bag up on it. Then he began running down the slope. He jumped the small creek and was making his way up the next hill to his hiding place, when two of his pursuers, saw his propped-up duffle bag.

"Stop!" the first man shouted. "It could be booby-trapped." Their attention was completely on the duffle bag, and they did not see Walt as he climbed the hill. The two men positioned themselves behind two trees, as the first man tossed a dead limb at the duffle bag. The limb hit the duffle bag and it fell flat to the ground. The first man walked up to the duffle bag, lifted it up with the barrow of his rifle, and tossed it to the side.

"Smart move," the second man said. "He went that way. He was just trying to slow us down, to give him time to get over that hill."

"Or find a hiding place somewhere over there," the first man said. "He could be armed. You stay here and cover me. When I get over the creek, then you come down."

"Roger that," the second man said.

Walt watched as the man moved cautiously down the slope toward the creek. Then Walt looked through his scope at the other man who was standing partially behind a tree. He had his rifle raised, waist level, and he was watching the hill for movement. His right side from his leg to his head was exposed. Walt scanned his right side. He could kill him or wound him. Then he aimed at the man's face. "This is for Rev. Zackery," he said aloud as he slowly squeezed the trigger. However, before the final squeeze Walt scanned his right side again. He did not see a sidearm. He pointed his scope at the man moving down the slope. He did not have a sidearm either.

"They could not have killed Rev. Zackery. They don't have pistols," he said to himself. "Rev. Zackery just save your lives," Walt said aloud pointing the crosshairs of his scope on the leg of the man next to the tree. "He would want me to have mercy on you. I hope I don't regret this, Rev Zackery."

However, before he could shoot, he saw something move behind the man's leg. He raised the scope. Two other persons had come up behind the man. Walt focused in on their faces. One was a man. The other was a woman and she had a pistol in her hand. "She killed Rev. Zackery," Walt said. Her face was a very, familiar, face. It was a face that had been indelibly imprinted in his mind.

As he remembered the past, he could see Pam reaching out to that face as Pam balanced herself with her feet on the edges of the opposite sides of an open trapdoor. Just as Pam was about to reach the extended hand of that same face, the hand was jerked away and the foot of that same face kicked Pam's foot, causing her to fall on a bed of long sharp spikes. It was that face, that transplanted face, of Sibal. In his mind he could see Pam fall to her death. He could see that face with an evil smile of satisfaction as the image in his mind faded.

"Sibal." Walt said to himself, "How could she have survived the fire. You won't escape this time," he said as he took aim. However, before he could shoot one of the men with her, blocked his view. The man's face was directly in front of hers. Walt shot anyway. Both persons went down.

The first man, who had just jumped the creek he heard the gunshot, ducked behind a small bush, and he looked up in Walt's direction. That was a mistake. It gave Walt the shot he wanted. Walt's bullet hit him between his eyes. His body landed halfway on the bank of the creek and halfway in the creek. Then Walt raised his scope back to where he had shot the man and Sibal. He could see the man who had been beside the tree pulling the dead man off Sibal's body. Then to his dismay, he saw Sibal move. She was not dead. Walt chambered another round and quickly raised his rifle in her direction. In his scope he could see the last man holding the dead body up in front of him and Sibal as he backed into the trees. Walt shot, hitting the dead man just below the bottom of his flak jacket. Both men went down, but Sibal ran into the trees.

Immediately, Walt started moving down the hill. He had to catch her. Walt overlooked one thing. The man that had been holding the dead man was not dead. The bullet that Walt shot, had passed though the dead man's body, however, it had hit the other man's flak jacket. When he went down, he had remained motionless, hoping that he would not be shot again. Then when he saw Walt going down the hill, he crawled from beneath the dead man. He laid his rifle across the dead man's body and took careful aim at Walt. He waited till Walt reached the creek where the body of his friend was. He fired, hitting Walt in his heart. Walt fell straight back, his arms stretched out wide as he lay on the ground next to the other body. The man fired another shot. It rocked Walt's body. Then the man got up, pulled his radio from his belt, and ran through the trees back toward the house.

"Miss Sibal, come in," he yelled.

"Yeah," she moaned.

"I got him. He's dead."

"Okay. Get back here ASAP. I'm bleeding. I'm at the car. I need to get to my doctor."

"Roger," he said. "I'll be there in three minutes."

Sibal held the two manilla folders out in front of her. "So, you think you'll be safe in Chicago and Andersonville. Well, you don't know Sibal very well. There is nowhere you can go to get away from me," she growled as she applied pressure to the bloody stitches on the side of her new face.

Chapter 7
Family History

(Wednesday 7:30 PM)

Jason walked into his three-bedroom house, turned off the alarm, locked the door, and went directly to the nightstand beside his bed. He opened the top drawer and pulled out his thirty-eight revolver. He checked to see that it was loaded, then he walked to the kitchen, gun in hand. He took the phone off the wall charger, walked over to the kitchen table, laid the pistol on the table, sat down, and dialed the phone. A woman answered.

"Mom, I just wanted to let you know that I was back."

"I thought you were going to stay two weeks. I knew it. You couldn't take all that voodoo mess, could you?" a lady's voice replied through the phone.

"It was pretty weird mom, but something bad happened to Gramma," Jason said softly.

"What happened? Is she all right?"

"No ma'am, she's dead," Jason said.

"What happened to her? How did she die?" his mother asked.

"She was killed, murdered," he said as he got up and walked to the cabinet. "These hicks tied her up and set her house on fire with her inside. She was alive when they burned her home down."

"Lord, have mercy. Did they arrest the people responsible?"

"Two of them were killed in the fire, the other ones were killed later. So, they did pay for the crimes." He took a pint of Cognac and a glass out of the cabinet.

"How are you doing, Jasse. Do you need for me to come over and fix you something to eat?"

"No ma'am. I'm going to take something and then I'm going to get me some, much needed sleep. Gramma's body is at a funeral home in Tipton. This pastor who knew her is going to do her funeral Saturday."

"She knew a pastor?" the woman asked in amazement. "That's a big surprise."

"He told me, that Gramma gave her life to Jesus not long ago. He said she was saved, mama."

"Are you serious? I never thought she would change her ways."

"He told me, how he led her to salvation. He tried to lead me to salvation, too."

"He tried?" she said. "I'm guessing that means he didn't succeed."

"I was too angry at the time. All I had on my mind was hate and revenge. Those two mindsets are not very conducive for salvation. You have to forgive to be saved."

"Yeah, that's right, son. Sometimes forgiving is very, hard to do," she said sadly. "For the longest time, I couldn't forgive your grandmother for your father's death."

"I knew you didn't like her, and you told me to stay away from her because she was into roots and voodoo, but why did you blame her, for daddy's death?" There was a pause. "Do you still blame her for his death?"

"I try not to think about that," she replied. "I guess I shouldn't blame her. I don't believe in that witchcraft stuff, but for some reason, I have felt she was responsible."

"Why? What did she do?"

"She didn't like me." His mother was beginning to get emotional. "Because I had come between them, because I didn't want him to be involved with her and her lifestyle."

"Mama, what did she do?"

"She spoke his death. The day your daddy died, she called me. She told me that he was going to die. She said that I should keep him home. She told me to do whatever I needed to do, but I had to keep him home. She said he was going to die if I didn't. I told her she was crazy, and I hung up on her. I did not say anything to your daddy, and like she had said, he died. She spoke it over him. She made me feel guilty for not keeping him home. I keep thinking if I had kept him home, he would not have died. Even though I know in my mind, she couldn't have caused his death, but in my heart, I believe your daddy died because of something she was involved in. I believed he died because someone put a curse on him because of her."

"I see," Jason said. "Mom, Rev. Zackery would tell you that you need to forgive Gramma, so that God can forgive you. You can't go to heaven with unforgiveness in your heart."

"Rev. Zackery? Who is that?" she asked.

"He's the preacher I told you about. He led Gramma to Jesus. He's a good man. Maybe, when I get back there, I'll let him lead me to Jesus, too. I want to see Gramma in heaven. I want to see you there, too. So please, forgive Gramma."

"I say I forgive her. I've prayed to God to help me forgive her, however in my heart, I still feel this animosity against her. Maybe now that she has passed away, I can let it go."

"Rev. Zackery would say," Jason changed his voice to imitate Rev. Zackery. "It's not about feelings, your feelings can fool you. It's about faith. If you asked the Lord to help you, believe in your heart, and it will be done. In fact, He'll do it before you even ask, because He knows what you're gonna ask, even before you ask it."

"I like this Zackery fellow," she said. Jason could hear happiness in her voice.

"Yeah, it will be good to see him again. I've got to go back down there Friday to settle up with the undertaker, and like I said, the funeral is Saturday."

"You're going back Friday?" she asked. "Why didn't you just stay down there. Why come back here, then go back down there a day later, and then come back here a day after that. That's a lot of unnecessary traveling."

"You're right mom. Anyway, I'm tired. I'm going to get in bed now. I'll call you in the morning and answer all your questions then. Okay?' he said.

"Okay, get some rest, honey. Call me when you get up or whenever you need to talk," she replied. "I'm so sorry this happened, Jason."

"Talk to you in the morning, mom," he said and pressed the button to end the call. Then he poured himself a large glass of Cognac and walked to his bedroom, drink in one hand, gun in the other.

Chapter 8
Out of Restraint

(Wednesday 9:30 PM)

Dave left his hotel room, went down on the elevator, passed through the lobby, and went into the hotel bar. He needed a drink, badly. However, Dave did not notice that he picked up a tail when he went through the lobby. This person, wearing a long black trench coat and a wide brimmed hat, followed him into the bar. Dave stopped sat down at the bar. His tail went to a corner table and sat down.

Since Dave knew very little about mixed drinks, he ordered the James Bond special, a martini on the rocks, shaken not stirred. The bartender smiled as he sat the drink in front of Dave. Dave put his ID and room keycard on the bar.

"I'm going to run a tab. Charge it to my room, please," Dave said.

"Let me know if you need anything else, Mr. Bond," the bartender said taking the keycard and his driver's license.

Dave raised one finger up toward the bartender with one hand and the drink up to his lips with the other. He drank the martini completely, sat the glass back down on the bar, waited for his stomach to stop burning, looked up at the bartender, and tapped the top of the glass.

"Rough day?" the bartender asked.

"Very," Dave replied.

"Let me guess? You either got fired or your woman left you," the bartender said as he poured another drink.

"Both," Dave replied as he rested both elbows on the bar in front of his drink.

"This one is on the house, provided that you drink it very slowly."

"Thank you, Mr. bartender," Dave said. "I perceive that you are very astute at your craft."

"You perceive correctly, my friend. So, heed to this bit of wisdom. Alcohol is just a salve, not a solution." The bartender looked toward the door. "Looks like you have company, the blue kind." Dave turned and saw two policemen looking directly at him, as they came directly toward him. "On second thought, maybe you should finish that drink as soon as you can, while you can."

Dave turned his glass up quickly as one of the officers grabbed his free hand and cuffed it. The other officer waited until he had put his glass on the bar before grabbing his hand and putting it behind his back so the other officer could cuff it.

"Officer Pender," Dave said smiling, "it's good to see you again. I never got a chance to thank you for letting the judge know about my wife making false charges against me."

"Just doing my job, sir, then and now."

"So, officer Pender, what crime have I committed, now?"

"Mr. Parker, you were warned by me, that you could not be within a hundred feet of you wife. You violated your restraining order, so, I'm going to have to arrest you," Officer Pender stated.

"I have not even seen my wife, much less be within a hundred feet of her. Why would you say that?"

"She called us and told us that you followed her here," Pender said.

"Here?"

"Yes sir," Pender said pointing.

Dave looked at a table in the corner of the bar. There was a person sitting at the table with her back turned. She was dressed in a short black dress with spaghetti straps. She had a wide brimmed black hat that was pulled down so far on her head, that it covered half of her face. As Dave watched the person's head turn around, he saw it was Carol.

"Excuse me, officer. This man is a patron of this hotel," the bartender said holding up Dave's license and room keycard. "He did not follow anybody in here. In fact, that person came in after he got here, right after he got here. I would be willing to testify to that in court, if necessary."

Officer Pender took out his pad and began writing. "That's good enough for me," officer Pender said as the other officer unlocked the cuffs on Dave's hands. "Look Mr. Parker, I think she may be following you. She is trying to get you put in jail again. I heard what happened last time you got locked up. The jailer almost lost his job for putting the dude in your cell."

"What are you doing?" Carol screamed as she ran up to police officer, who had taken the handcuffs off Dave's hands. "I am filing charges against him. He has been following me, and he is not supposed to be within one hundred feet of me. Does this look like one hundred feet?"

"Ma'am," officer Pender holding his hands out to stop her from getting closer to Dave. "The bartender says that you came here after Mr. Parker arrived. Therefore, I could charge you with making false statements to a police officer. Mrs. Parker you could be arrested and locked up for that."

"Somebody has been following me. It looked like him." Carol said with nostrils flaring and fire in her eyes. "Either way, he is within one hundred feet of me now, isn't he? He should leave."

"Ma'am," officer Pender said calmly. "Mr. Parker has a room here at this hotel. Why are you here?"

"Like I said, somebody was following me, so I stopped here to call the police. Anyway, this is a free country. I can come here if I choose to."

"Do you have a room, here, Ma'am?" officer Pender asked.

"No! I came in this bar for a drink," she replied.

"Well, Mrs. Parker," officer Pender said, "we are not going to ask him to check out. We will escort him back to his room. However, since you don't want him to be within one hundred feet of you, we advise you to leave this hotel after you've had your drink."

"I'm leaving now," Carol said to officer Pender. Then she turned to Dave. "You had better stop following me. Next time, I'm not going to call the police. I'll handle it myself, my way."

"Good night, Carol. I'll see you tomorrow at our mediation session," Dave said cordially.

They all watched as Carol strutted out of the bar.

"I've never seen her like this before," Dave said. "Has anything else happened since I've been gone?"

"Well, that guy, you caught in your house, Charles Norris, was locked up for selling insurance without a license. Currently, he has not been able to come up with enough money to get out on bail. At court, your wife got really, belligerent with the judge for not dismissing the charges. The judge got so angry that he raised the bail from a thousand, to ten thousand dollars. The judge almost charged her with contempt of court, instead he had his officer put her out of the courtroom." Officer Pender paused. "I hate to say it, but I think your wife has lost it."

"Do you think she is dangerous?" Dave said concerned.

"I don't know, Mr. Parker. Has she ever had a drug problem?"

"No," Dave said. "We've been married for over five years, and I've never seen her take drugs. She doesn't even smoke pot."

"Has she ever been treated for depression," officer Pender said. "She is exhibiting some characteristics of manic depression. You need to be careful whenever you come within a thousand feet of her."

"Thank you, again officer Pender, you have saved me again," Dave said sincerely. "Do you do security work on the side?"

"Actually, we can get authorization to work as off duty police officers. Contact the office and let them know what you need."

"I may just take you up on that. I think I'll seek the safety of my room, for now. Good night, gentlemen," Dave said.

"Mr. Parker?"

"Please, call me Dave. I'd be in jail if it wasn't for you."

"We interrupted your bar time," Officer Pender said. "I feel it's only right that I recommend a place where you can go and have a drink in peace."

"Peace and a drink, that's a combination that's hard to refuse."

"It is on the other side of town, but I'm sure you won't have to worry about Mrs. Parker finding you," Officer Pender said smiling.

"Hey, that sounds great to me. After all I've been through today, I really need some drinking thinking. Thanks, Officer Pender."

"Call me Calvin, Dave," Officer Pender said as he gave Dave a piece of paper with an address on it. "My vacation starts when I get off today. If you come, I'll buy you a drink."

Dave and the two officers left the bar and went to the hotel lobby. Officer Pender and his partner got in their patrol car and left as Dave waved.

There was *a* person sitting in *a* car in the parking lot watching them leave. It wasn't long before a taxi pulled up. Dave got in and left. The person, dressed in black slacks and a black hooded sweatshirt, who had been watching, got out of their car, walked inside the hotel, went to the hotel lobby house phone, and dialed.

"This is Dave Parker," the person said in a very deep voice. "I just left the bar, and I forgot my room number. Could you give it to me, please? I really need to use the bathroom, and I've already tried two doors. Please hurry!"

"Yes sir. You are in," the attendant paused, "room 407."

"Thank you. Oh no! I'm going to need some extra towels. I just had an accident. Just tell them to put them on the bed. I'm sure I'll be in the bathroom."

"I'll have some sent up right away, sir," the attendant said shaking her head. "If you can't hold your liquor, you shouldn't drink," she said to herself after hanging up.

The person dialed again. An answering machine voice was heard. When it was time to leave a message, the person began to speak, once again in a deep male voice. "Come back to the hotel, room 407. It is very important. We need to talk about mediation. I am willing to give you the house free and clear, but I want something in return. Please come, now."

Chapter 9
Design Protection

(Wednesday 10:30 PM)

The severe pain in his chest was beginning to subside. Walt could finally take deep breaths. For an hour he had been lying still, watching for any movement on the slope above him. Finally, it had become dark in the woods, so he slowly rolled over until he hit the body of the man he had shot in the head. The three-quarter moon overhead provided enough light for him to find his rifle. He could see the tactical gear the dead man was wearing. Walt began to take every piece of amor, every weapon, and every ammo clip. He even undressed him, taking his uniform, even though the pants were wet. The man's body was left with nothing on it but underwear, and boots. The man's helmet was full of blood and brain matter. Walt rinsed it out in the stream. Water flowed out the bullet hole in the back of the helmet when he lifted it.

He then jumped the creek and made his way up the slope to his other victim. He went by him, looking for his duffle bag. When he found it, he loaded everything he was carrying into it. Then he returned to the other dead body and took his gear also. In all, he had two flak jackets, two ammo belts, with hand cuffs and radios, two uniforms, and one damaged helmet. Walt looked at the back of this man's helmet and he knew why Sibal had escaped. His bullet had not penetrated the outside of the helmet. There was a large dent in the back where the bullet had hit it but had not gone through.

"I should have waited for a better shot," Walt said to himself as he started back to Rev. Zackery's house. He had made two mistakes that could have cost him his life. He was going to have to be more careful. Killing Sibal was going to require a detailed and well executed plan.

Walt had parked his car in the woods across the highway in front of Rev. Zackery's house. He hoped it was still there. When he reached the back of Rev. Zackery's house, the lights in every room were on. He ducked down and approached cautiously. When he was ten feet from the window he had earlier jumped out of, the bathroom light went out. He dropped the duffle bag, pulled his pistol, and went up to the house next to the living room window and peeped inside. There inside to his utter amazement was Rev. Zackery. He was shirtless, with ace bandages wrapped around his chest from his armpits to his belly button. Gladness he had never felt before, filled Walt's heart. He wanted to yell to Rev. Zackery, however, he needed to patrol the area.

Carefully, he searched the perimeter of the house, he located and checked his car, then he returned to the house, looking in all the windows. After he was sure it was safe, he called out to Rev. Zackery.

"Rev. Zackery, it's Walt. Don't shoot," Walt yelled. "Look out the window, in the back, by the big pine tree."

Rev. Zackery moved the curtains and peeped out of the window. He saw someone behind a tree waving their arm.

"Come out, so I can see you," Rev. Zackery yelled back.

"I'm coming out. Don't shoot," Walt said as he came from behind the tree with his hands up. He walked up to the window so Rev. Zackery could see him clearly.

"Walt!" Rev. Zackery shouted joyfully. "Come on in here, son."

"Yes sir. Let me get my bag."

The two men met at the busted kitchen door. They were about to hug, however, because of their injuries, they grabbed each other's shoulders and touched their foreheads together.

"Thank You, Jesus," Rev. Zackery said softly.

"Amen, reverend," Walt replied. "You had on the vest."

"Yes, I did. Thank you very much," Rev. Zackery said. "I wanted to see if wearing it was very noticeable. When I came out and you didn't say anything, I figured you couldn't tell that I had it on. Then when that lady police officer shot me, I guess she couldn't tell either, otherwise, she would have shot me in the head."

"That was no police officer, and she definitely was not a lady. That is the witch who killed Pam," Walt said angrily. "I thought she had been killed in the fire with the others. Reverend, I know you don't believe it's okay to murder, but I've got to stop her before she goes too far. If she came here, she was probably looking for Dave and Jason."

"Yeah, and like an idiot I told her they had gone home."

"Why did you do that?" Walt asked.

"When she put her pistol to my head and asked me where they were. I panicked. I thought she was going to blow my brains out. I got scared and I told her."

"Why didn't she shoot you in the head after you told her?" Walt asked.

"She had the gun to my head, but then there were gunshots behind the house. When she heard it, she ducked down and pointed her gun toward the back. One of her men said you had jumped out the window. That's when I started backing away, so she shot me two times in the chest. I fell and she shot me two more times in the back. Then she went after you."

"Rev. Zackery, you really lucked out this time."

"No, Walt, the Lord blessed in a mighty way."

"Yes, He did. He blessed you, and me, too. I took two in the chest myself."

"Well, say 'Thank You Jesus' then."

"Reverend, let's say it together?"

"Thank You, Jesus," they said together.

"These vests might stop bullets, but they definitely don't stop the pain," Rev. Zackery said taking a slow painful breath.

"I'll wrap some ice on the sore spots," Walt said walking to the refrigerator. "I need to get you somewhere safe and then I'm going after Sibal," Walt said.

Chapter 10
Planning to Harm

(Wednesday 11:30 PM)

When the night maid left Dave's room after leaving the towels on the bed. The door closed behind her. However, it did not lock. The person who had made the call for towels walked to the door, pushed it open, removed the paper blocking the latch, let the door close and lock, and then dropped the large bag on the floor. The person looked around the room and eventually faced the mirror. The reflection revealed an ominous expression.

"Hell hath no fury like Carol scorned," Carol said as she frowned into the mirror.

She quickly dumped everything in her bag on the bed. There was the dress, hat, and high-heel shoes she had worn earlier. There was a roll of duct tape and a pair of bloodstained panties. She quickly took off the clothes and shoes she had on and put them in the bag. Then she put on the dress, hat, and heels she had worn earlier. After blocking the door from closing with a ball point pen, she took the bag and put it in a dumpster behind the hotel.

When she got back to the room, she began to go through her planned story for the police.

"Dave called me. He apologized for everything. He said he needed to talk to me, face to face, before we go to mediation. He asked me to come to his room. I told him, no. But then he promised, if I would come, he would give me our house, and he would pay off the mortgage. I should have known better, but I thought he was sincere," she said as if she was talking to the police. She backed up to the door. "However, when I got inside, he went mad. He grabbed my head and push it back into the door." She dropped her hat on the floor and banged her head against the door. "That almost knocked me unconscious. While I was in a daze, he wrapped duct tape around my head covering my mouth. Then he grabbed my hair and pulled me over to the bed. I tried to hold on the closet door but," she said as she bent over as if someone was pulling her hair. She kicked off one of her shoes. She grabbed the sliding closet door and jerked it partially loose. "The door broke, and I lost my grip. Then he threw me on the bed and jumped on my back." She kicked off her other shoe, fell across the bed, and pulled the bedspread down on both sides of her body. "He twisted my arm back and wrapped my wrist in duct tape. Then he held my other arm while he wrapped the tape around me." She put both hands behind her back. "Then he said he was going to do me like Chuckie did me." Then Carol changed her tone. "I don't know why he thought I was having sex with Charles?" Carol's voice became frantic. "Then, he pulled me halfway off the bed, and he, he, he raped me." Carol sat on the bed and smiled. "Then after brutally raping me, he duct-taped my legs together and left me here on the bed. I figured he was going to kill me when he got back. I managed to kick the phone off the nightstand." She kicked the phone off the nightstand. It fell to the floor and the receiver fell off. She noted where it was before she put the receiver back on the phone. "Then, I pressed the front desk key with my nose and mumbled into the phone and finally someone came to the room and found me." She smirked. "That should do it," she said taking the duct tape from the bed. She unrolled a foot of the tape, covered her mouth, grabbed a handful of her hair at the top, and then rolled the tape around her head two times, before tearing the tape. She taped her right wrist then she rolled out ten feet of tape, sticky side up, across the floor. She sat down on the floor and taped her ankles. Then she pulled her panties down to her ankles. Then, she laid down on the floor with her arms behind her back and rolled over the tape. As she rolled, she bound her arms to her body. Finally, she began rolling and squirming back to the phone. It took longer than she thought it would.

Chapter 11
Caught in the Act

(Thursday 12:15 AM)

The telephone on the nightstand of the dark bedroom rang several times before Jason awoke. He slowly picked up the receiver and put it to his ear.

"Hello," he said disgustedly.

"I see, you decided, not to let me know you got back," a woman said angrily. It was his lady friend, Laverne.

"I was going to call you first thing in the morning," Jason replied. "I needed. I need to get..."

"What's her name?" she said cutting him off.

"What?" Jason asked.

"What's her name. I know you have some woman in bed with you right now," she said. "So, what's her name?"

"Laverne, believe me, there is no one here in bed with me, now."

"Oh, so she left already and that's why you are so tired that you didn't have enough energy left to pick up the phone and call," she said.

"When my plane landed, I came straight home, called my mother, and then went to bed. Nobody has been here since I've been home. Stop tripping," Jason said. "Anyway, didn't you say that you were going to date other men?"

"Well, you said you were going on a two-week vacation without me. What did you think I was going to say?"

"I said I was going to visit my sick grandmother, who wanted to see me before she died," Jason said loudly.

"Well, since you've been gone, I bet you spent time with another woman, other than your grandmother." There was silence for a few seconds.

"If you must know, when I got to my grandmother's house, she did have house guests," Jason explained. "A couple, Dave and Pam, were staying with her. So, technically I did spend time with another woman while I was there."

"So, your sick grandmother, who was on her deathbed, had house guests," Laverne said incredulously. "Is your grandmother better, now?"

"No! She's dead," Jason shouted. "And the woman that I technically spent time with, she is dead, too."

After a long pause Laverne spoke. "How did they die?" said arrogantly.

"Some hillbillies and witches killed them," Jason said bluntly. The phone went dead. Laverne had hung up on him.

Jason hung up the phone and grabbed the bottle next to it. He removed the top and drank from the bottle. He sat on the side of the bed and took a big gulp. "If it ain't witches, it's bitches." After his stomach stopped burning, he laid back down.

Just before he was about to fall asleep, the phone rang, again. He answered quickly.

"Yeah!"

"You lying sack of…" Laverne yelled.

"What is your problem?" Jason said, cutting her off. "Nobody is lying to you."

"I thought you said you were alone in bed?"

"I am alone in bed," he said.

"Well, why do I see someone with a flashlight in your living room?" Laverne said angrily. "Tell her, she might as well turn on the lights. She's not fooling nobody."

"Are you outside my house?" Jason asked angrily. However, his anger turned to concern as he looked at his bedroom door. "Where is the light now?" he asked picking up his revolver.

"It's moving toward your bedroom," Laverne said, watching from her car as the light went into the bedroom. To her amazement there were several gunshots with the corresponding flashes of light coming from both sides of Jason's bedroom.

"Jason! Jason!" she screamed. The line went dead. She was about to call Jason again when a black van slowly came pass her car. She ducked down in her seat. The van parked two cars ahead of her, directly in front of Jason's house. She decided to call 911. While she was talking to the 911 operator, a man dressed in black came out of the house with a long, lumpy, black bag over his shoulder. He threw the bag in the van, got in, and the van drove away.

Laverne could barely see the license plates. She only got the first three letters, BKQ.

"Police officers are in route to your location now. ETA is less than ten minutes," The 911 operator said. "Please remain where you are until they speak with you."

Chapter 12
Foiled Again

(Thursday 12:45 AM)

Dave and Calvin, the police officer, got off the elevator and walked toward Dave's room.

"You were really getting down on the dance floor," Calvin said smiling. "What was that, the Boogaloo?"

"Man, I thought you were hip to the new dances," Dave replied. "That was the Funky Chicken."

"Oh yeah!" Calvin said flapping his elbows. "That was the chicken trying to fly. Then, when you did the James Brown, that was so funny."

"Well, the DJ said, 'Wave your hands in the air, and do the James Brown like you just don't care.'"

"I guess we hear what we want to hear sometimes," Calvin said. "You evidently wanted to hear, 'do the James Brown', however I think he said, 'and wave em all around like you just don't care.'"

"All I know is, I had a ball. It was just what I needed."

"Was it your first time going to a black club?" Calvin asked.

"Me and my main man Slick, use to go to this black club, called the Hole in the Wall, all the time when I was in college. That was a long time ago."

"Slick?" Calvin said. "He sounds black."

"Yeah, he was one my best friends while we were in school. He dropped out."

"Okay, so, some of your best friends are black?" Calvin said.

"I know it sounds like a cliché, but in reality, my best friend now, is a black man. We have been through more in a week, than most friends experience in a lifetime."

"Wait, listen," Calvin stopped and held his hand out to stop Dave. There was beating sound coming from the door ahead of him.

"That's my room," Dave said.

"Give me your keycard. Let me check it out," Calvin said as he pulled his pistol from his side holster under his shirt. He unlocked the door and pushed until he hit something. He ducked down and pushed harder. Now he could see Carol's head. He went through the door, passed Carol, went into the bathroom, checked it, came out and checked the rest of the room. It was clear. He came back to Carol. She was lying on her back, looking up at him pitifully. Her dress was well above her hips, exposing her naked body from the waist down. He knelt beside her and began to pull her dress down. However, just before he covered her, she opened her legs. Calvin covered her legs and looked up at her again. This time, her look was seductive. He carefully took the tape off her head and mouth. Immediately, Carol began to speak.

"It was Dave Parker," she screamed. "He attacked me and raped me. He's coming back to kill me."

"Mrs. Parker, are you taking any medication?" Calvin said as he removed the tape from her ankles.

"Why are you asking me about medication?" Carol asked and then began to scrutinize his facial features. "Aren't you that police officer who said I made false statements against my husband?"

"Yes ma'am. I am officer Pender, and yes, I reported that Mr. Parker did not hit you. I also reported that Mr. Norris disputed your claim that Mr. Parker forced you and him to take off your clothes. Mr. Norris also admitted that he had spent the night with you three times. Your neighbor, Mrs. Simmons also, corroborated that."

"He did not spend the night at my house," she yelled. "They are lying."

"Ma'am, earlier, you said that Mr. Parker was following you. The bartender said you followed Mr. Parker into the bar," Calvin said and then took a deep breath. "Ma'am, how did you get in Mr. Parker's room?"

"He called me after I left the bar, and he told me he wanted to talk to me. He said it was very important. So, I came. That's when he attacked me."

Officer Pender walked to the door. "That's not possible because Mr. Parker was with me," Pender said as he pulled open the door revealing a sympathetic Dave. "I'm going to ask you again, Mrs. Parker, have you been taking any drugs or medication."

Carol tried to move her arms, but they were still taped to her body. She looked up at officer Pender anxiously. "I may have taken a mild antidepressant earlier today."

"Have you had any hallucinations or panic attacks."

Carol shook her head 'no.'

"Are you okay now?" officer Pender asked slowly.

"Yes, officer Pender, I'm okay."

"You can call me Calvin, ma'am," Calvin said and paused. "I need to ask you one more question before I remove the tape from your arms."

"Okay," she said.

"Do you still want me to charge Mr. Parker with assault, battery, and rape."

Carol sat there for a minute before speaking. Tears began to roll down her cheeks.

"I was angry and ashamed. He," she looked at Dave, "let this man insult me and he didn't do anything about it. I was mad and I wanted to hurt him, so, I had an affair. Then, when he found out, I was ashamed. I didn't want anyone else to find out, so I lied and tried to cover it up. I had him put in jail and I convinced myself that I had no other recourse. When he got out, I felt I had to do something to prove to everyone that he was a bad person. I followed him here. I got into his room, tied myself up and was planning to accuse Dave of raping me, but when I kicked the phone off the nightstand, the cord on the receiver became disconnected from the phone. I could not call the front desk as I had planned, so I crawled to the door and began kicking on it. Fortunately, you came instead of the hotel personnel. You kept me from making matters much worse. I was wrong. I admit it, and I'm so sorry." She paused. "Are you going to lock me up.?"

"That will be up to Mr. Parker. If he presses charges against you for breaking and entering, I will have no choice," Calvin said. Then he turned to Dave. "What do you want to do?" Calvin began to remove the tape from Carol's body.

Dave dropped to one knee so that his face was near hers. "Can we talk for a minute?" Dave said as he grabbed her freed hands and pulled her up to her feet.

While Dave and Carol talked with officer Pender sitting across the room at the hotel, Chuck was walking into the open garage at Carol's house. Earlier that evening, the judge had lowered his bail and he had been released from jail. However, he had spent several hours at the bail bondsman office, working out the terms of the bail. He was tired, and angry when he got to Carol's house. When no one answered the doorbell or his knocks on the door inside the garage, he took the key under the floor mate, and let himself in. He turned off the alarm and went up the stair to Carol's bedroom. When he went through the door, he was hit in the back of his head. As he was falling to the floor, the same person that hit him, caught him by the waist, and was holding him up. Another person, who had also been waiting in the room walked in front of Chuck. He had a needle in his hand. After he had rolled up Chuck's sleeve, he stuck the needle into the vein of his left arm. The men waited for the drug they had administered to circulate. Then one of the men grabbed Chuck's chin with one hand, and the back of his head with the other, then he twisted Chuck's head roughly, breaking his neck. Then the two men, both wearing black stockings over their heads, each grabbed one of Chuck's arm, drug him to the edge of the top stair and threw him into the air. His heels hit first, then his butt, then the back of his head. He rolled over once and ended up lying face down on the bottom steps.

In the hotel room, Dave and Pam sat on the bed, each one looking at the floor waiting for the other to speak. They both spoke together.

"I'm sorry," Dave said. "You go first."

"When did you install cameras in our house," she asked.

"There are no cameras in our house."

"Well how did you know about me and Chuckie, I mean Charles," she said in a louder voice.

"You wouldn't believe me if I told you, so I'll just say I found out the day after I left."

"So, you didn't see us. Somebody told you about us," she said even louder.

"No, I saw you all right," Dave said, his voice now getting louder. "Not long, before I called you, I saw him slap you and bust your lip. I also saw you do things to him that you never did to me."

"You had cameras put in our bedroom to spy on me. That's despicable."

"Despicable? What's despicable is you bringing another man into our bedroom and screwing him in our bed. That's despicable! And for the last time, there are no cameras," Dave shouted.

"Well, how did you see me, Dave? Tell me!"

"I saw you in a fortune teller's crystal ball," Dave yelled.

"Maybe, we need to end this conversation," Pender said. "Tempers are beginning to get out of control."

"That's the best lie you could come up with." She said getting up to get her shoes. "You are a pitiful liar, a pitiful husband, and a pitiful lover."

"You never gave me a chance to be a husband or a lover. You never loved me, you only wanted someone to control and use," Dave said. "It took all these years, but I have finally learned my lesson." Dave looked at Pender. "You did say I could file charges against her for breaking into my room, didn't you?"

"Yeah, that's right," Pender said. "Is that what you want to do?"

"Are you going to file a police report of what happened here tonight?" Dave asked.

"Yes I am."

"I thought you said you were not going to press charges," Carol interrupted. "You changed your mind because I got upset because you put cameras, I mean, because I didn't believe that stuff about crystal balls?"

Dave thought for a moment. "Okay, I won't press charges, now. However, if you continue to follow me, harass me, or if you make any other false accusations against me, I will press charges. And you must agree to allow officer Pender to follow you home tonight to make sure that nothing happens to you between here and there, because I'm sure I will be blamed if it does."

"Okay, Dave," she said agreeably. "I'll do that and thank you for not filing charges." She gathered all her belongings. "I'm ready when you are, officer Pender."

"All right. Let's go."

Chapter 13
Crime Scenery

(Thursday 1:15 AM)

Laverne was becoming frantic. She had been sitting alone in the police car for about twenty minutes. She felt like a trapped animal as she looked through the cage. She tried the back doors several times. Still, they would not open. The back windows were closed, but a cold breeze was blowing through the front window. She wished now that she had worn a coat when she left her apartment. Four police cars and a CSI van were at the house now and police officers were moving in and out of the house. One came close to the car she was in.

"Hey!" she yelled. "You need to let me out of this car. I already gave you a statement. Why am I still locked in this car?"

The policeman walked to the window. "Ma'am," he said sympathetically, "a detective is on his way. He has a few more questions to ask you."

"Okay, but can you at least tell me if Jason is all right?"

"Ma'am, I can't give out any information at this time. The detective," he stopped talking and then he looked up at a black sedan that had just driven up, "is here. He just arrived. I'll go get him." The officer took his clipboard from the front seat and then he walked to the black sedan. He gave his clip board to the detective, they talked for a minute as they looked through the pages of the clipboard, and then they walked to the police car, where Laverne was pulling on the door handle impatiently.

The policeman opened the door and helped Laverne out of the car.

"Thank you for being so patient, Ms. Dix. I know you have been waiting a long time and I thank you for calling us when you did and giving us the info about the tag. I am detective Charles of the CPD. I understand that you were the girlfriend of Mr. Scott," detective Charles said politely.

"Yes, were?" Laverne said. "Is Jason hurt? Was he shot? Is he dead? I heard so many gun shots."

"There was a small amount of blood on the bed covers, but we didn't find any bodies in the house. It may be that his body was in the lumpy black bag you saw the man put in the van. We just don't know anything conclusively yet."

"They took his body?" Laverne moaned. "Why would they take the body?"

"We think either he was assassinated, and the body was taken as proof of death, or maybe he is still alive, and he was taken hostage." A policeman beckoned detective Charles. "Give me a minute," he said, as he walked away. Five minutes later he returned. "They found skull bone fragments in that blood on the bed. It doesn't look too good for Mr. Scott. However, there is still a possibility that he is still alive. Therefore, we will be classifying this case as a missing person and possible homicide, until we find any other evidence to indicate otherwise. Do you know any relatives of Mr. Scott?"

"His mother lives here in Chicago. His father is deceased. He doesn't have any brothers or sisters, or children," Laverne said as tears rolled down her face. "I just found out his grandmother died recently." She leaned over the hood of the police car and sobbed in anguish.

"Do you need medical attention," detective Charles asked.

"No. I just need a minute."

"Of course," detective Charles said compassionately. "I just have one more question and then you may leave."

"What is it?"

"Do you have a name, address, or phone number for Mr. Scott's mother?"

"No," she said sadly. "I only met her once. I don't think she likes me very much."

"Okay ma'am, you are free to go. Here's my card, you can contact me if you remember anything else that you think is important."

"Thank you, detective Charles," Laverne said taking the card.

The two policemen watched as Laverne got in her silver Lincoln Mark IV two-door Luxury Sports Coupe.

"That's one fine ride," the patrolman said to detective Charles as she drove away.

"That's one fine woman," detective Charles replied.

"There is one more thing, detective Charles," the patrolman said.

"What's that?"

"There were several shots through pillows covered up to look like someone sleeping."

"So, the perp thought Scott was in the bed and shot the pillows," detective Charles said.

"Yeah. The girlfriend said she was talking to Scott when the shooting occurred. She said she told him that she saw a light in the living room, possibly a flashlight, moving toward the bedroom."

"That would have given Scott a chance to get up, setup the pillows in the bed, and get ready for what now seems more like an attempted assassination," Charles said. "I need to get in there as soon as the CSI gets through."

"Do you think it is drug related?"

"Don't know, but I want the house checked from top to bottom for drugs. There's a good chance our Mr. Scott is not dead. If he is a drug dealer, he may just be on the run," Charles said.

Chapter 14
Scene at the Crime

(Thursday 2:00 AM)

When Carol got to her home, her garage door was already open, so she drove inside. Officer Pender stopped his car behind hers. She got out and waited by her car door. He got out of his car and went to her in the garage.

"Are you going to be all right, Mrs. Parker?" Calvin asked.

"Calvin, you did say I could call you that, didn't you?"

"Yes, ma'am. You can call me Calvin."

"Well, Calvin, I wish you wouldn't call me that," she said.

"Call you what, ma'am?"

"Mrs. Parker," she yelled. "I'm not going to be that person anymore. Please, just call me Carol, or if you must use my last name, call me by my maiden name, Ms. Thompson."

"All right, Ms. Thompson," he said calmly.

"I would prefer Carol."

"Okay. Carol, let me be very clear. If Mr. Parker has any more problems with you, whether it is making false statements or following him, or any other illegal act, I will have to arrest you, and put you in jail. You would not want that to happen, would you, Carol?"

"No, I wouldn't. I was upset. I'm better now. You don't have to worry about me doing anything else, Calvin," she said apologetically. "Thank you for being so understanding."

"You are very welcome, ma'am."

"Calvin?" she asked sweetly. "Would you mind coming into the kitchen and waiting there for a minute while I make sure my house is safe. I could make you a cup of coffee while I checked everything out. I know you don't believe me, but I did think someone was following me."

"I don't want any coffee, but I will walk you in your house and check to make sure nobody is here."

She grabbed his left arm and pulled it against her breast. Since she did not have on a bra, he could feel her nipple against his arm.

"Thank you so much, Calvin. You can't imagine how much I appreciate this. Being in this house alone can be very frightening," she said unlocking the door. She went to the alarm, but it wasn't beeping. "I thought I set the alarm when I left," she said. "Maybe I didn't."

He walked in behind her as she walked to the coffee maker on her counter. He peeped his head through the entrance to the dining room. Nobody was there. She took two cups from her cabinet as he walked pass her. He walked pass the foyer into her family room admiring the elegant décor and the romantic soft lighting of the room.

"Everything looks good down here," Calvin said as he watched her place two cups of coffee on her coffee table in front of a long white leather sectional sofa in the family room.

"Please, just have one cup of coffee with me, please Calvin please," she begged. "I'm still very nervous."

"Okay, Carol, one cup," he said sitting down in front of his coffee. He took off his jacket and laid it on the sofa. Then he removed his pistol from the side holster and slid it under his jacket. "Are you sure this coffee isn't going to keep you up all night."

"No. I'm going to take something to put me to sleep. I hate being alone, I can't sleep by myself unless I take something."

"This coffee is really good," Calvin said.

"It's my special Columbian blend," she said

"Can I ask you a personal question?" Calvin asked.

"Okay. But first, will you help me get out of these shoes," she said pulling her dress up to her knees, crossing her legs, and pointing her foot at him. "Those straps are so hard to undo."

He grabbed her ankle, sat her foot on his knee, unstrapped her shoe, and removed it. Then she pulled down her dress between her legs and put her other foot on his knee. He removed that shoe. This time she let her foot remain on his knee.

"Free at last, free at last, thank God Almighty 'theys' free at last," she said smiling a beautiful, inviting smile at him. "Would you do me a really big favor Mr. Calvin?"

"What's that," Calvin said mesmerized by her pretty bare foot on his knee.

"I would do anything you ask, if you would rub my feet," she said sexily as she slid the other foot on his knee.

"Foot massages are my specialty," he said as he instantly began to massage her feet.

"Oh, Mr. Calvin, oh, that feels so good," she moaned as she laid back, sliding the spaghetti straps of her dress down over her shoulders. He felt dizzy as he looked at her fine sexy body lying there inviting him to have sex with her. Then before he knew what was happening, she pulled her feet back, straddled him, took his head in her hands, and pulled it to her breasts.

"You put something in my coffee," he said pushing her up.

"The truth is, the police report is going to say, you came over here, slipped some Eustacy in my coffee, and then you took some Eustacy and Viagra. However, I was able to fight you off and call the police."

"Ecstasy and Viagra!" Calvin shouted as he ran to the kitchen table. He grabbed the saltshaker, opened it, and dumped it into his mouth. Then he went to the sink and drank water from the faucet. He then went to the bathroom and immediately began to throw up.

Carol took the pistol from beneath Calvin's jacket and was backing toward the foyer when Calvin came out of the bathroom.

"What are doing with my weapon," Mrs. Walker.

"I said don't call me that," she screamed.

"Okay, Carol," Calvin said softly. "What are you going to do with my gun?"

"I want to make a deal with you. If you agree not to file a report about me breaking into Dave's room, I won't call the police on you now. However, just to make sure you keep your end of the deal, I'm going to hold on to your gun," she said and then waited. "Do we have a deal?"

"Okay, I won't file a report about the break-in, but I can't leave here without my weapon."

"I'm going up to my room now. If you break my door down, I'm going to shoot you, kill you," she warned. "Now, you wouldn't want that to happen would you, officer Pender?"

"No ma'am, I wouldn't," he said shaking his head 'no.'

"If you had just had sex with me, none of this would have been necessary. I could have used that to stop you from filing your report," she said. "You missed out. I was going to be good to you."

"Give me another chance. I choose option two. We can make love and you give me my pistol. I promise I won't file a report," Calvin pleaded.

"Good try. Now, get out!" She walked backwards to the front of the foyer. Suddenly she dropped the pistol. She saw Chuck's body lying face down at the bottom of the steps. Calvin ran quickly and picked up his pistol.

"Chuckie," she screamed as she ran toward the body.

"Wait!" Calvin shouted as he grabbed her arm and stopped her. "Don't touch the body. Let me check him." He turned her body toward his. "I'll do whatever is needed for him. You call 911." Calvin went to the body while Carol went to the phone. While Carol was talking to the 911 operator, she walked toward Calvin.

"Is he dead," she asked.

"Yes," Calvin said sadly shaking his head. "His neck is broken. It looks like he fell down the steps."

"Fell down the steps," she said disbelievingly. "He was most likely pushed."

"That's a possibility," Calvin said. "Let me speak to the operator." Calvin took the phone from Carol. "This is Sargent Pender, send a police car, an ambulance, and a crime scene unit to," he paused.

Carol told him the address and he relayed it to the operator and then he hung up.

"Are you sure you were with Dave all night," she asked.

"I was there with him and you earlier, while we were at the hotel bar. I told him about this club where he could go to get away from you, then I left and went by home to change clothes. When I got to the club, Dave was already there."

"So, you were not with Dave the whole night."

"Well, no," he said. "It took about thirty-five minutes for me to get home, get changed, and get to the club."

"Was that time enough for him to get over here and do this," Carol asked.

"That's very unlikely, Mrs. Parker. The time it would take Dave to drive form the hotel to here, and then to the club, would take at least forty-five minutes."

"You have never seen Dave drive," she said as if she had proven her point.

"Dave took a cab to the club. It will be easy enough to check with the cab company to verify where he went."

"Oh, yeah," she said disappointedly.

"You never give up. Do you?" he asked. "Why do you hate Dave so much. What did he do to you?"

"I don't know!" she screamed. "Maybe it's because my father bribed Dave into marrying me. My father made me marry him. My father said that nobody would want a woman who had been caught having sex with the whole baseball team."

"What are you talking about?" Calvin asked.

"He didn't believe that I had been drugged and taken advantage of by one of my boyfriends and some of his team members. He said that I was a prostitute. He showed me pictures that they had taken of me. He paid them money for the pictures and to not say anything about what had happened." She began to cry as she leaned against Calvin holding his biceps with both hands.

"You were gang raped, and your father didn't believe you."

"No," she said. "He looked at the pictures. He said that the picture showed that I was a willing participant, that I was enjoying it. I told him that I was drugged, and I didn't know what I was doing. But the picture seemed to show that I was not being forced, and that I was doing things on my own, so, he refused to let me file charges."

"I'm so sorry that happened to you. Does Dave know anything about this?" Calvin asked pushing her away gently.

"I don't know. I don't know what my father told him to get him to marry me. I do know my father made him a manager after we got married," she said, refusing to be pushed away.

"I don't think Dave knows anything about that. When we were at the club, he said that he had tried to be a good husband, that he had tried to make you happy. He said you just don't want him."

"He's right. I don't want him," she said. She had become calm. "I tried one time, a long time ago, but he said I was being freaky. So, from then on, I just laid there. Dave and I are sexually incompatible. He has a very low sex drive. He's not like you."

"Me?" Calvin said.

"Yeah, I could tell you wanted me by the way you were looking at me at the hotel. You love sex, I can tell."

"It's better than food," Calvin said.

"Yeah, that's why Dave is not what I want. That's why we never had children. I don't want to have children and be stuck in a relationship with him for the rest of my life. My only problem is, I can't provide for myself the type of lifestyle that I'm accustomed to."

"Well, he has filed for a divorce, so what are you going to do?"

"If I can get my house, the Mercedes, and alimony of about six thousand a month, I will be able to survive," she said counting on her fingers.

"Wow! That's a lot," Calvin said. "How much did Dave make a month?"

"Almost ten thousand," she said suddenly confused. "What do you mean, how much did he make?"

"He was fired today."

She released his arm and stepped back in shock. There was silence as they stared at each other. The silence was broken by the sound of approaching sirens.

Chapter 15
Burning Revelation

(Thursday 3:00 AM)

Walt knocked on the motel door to the beat of one two, one, one two three. Rev. Zackery let him in. They were in Pam's hotel room where she and Walt had been two days before.

"Where did you go?" Rev. Zackery asked.

"I took the bodies to the burial site."

"What burial site?"

"Where the witches who died in the fire are buried," Walt said. "Something happened while I was there."

"What?"

"I thought I heard Pam screaming," Walt said holding his head as he walked aimlessly around the room. "It was faint, but I could have sworn it was her."

"Have you ever heard her scream before?" Rev. Zackery asked.

Walt thought about when they had made love and how she had screamed softly when she had reached her second climax. "No! Not really," he said.

"It was probably your imagination," Rev. Zackery said. "This burial site, you went to, were there many people buried there?"

"It was a mass grave where hundreds have been buried."

"Over the years, or just since yesterday," Rev. Zackery said concerned.

"Just since yesterday. The ground was still soft, it was very easy to dig the hole for those two I killed."

"Walt, how did Pam die? What did she, Dave, and Jason do?"

"How did Pam die? They killed Pam by dropping her onto a bed of sharp spikes. What did Dave and Jason do? They killed some very bad people, some of whom had tried to kill them, you, and me. I know I'm a bad person. I have killed many people, some for my country, some for the witches I worked for, and some for my own personal reasons. But these people, that Pam, Dave, and Jason killed, were not just bad, they were evil. They worshiped the devil, Satan. They sacrificed their own babies to him and drank their babies' blood in satanic ceremonies." Walt waited for a response for Rev. Zackery, but got none, so he continued. "So, when these evil witches, who were responsible for the death of Pam's aunt, were having one of their evil ceremonies in this large barn, Pam, Dave, and Jason designed a plan to trap them, and burn the barn down with all of them inside. Something went terribly wrong. The witches caught Pam and they killed her during the ceremony. So, Dave and Jason blocked the doors, and just like they burned Pam's aunt's house down with her inside, Dave and Jason burned their building down with them inside." Walt waited for a response again. Again, he got none. "I guess your God would not like what they did?"

"One time, God caused a great flood that killed almost everyone in the whole world," Rev. Zackery said.

"Yeah, that's the story of Noah. I thought that was a fairytale."

"It's a fairytale to non-believers, but to us, who believe, it is the truth," Rev. Zackery said as he walked over to the bed where his bible was lying. He picked it up and turn to the book of Genesis. When he had found what he was looking for, he began to read. "You want to know about God, listen to this. 'And God saw that the wickedness of man was great in the earth, and that every imagination of the thoughts of his heart was only evil continually. And it repented the LORD that he had made man on the earth, and it grieved him at his heart. And the LORD said, I will destroy man whom I created from the face of the earth; both man and beast, and creeping thing, and the fowls of the air; for it repenteth me that I have made them. But Noah found grace in the eyes of the LORD.'" Rev. Zackery looked up at Walt. "So, based on what

I read, it is abundantly clear, God does not condone individuals with evil hearts."

"Rev. Zackery, are you saying that you think God was okay with them killing all those witches?"

"I'm not saying that God was okay with it, but I know that God allowed it to happen, and because he did, the world is a better, safer place. On one hand, Jason was probably seeking revenge, that was not good, however on the other, Dave has a calling on his life, that is good. I believe God was using them to do His will. I believe God is using you, too, Walt. You saved Dave and Jason, and you saved me."

"You can't be serious," Walt replied.

"Listen Walt, God chooses whomever He wants. He looks at the heart, and you have a good heart. The bible is full of instances where God chose flawed people. Moses was a murderer. David was a murderer and an adulterer. Even father Abraham was a liar."

"I know about Moses and David, but I didn't know that Abraham was a liar," Walt said as he took from his duffle bag, the uniform of one of the guards he had killed.

"An Egyptian Pharaoh saw Abraham's wife and wanted her. Because Abraham thought Pharaoh would kill him and take his wife, he told Pharaoh that his wife was his sister, and he gave her to Pharaoh in exchange for sheep, oxen, donkeys, camels, and servants."

"Father Abraham," Walt said shaking his head. "How low can you go." Walt took off his clothes and put on the guard's uniform. It fit him loosely.

"However, God, being the understanding God that he is, and even though Abraham was totally wrong, God would not let Pharaoh touch Abraham's wife and God made Pharaoh give Abraham's wife back to him. My point is this, God has chosen some pretty suspect individuals, me included. If He chose me, He can choose you, or at least, use you."

"Okay, I can go with, 'He can use me,'" Walt said. "Did you get any sleep?"

"No. I've been praying since you left."

"I need to get a nap. I got to get back to your house before daybreak," Walt said as he laid down on the sofa.

"Why are you going back there?"

"I need to stakeout your house. I figure they will come to get the bodies. I want to be there when they come."

"Do you think the woman who shot me will be with them when they come?"

"I hope so," Walt said with hate in his eyes. "If not, I'll follow them and maybe they will lead me to her."

"Then what?"

"Then, hopefully, God will allow me to kill her," Walt said. "If He does, the world will be a better, safer place."

"If you fail, they will kill you."

"If I fail, they will kill you, Dave, Jason and possibly me. Sibal knows they set the fire. I need to stop her now, before she sends someone to kill Dave and Jason at their homes, because their families or friends could get caught in the crossfire."

"I didn't think about that," Rev. Zackery said sadly. "I never should have told her that they had gone home. It will be my fault if anyone else is killed."

"No, Rev. Zackery," Walt disputed. "It's standard operating procedure to find out where the targets live. When you told her, they had gone home, I'm sure she thought you were lying. It is not your fault. Don't waste your time guilt tripping. Use your time doing what you can, to remedy the problem."

"You are absolutely right, Walt. Thanks! I will do what I do best. God has given me authority over all the works of the devil."

"Okay reverend. Would you mind turning out the light," Walt said.

"I pray that the Lord will you give a restful nap, and that you will wakeup rested and focused on your mission and that all will go according to God's will, in Jesus name, amen," Rev. Zackery prayed and turned out the light.

Chapter 16
Crystal Dreams

(Thursday 6:00 AM)

"Are you awake?" Pam said softly. Ten seconds passed before there was a response.

"Yes, sister dear," Tamera said sarcastically. "I never went to sleep."

"That's too bad. I got a nice nap. I was exhausted after all the screaming," Pam said happily.

"I could tell by the sound of your loud snoring. I was very tempted to suffocate you."

"I'm sorry," Pam said. "Maybe now that I'm awake you can get a nap. I'll wake you up if I hear anything."

"Okay, maybe I could get a little sleep. When I was here alone, I wouldn't let myself fall asleep, because I was afraid, I would miss an opportunity to get out of here," Tamera said.

"Maybe you will have nice dreams like I did."

"You had dreams? About what?"

"I had two dreams. The first was a juicy dream about my lover. We had just made love and I was just lying in his arms, just enjoying the moment," Pam sighed. "That is the best feeling that I have ever felt." Pam took a deep breath and brew it out loudly. "I bet you have never made love or even had sex before. You have been so busy trying to kill me, you probably have never been anywhere either. You are so worried about me taking some of your power. We could die in this crystal. If we get out of here, you need to make love at least one time, and you need to see Niagara Falls before you die."

"What was the other dream about?" Tamera said softly.

"I dreamed about our mother," Pam said. There was a long silence.

"You remember her."

"No, but I know it was her."

"If you don't remember her, how do you know it was her," Tamera said incredulously.

"I just know," Pam snapped. "She was walking with us and holding our hands. She joined our hands together and then she disappeared. We were young children, and I got the feeling that she was teaching us to stay together, even though she would not be with us."

"That's so touching," Tamera said sarcastically. "You are going to make me cry."

"Do you remember her?"

"No, I only know what I was told about her," Tamera said angrily.

"What was that?"

"She abandoned me and when the seekers found her to bring her back, she killed herself. She hated me that much."

"That's not true," Pam shouted. "They lied to you about her, just like they lied to you about me. Our mother loved both of us."

"And how is it that you know so much about," Tamera paused, "this woman you call our mother."

"I know that when the leaders of your witch coven found out that our mother was going to have twins, they planned to kill the child born last, me. So, she ran away to save both of us."

"How do you know this?" Tamera snapped.

"Our mother told the woman she left me with, my play auntie, the one your assassins killed."

"What exactly did your play auntie tell you?" Tamera said softly.

"She said, our mother felt that the witches were going to catch her, so she hid me with Auntie, and she took you. She had planned to turn herself over to them if she got caught. She didn't think they knew she had delivered twins. However, when they caught her on the roof of this building, they asked her where the other baby was. She knew that they would force her to tell them where I was, so she put you down, went to the edge of the roof, and jumped." Pam waited for a reaction.

"You expect me to believe that?"

"It makes a lot more sense than believing your mother abandoned a perfectly normal baby girl and then killed herself to keep from seeing her again," Pam said. "You have got to be pretty dumb to believe something as ridiculous as that."

"They said, she left because she could not deal with the witchcraft and the ceremonies. Either way I was born first, and I am the rightful queen."

"How do you know you were born first. She could have just told them that. Maybe I am the rightful queen."

"Maybe we should decide right now," Tamera said ominously. "The one who is left alive will be the rightful queen."

"Look genius, if my people find us first, they will get us out of here, then I'll fight you. On the other hand, if your people, what's left of them, find us, they just may bury us deeper in the ground."

"My people will get me out of here. I'll make them," Tamera yelled.

"Yeah, I'm sure you will if you get a chance. You had better hope that my people find us."

"Quiet!" Tamera said. "I hear something. It sounds like heavy equipment."

"It is the bulldozer. The sound is getting louder. Maybe we are close to the surface."

"Let's make some noise," Tamera said politely. "Maybe they will hear us."

"Okay."

"Aaaaaaaaaaaaaa," they screamed.

Chapter 17
The Stakeout

(Thursday 7:15 AM)

A black van stopped in front of Rev. Zackery's brother's house. Walt was watching from the trees, as four men exited the van. All four were dressed in black like Walt, except two of them were only armed with pistols, and they did not have on vests. The two with just pistols went into the house, and the two with flak jackets and semi-automatic weapons went around the house into the woods. Walt was very disappointed that Sibal was not with them. Now, he would have to follow them and hope that they would lead him to her. He used his rifle scope to get a close-up view of their faces. One looked very young. The thought of putting a bullet through his head made Walt sad. That was a new feeling for him. 'Is the thought of killing them causing me to be remorseful,' he thought. "They wouldn't have any remorse killing me," he said to himself.

After fifteen minutes, the two men who had gone into the woods, came back. The other two men had finished up in the house were waiting on the porch.

"We did not find any bodies. There were supposed to be three," the first man that had come from the woods said.

"We didn't find the one that was supposed to be in the house either," said the man closest to him who had been waiting on the porch.

"We better call this in," the first man said pulling his radio from his belt.

When Walt saw the man put his radio to his mouth, Walt turned on the radio he had taken from his dead enemy.

"Ms. Sibal, come in. Ms. Sibal, this is Slim, come in."

"Yeah, this is Sibal, go head," was the reply.

"All the bodies are gone. The one you shot, the one I shot, and our two guys, they are all gone," Slim said. There was a long silence. "What do you want us to do?"

"Send the van and two guards back to my house. Pick you one man to stakeout the house with you. I want to see if anybody comes back to the house. The preacher may have lied to me. Parker and Scott may not have gone back home. They may be still here. They may have taken the bodies. Be very, cautious. Don't let anyone sneak up on you. I'll go to the grave site to see if anybody from there went to get the bodies. You stay there until I send someone to pick you up."

"When will that be?" Slim said impatiently.

"It will be when I send someone to pick you up," Sibal snapped. "Any more questions?"

"No ma'am," Slim said humbly.

Walt made his way to his car. He did not have to follow them now. He knew Sibal was going to the grave site.

Slim picked one of the men to stay with him. The others took the vehicle and left.

"You go to the bedroom window and watch from there. Stay out of sight. I'll watch from the dining room. Hopefully, this won't take too long. Hopefully, nobody will come. However, if somebody does, be prepared to take them out."

"Roger, I'll be ready, sir."

"You appear to be pretty young. Is this your first security assignment?" Slim asked.

"Yes, sir," the young man answered.

"How did you manage to get assigned to security so quickly?"

"Ms. Sibal chose me. Yesterday, we were taking her to her doctor. I was attending to her. I am a paramedic. So, she stopped me, and asked me if I could fight and shoot. I told her, I could. She said she liked how big I am, and that I had first aid training. She said she needed some good men with my skills on her personal security team. Then, today she asked me if I wanted to work for her. I said yes, and here I am."

"I hope she warned you how dangerous working for her can be. We loss two highly trained, experienced, men yesterday. We almost lost a third, me. Like you, it was their first day working for her."

The former paramedic turned and walked toward the bedroom. "Are there any other instructions," he said without looking back.

"After you get in position where you can see, don't move the curtains and don't get too close to the window," Slim said.

CHAPTER 18
WAS LOST BUT NOW FOUND

(Thursday 8:45 AM)

Sibal and two bodyguards got out of a black sedan which had arrived at the site of the mass burial. All the cars that had been left on the night of the fire, were gone now. The bulldozer was gone, too. There was a bobcat with four large tires, pushing the debris of the burned down building into a trench and covering it with dirt.

All the right side of the building had been cleared and buried. Sibal watched as the bobcat made its way toward the place where the trap had been built to kill Pam. She remembered how Pam had reached out her hand for her help, and how instead of saving Pam, she had kicked Pam's foot causing her to fall into the pit of spikes. In her mind, she could see Pam's robe, which Pam had thrown off, floating down over the spikes hiding Pam's body. The half full bucket of the bobcat was stopped when it hit the bed of spikes embedded in concrete. The driver lifted the bucket just in front of the spikes of the trap. When he did, a piece of the metal roof was pushed back, exposing the bed of spikes. The driver emptied the bucket in the pile, and then continued to work around the bed of spikes.

Sibal could see the black robe the Pam had thrown off as she had fallen into the pit, but there was no sign of her body. The robe laid draped over the spikes with some of the longer ones penetrating it. 'How could they have gotten a body out of the pit without removing the robe?' Sibal thought.

When the piece of metal was removed from the pit, the sun light hit the crystal. Pam and Tamera could now see. The sudden brightness was almost blinding for a while. They both shaded their eyes from the direct sunlight and immediately began screaming. However, the sound of their screams was drowned out by the noise of the bobcat.

Sibal and her two bodyguards walked toward two men in black suits. The men turned and faced Sibal's group. One of the men raised his hand in a stop motion. Immediately, the group froze. Then with one finger he pointed at Sibal and signaled for her to come forward. She alone, immediately moved forward. As she got closer, his stern expression became warm.

"Sibal, how are you feeling? Sergio told me that he took you to your house. He said you didn't want to go to the hospital," the man said.

"No. I called my personal doctor. He came to take care of me, and he brought me a car," Sibal said. "But you probably knew that."

"Why would I know that?"

"I figured you would send some more of your people to make sure I was safe," Sibal said.

"Safe? I assigned five guards to protect you. Sergio said you also ask for my paramedic and I gave him to you as well," Richard said. "Did you need more protection than that?"

"No. I just thought I saw a car following me yesterday."

"If someone was following you, it wasn't any of my men. All of my remaining security is here with me," he said suspiciously. "Now, you can keep the van and my men for two weeks, no later. Are you sure you are all right?"

"I'm much better, Richard. Thanks for asking, thanks for the guards, and thanks for not killing me, too," Sibal said.

"It's a good thing you spoke up when you did. If I had not recognized your voice, you would be pushing up daisies, now," Richard said nonchalantly. "I never took you to be vane. Why did you get a face job?"

"Someone tried to kill me with a stick of dynamite. Half my face was blown off. So, since I had to have something done, I picked the face of someone that I felt was attractive and young."

"You took someone's face," Richard said surprisingly.

"She didn't need it anymore."

"I'm sure she didn't," he smirked. "Quick question?" Richard said with a little smile.

"Okay."

"When my men found you in the storm cellar, there were two guards down there with you, who had bullet holes in the back of their heads. You had to have done that, why?" Richard asked.

"They were breathing too much of the air. If I hadn't shot them, we would all be dead," Sibal said. "Wouldn't you have done the same thing."

"Yeah, I guess so," Richard said shaking his head up and down with a little smirk on his face. "Enough small talk. What happened here? This is a big mess. Who did this?"

Sibal turned and watched the bobcat for a few seconds. Then she turned and looked into Richard's eyes. "Did you know that Tamera had a twin sister?"

"What? Are you serious? Tamera had a twin sister."

"Yes. Tamera discovered it herself. The twin was somehow taking some of Tamera's powers. Tamera went to kill her twin, but the twin killed Tamera. Then the twin tried to take control of the coven at the seeding ceremony. We killed her when she tried, but when we did that, her people did this. There were four of them. They trapped us in the barn and then set it on fire. Every important member and practically everyone else in our coven were killed in the fire." Sibal paused. "Yesterday, I got authorization to have agents from the national office, sent to eliminate two of the men who did this. The other two were killed yesterday. One of the guards you loaned to me killed one, and I killed the other one."

"So, you have taken care of everybody responsible?" Richard asked.

"Yes. I got word that one of the teams I sent was successful. That man is dead. I have not heard anything from the other team, yet. I'm sure all went well. They are the best of the best."

"Okay. Keep me informed. When he finishes," Richard said pointing at the bobcat driver, "our work will be done. I'll let the national council know that everything has been resolved. However, I am sure at some point, you will have to come and meet with them," Richard said. "If there is nothing else that you need to tell me, then we are going to start back home."

Sibal thought about the two guards, whose dead bodies had been stolen. "No, that's it," she said.

Richard raised his finger and circled it in the air and whistled loudly. Then Richard, Sergio, the other man in the black suit, and two other armed guards standing nearby, got into the large black sedan. Several other guards, who seemed to appear out of nowhere got into the van and they all drove away. That left only the bobcat driver, Sibal, her two guards, and one person, a thousand yards away, in a tree, with a rifle, with its crosshairs trained on Sibal's head.

The person in the tree was Walt. He had arrived thirty minutes earlier and had finally gotten in position. He was waiting for just the right moment. He needed to wait for the black sedan to go beyond the sound of his rifle shots. His plan was to take out Sibal first. Then, when the guards reacted to her falling, he would take out the slowest guard. The last one would be harder. He would probably locate Walt in the tree and take cover, most likely, behind the sedan. Therefore, he decided he would leave the tree after the second kill. He watched as the motorcade disappeared through the trees. Then he remembered the bobcat driver. He remembered him because he had driven his bobcat in front of Sibal and cut the engine off. He no longer had a clear shot. In his past life, life before Zackery, he wouldn't have given a second thought about killing the bobcat driver. Now, after meeting Rev. Zackery, and wanting to go to be with Pam in heaven, he decided to wait, hesitate. 'Hesitation always means trouble,' Walt thought.

"I hope I won't have to kill you, dude," Walt said to himself. "I'd hate to have to explain it to Rev. Zackery."

Inside the crystal, Pam and Tamera were resting from all the screaming they had been doing, when they realized that the noise of the bobcat motor had stopped. Immediately, they tried to scream again. Unfortunately, their voices were screamed out. They could barely hear each other, and they were both exhausted.

"I can't drive over those spikes with my tires," the bobcat driver said to Sibal. "All I can do is possibly catch it at the bottom of the concrete and turn it over, so that the spikes will be facing the ground. Then I can push the spikes in the ground."

Sibal looked at the newly cleared area. In the middle, was a square slab of concrete, with sharp steel spikes of different lengths protruding from it, and in the middle of the spikes was a partially burned black robe lying on the spikes.

Walt watched helplessly as Sibal moved along side of the bobcat toward the spikes, the bobcat blocking his opportunity for a shot at Sibal.

Walt turned his attention to the spikes as well. He also remembered the last time he saw Pam alive. The loft door closed as Pam was falling onto the bed spikes. "Where is her body," he said to himself softly. Then, he heard it again, the sound of Pam screaming. It was very faint, yet he was sure, well almost sure, it was her, or someone, screaming. He focused the sights of his rifle closer in on the spikes. He could see something in between the spikes. He couldn't make it out. As he focused closer. Then, he saw a hand reach between the spikes and pick up what he had been trying to see. It was Sibal's hand. She had removed the burned black robe and was holding something in her hand. Walt refocused, and he could see it. It was a round glass ball. Quickly, Sibal wrapped the black robe around the glass ball. Then before he realized what was happening, the black sedan pulled up beside the bobcat, Sibal got in, and the car drove past Walt. The sound of the screaming grew louder as the car approached his position. When the car passed him and drove away, the screams faded until he could no longer hear them.

Inside the crystal, Pam and Tamera stopped screaming. They were in the dark again. They knew they were not in the barn rubble anymore. They knew that someone had found the crystal. They could hear the car motor, but they could hear nothing else. They listened for several minutes hoping to hear something that would give them some indication who had them. Finally, Tamera whispered. "Did you see her?"

"Yes," Pam whispered back.

"Well, is she one of your people?"

"No! Since you asked, I assume that she is not one of yours either," Pam said.

"Never seen her before," Tamera said sadly.

"This could be tricky," Pam said. "Did you move when she looked at us?"

"No. Did you?"

"No," Pam said. "We don't want to scare her. She might throw the crystal out the window. How do you want to play this?"

"I could push her and make her take the crystal to one of my people," Tamera said.

"One of your people?" Pam said indignantly. "Like who?"

"I could have her take it to Dutchman."

"No. That won't work. He's dead," Pam said. "Jason killed him."

"Him again," Tamera said angrily. "Okay, I'll have her take it to one of the members of the head council."

"Dead," Pam said. "They all burned up in the fire."

"What about Sibal?"

"She was in the barn when it burned down," Pam said.

"So, you killed all my people," Tamera said angrily.

"Pretty much. All your people were trying to kill me," Pam responded equally as angrily. "I guess they, and you should have left me alone."

They both stopped talking. The only thing that could be heard was the car engine and the sound of their heavy angry breathing.

CHAPTER 19
SLIM CHANCES

(Thursday 10:00 AM)

A black van turned off the highway and came down the driveway slowly. Slim and the young paramedic watched intently as it came to a stop about thirty feet from the front door.

"This is Slim at the stakeout. Ms. Sibal, come in, Ms. Sibal come in, come in," Slim said into his radio.

There was only static.

In the car, several miles away, Sibal heard the first few words that Slim had said before she hurriedly turned down the volume on her radio. What she had heard was, "This is Slim at the stake out. Ms. Si…"

"Hold up, Slim. Give me a minute," Sibal said looking down at the crystal, wondering if her two captives in the crystal could hear at all, but more importantly, if they had heard him say her name. Sibal continued to hold the speak button down on the radio as she told her driver to pull over. When he did, she got out with her radio. "Okay, go ahead," she said and released the speak button.

"Ms. Sibal come in. Ms. Sibal," Slim said almost pleadingly,

"What do you want?" Sibal shouted angrily.

"A black van just pulled up at the house. It is just sitting there with the motor running. I was calling to see if you sent it to get us."

"A black van. No, I didn't send it, and they are not Richard's men. They must be the ones who took the bodies," Sibal said.

"What are your orders?" Slim asked.

"If they get out. Find out who they are and tell them to stay put until we get there. We are on our way. ETA thirty minutes," Sibal said as she jumped into the sedan.

At the mass grave site, Walt was standing next to the concrete slab. He had just picked up a small piece of the black robe Pam had worn the night she was killed. He noted that there were no bloodstains on it. That's when he heard the conversation on the radio he had taken from the dead guard.

"So, you will be back to the house in thirty minutes," Walt said aloud. "I'll be there waiting on you." He immediately began running to his car.

"You ready, in there," Slim said just loud enough for his companion in the bedroom to hear.

"Yeah," he answered. "What do you want me to do?"

"Follow my lead," Slim said. "If I shoot, you shoot. Shoot to kill. I see two men in the front seat. I'll take the one on the right, you take the one on the left. Don't let the van leave. Take out the tires if it tries to leave."

"The driver is getting out," the former paramedic said.

"Ms. Sibal said if they get out of the van, to find out who it is, so that's what I'm going to do. Hold your fire for now but be ready. Ms. Sibal and her bodyguards are on the way. We are to keep them here till she gets here," Slim said moving back from the window, while aiming his pistol at the van driver.

"He is moving this way."

"Hey, you, by the van," Slim yelled. "Who are you and what do you want?"

"We are looking for Rev. Zackery. We work for the construction company that did the repairs on his church," the van driver said. "Is he available?"

"No, but he will be here in a few minutes. Just wait right where you are. He just called. He is on his way," Slim said.

"We just tried to call. His phone is out of service," the driver said repeating the words that were whispered to him from inside the van. "We'll come back later." The driver repeated once more the words he heard as he turned to get back in the van.

"I said stay where you are," Slim shouted.

A curtain in the bedroom moved slightly as the guard in the bedroom placed his pistol on the window ceil and aimed it at the passenger on the front seat. The former paramedic had made a fatal mistake. He revealed his position. The person in the back of the van placed the sights of his M16 rifle slightly above the window ceil where the pistol was.

"Hurry up. Get back in the truck," the voice whispered.

The driver made a dash to get in the open door of the van. As soon as he moved, several shots rang out from the house. The driver fell to the ground as shots penetrated the windshield on the passenger side of the van striking the dead body that was securely duct taped to seat. There were also bulletproof vests taped to the back of the seat. Immediately, after the firing started, three shots were fired by the person kneeling behind bulletproof vests taped to the seat in the van. His shots went through the bedroom window slightly above and slightly below the window ceil. When the shooting ended, the former paramedic was holding his neck as he lay against the wall of the bedroom.

"Are you all right in there," Slim shouted. There was no response. Slim carefully watched the van for several minutes. He saw no movement. "Hey youngblood, are you hurt? If you are alive, make some noise." There was nothing. Slim ran to the bedroom and confirmed his worse fear. His young partner was sitting against the wall with the saddest expression on his face. "You were so proud to be chosen as a guard. That proud look is gone now."

Slim said as he walked over to him, laid him on the floor, closed his mouth and his eyes. Then he looked out the window at the van. It was still the same, no movement, just the sound of the engine running. The sound of the engine was getting on his nerves.

While Walt was hiding his car in the woods near Rev. Zackery's house, he had heard all the shooting. He found a good position to see the front yard and to shoot Sibal if she went inside the house. However, he had no idea what had just happened. So, he just watched and waited.

Slim went to the front door and pulled it open. He peeped out for a second. Then he slowly walked out with his pistol aimed at the bloody face of the person who was still sitting on the passenger side of the van. Slim shot him one last time to make sure there was no life left in him. Then he ducked down in front of the van. Then looked cautiously over the dash and saw that it was a cargo van with no seats in the back. Confident that it was safe he went around the door, laid his pistol on the driver's seat, and reached inside to turn off the ignition. When he turned the key, he saw movement and heard a voice.

"Don't do it," the voice said from the behind the seat where the dead man was sitting.

Slim didn't want to, and he knew he should not have, yet he did it anyway. He grabbed his pistol and tried to bring it up to take a shot. He only succeeded in seeing the person who ended his life. Before Slim hit the ground, the man inside the van, quickly opened the side door and made a dash for the trees. He was surprised that he hadn't heard any shots, as he knelt down behind a tree. He peeped around the tree at the house, not noticing the figure coming up behind him.

Walt got behind a tree and aimed his rifle at the man he had seen shoot one of Sibal's men.

"Don't do it," Walt said threateningly.

The man froze, dropped his weapon, and raised his hands.

"Somebody once said, the enemy of my enemy is my friend," Walt said. "Why did you and your men kill those men."

"They were not my men," the man said. "Those men in the van were sent to kill me. They failed, I killed one, captured the other one and I made him bring me down here. I figured if someone was sent to kill me, then someone might come to kill my friend who lives here. I guess I'm too late." Jason turned his head halfway back toward the voice behind him. Jason could only see a head buried in the sights of a semi-automatic weapon and an arm covered by a black shirt that looked exactly like the shirt the men in the house were wearing.

"You know Rev. Zackery?" Walt said.

"Yes, I knew him. He is, more than likely dead, now," Jason said turning his upper body slowly around.

"No. He's safe, Jason. It is Jason, isn't it" Walt said.

"Yeah. Can I turn around?" Jason said as he put his hand on the pistol stuck in his belt.

"Yeah, but first take that pistol and throw it away from you," Walt warned. "I'd hate to have to tell Rev. Zackery that I killed you for being stupid."

Jason threw the pistol on the ground. "I have a question? Why do you have on the same uniform as those men in the house?"

"Slim! We have arrived. What is your status?" a female voice said in a low volume on the radio on Walt's belt.

"I guess the same reason you are wearing the uniform of the people who were trying to kill you," Walt said. "That person, you just heard on the radio came here with her men, to kill Rev. Zackery. They were also looking for you and Dave. They failed, but we will have to talk about that later. She is back, and I'm going to kill her."

"Walt! It's you!" Jason said relieved.

"Pick up your guns and get in position. She may have a small army."

"Slim! Come in! Slim!" the radio said.

"Who is that?" Jason asked.

"It's Sibal."

"How?" Jason said.

"It was the Lord's will."

"What?" Jason said louder than he had planned.

"Rev. Zackery told me that the Lord had chosen to use me. God has given me the task of making the world a better safer place by putting a bullet in Sibal's head."

"One of her men is coming toward the van," Jason said.

"Don't shoot," Walt said quickly. "I want Sibal. The rest don't count."

The man had simi-automatic rifle waist level as he slowly walked up to Slim. "Slim," he said. There was a loud feedback noise on Slim's radio, Sibal's and Walt's, too. The guard reached down and turned Slim's radio off. "Slim is dead, ma'am. I'm going to check the other body," Walt's radio said softly.

The man checked the wallet of the dead van driver. "Ma'am, he's from enforcement, our Chicago district. This is the two-man team they sent in Chicago. They are both dead."

"Okay. Get back to the car," the female voice said.

"She's not going to come," Walt moaned.

"And she knows I'm here, and I killed the men she sent to kill me," Jason said. "I guess I messed up your plan."

Walt held up his hand, put his finger to his lips, and then waved for Jason to follow him. Quietly and quickly, they moved through the trees to the side of the house. "I didn't feel comfortable there, especially since my radio made that noise," Walt said. "We need to get back to the hotel and check on Rev. Zackery."

"Did you save his life, too," Jason said.

"No, I didn't save his life, it was his God. Sibal shot him four times, twice in the chest and twice in the back. I had given him the vest he was wearing, but the miracle was she didn't shoot him in the head."

"Rev. Zackery is one..." Jason stopped speaking when he saw a black sedan speed down the driveway and stop behind the van. Two men jumped out. They both had automatic weapons with bipods. One setup on the hood. The other setup on the trunk. They both immediately began firing in the general area where Walt and Jason had been. After they had swept the area in front of them, then they picked up their weapons, holding them at waist level, and moved out from the car in opposite direction and toward the trees, spraying the same area with bullets from two different directions. The trees and brushes were riddled with bullets, as the sedan backed out to the end of the driveway. The men had reloaded for at least the fourth time, when Walt tapped Jason on his shoulder. Jason was on one knee and Walt was standing behind him. Both of their rifles were propped against the house.

"Three, two, one," Walt counted. They shot at the same time. The men, firing the automatic weapons were each hit in the head. They fell together. Even though they had died instantly, their fingers became frozen to the triggers, and their weapons continue to fire until there were no more rounds to fire.

The sedan that had been at the end of the driveway, quickly backed out onto the highway and sped away.

"That van still works, doesn't it?" Walt asked.

"Yeah, the motor was still running after the shootout, and the tires were not hit, so it should be good," Jason replied.

"Let's get all those bodies and those automatics weapons in the van before someone else comes."

"We will take them to the mass grave site and bury them. Then I'll take you to Rev. Zackery," Walt said moving cautious to the front door of the house. Jason followed. They were on opposite sides of the front door, ready to enter when it happened.

"Hey, I know you are listening," the voice from the radio said.

Walt and Jason went through the door quickly.

"I knew I should have ripped your balls off when I had the chance," the female voice said.

Walt turned the volume up on his radio and sat it on the dining room table. Then he and Jason began to move throughout the house together checking everywhere.

"I under-estimated your power. Your desire for revenge has destroyed almost everything and everybody that was important to me. However, as you see, I am still alive," the voice said.

Walt and Jason found the body of the young paramedic lying on the rug in the bedroom.

"I have to commend you. You killed the team I sent to Chicago. You either have skills, or you are the luckiest man in the world," the voice said.

They continued to search the house. Then they returned to the bedroom. They dragged the rug with the body on it down the hall, out the door, toward the van.

"You are a lot luckier than that friend of yours, David Parker," the voice chuckled.

Jason dropped the corner of the rug he had been holding and ran back into the house. Walt followed.

"The team I sent for him completed their mission. Mmmmmm, their report says, they shot him full of drugs, broke his neck, and threw him down a flight of steps."

Jason and Walt stood at the dining room table looking at the radio. Tears began to roll out of Jason's fiery eyes. The hate radiated out of Jason's head, as he took the radio from the table.

"I should have killed you when I had the chance, and you should have died in the fire, but since you didn't, I want you to know, this," Jason said ominously. "When we meet again, and it won't be long, I'm going to make you wish you had died."

"Jason, Jason, calm down. You're going to bust a blood vessel and spoil our reunion," Sibal said. "Oh yeah, you can't imagine who I have with me. I can't imagine why they are so quiet now. They have been screaming in my ear all afternoon. Say hello, girls."

In the car on the side of the highway, Sibal put the radio up to the crystal ball which she had put on the black robe on the seat beside her. Pam and Tamera just looked at Sibal.

"Pam, if you want to get out of there, you had better say something to your boyfriend," Sibal said.

"Jason," Pam screamed. "Don't trust her and don't turn your back on her."

The robe was thrown over the crystal.

"Was that voice familiar," Sibal said. "We will talk again at five o'clock. At that time, I'll tell you when and where I want you to meet me, over and out."

Jason and Walt couldn't believe what they had heard. Was it a trick or was it really Pam that they had heard?

"She must be in the crystal," Jason said, "with Tamera."

"She's alive!" Walt shouted as tears of joy filled his eyes.

"For now," Jason said.

Chapter 20
In the Wrong Hands

(Thursday 12:30 PM)

Pam and Tamera are inside the crystal on the front passenger seat of the black sedan. It is mostly dark because the black robe is covering the crystal. However, there is a little light coming in from the bottom of the seat where the robe is not completely covering the crystal. Pam and Tamera can now distinguish each other's features and attire. Tamera is wearing a black hooded robe, with flat black shoes, and Pam is wearing military fatigues, a flak jacket, and black combat boots.

"I thought you said you didn't know this person," Tamera said. "She knows you and your boyfriend."

"I don't know everybody that knows me," Pam snapped. "I was on the stage in front of three or four hundred people. She probably saw me at the ceremony, and she doesn't know what she is talking about. Jason is not my boyfriend, he's just a friend."

"She knows Jason and they have history. You could tell they hate each other. So, what is she up to? She evidently wants to allow him to get us out of this crystal ball," Tamera surmised. "But what is she getting in the deal?"

"You," Pam said. "She is one of your people."

"One of mine," Tamera said happily. "I'll make her get me out of here. We don't need him."

"You need to let Jason get us out. She might screw it up."

"Shut up," Tamera ordered. "I'm getting out of here, now. Aaaaaaaaaaaaaaaaaa," she screamed.

They could hear the car come to a stop. Then suddenly the black robe was removed from above the crystal. They could see Sibal clearly as she picked up the crystal and held it close to her face.

"If you don't stop all that screaming in my ear, I'm going to throw you both down in a well so deep nobody will ever find you," Sibal screamed. "Did you hear that?"

Tamera and Pam silently shook their heads 'yes.'

Sibal wrapped the crystal in the black robe and threw it in the trunk of the sedan.

Tamera and Pam, however, were not in the total darkness because the crystal had rolled out from beneath the robe and there was a little light coming into the trunk where the taillights were.

"I know that voice," Tamera said.

"I still think our best chance is to let Jason get us out," Pam said.

"You just told me how much he hates me for sending Dutchman to kill his grandmother," Tamera said. "And, you said he won't be satisfied until one of us is dead. Well, that one is not going to be me. The first thing that I am going to do when I get out of here is kill him."

"I don't think so," Pam said. "Like I said, Jason is my friend. You are going to have to go through me first."

"Like that's going to be a problem," Tamera snarled.

"Look! We need to come to an agreement," Pam pleaded. "When we get out, you leave us alone, and we'll leave you alone."

"He's got to pay for putting me in here."

"Before you go and say too much," Pam said calmly. "Why don't we just get out of here, first. Then, we can handle any and everything that needs to be handled."

"I agree, sister dear," Tamera said. "Now, I'm going to get some sleep. I need my rest and my strength. Wake me up if anything interesting happens."

CHAPTER 21
QUESTIONING MY LIFE

(Thursday 1:00 PM)

Dave had been sitting alone in the interrogation room at the police office for at least an hour when the door opened. Two police detectives walked in. One had on a navy-blue blazer with a detective badge on the front pocket. He was middle aged, in his fifties, tall, around six feet, and weighted around two hundred and thirty pounds. He had an angry expression. He immediately sat down at the table in front of Dave. He dropped a folder on the table and they both looked at it.

The other man was younger, in his thirties, around five feet nine inches, and very muscular. He was wearing a white shirt, his muscles sculpturing the shirt. He had a shoulder holster with what appeared to be a thirty-eight-caliber pistol. He was standing next to the table constantly staring at Dave.

No one spoke for five minutes. The detectives seemed to be waiting for Dave to say something. Dave refused to be the first to speak. Finally, the detective sitting in front of Dave spoke.

"Mr. Parker, looks like you have spent time with us before." Dave did not respond. "You were arrested for assault with a deadly weapon and battery, hitting your wife." Dave did not respond. "You were locked up and while you were in jail, you got into a fight and put an inmate in the infirmary." Dave did not respond. "Do you have anything to say about this," the detective said.

"Could I have your names, please?" Dave asked politely.

"I am detective Johns, and this is detective Lemons," he said.

"I shot a hole in my bedroom wall when saw a man about to have sex with my wife in my bedroom, in my bed. So, yes, I assaulted my wall. As for the charge of battery, I never hit my wife. She lied. Those charges were dropped. Last, but not least, your jailer put this man in my cell to force me have oral sex with him. I didn't comply," Dave said. "I defended myself. No charges were filed." The two detectives looked at each other. "Why am I here, detective Johns?"

"Last night, the man you caught in your home, Charles Norris, was found dead in your home. It appears that he let himself in, took drugs, fell down the stairs and broke his neck."

Dave looked sternly from one detective to the other.

"We checked out the statement you gave concerning your whereabouts last night. You have a perfect alibi," detective Johns said.

"Too, perfect," detective Lemons said. "You were with one of our officers and your wife in your hotel room at the time of death. Why were the three of you in your hotel room at one o'clock in the morning, especially since your wife had a restraining order against you."

"Sargent Pender told me about this club," Dave said. "I met him there. We came back to the hotel, and she was there. She wanted to talk about the divorce terms. She said it was very important to her, to come to an agreement before we got to mediation. So, Sargent Pender agreed to stay there while we talked."

"Then after talking to you wife," Johns said, "you asked our officer to escort your wife home where they conveniently found the body."

"Are you saying that you think I had something to do with his death?" Dave said. "I thought you said it was an accident."

"Everything points to accidental death brought on by drugs, except one thing," detective Lemons said and waited for a reaction from Dave.

"What?" Dave asked.

"Your neighbor Mrs. Simmons said she saw two men in black on her street earlier that night. She also said that your wife and officer Pender were at the house forty-five minutes before the ambulance and police arrived," Lemons said.

"So, you think I hired someone to kill him?" Dave asked.

"No. He was in jail until late yesterday afternoon. No one would have known he would be out. They probably came to kill someone else," Johns said.

"Me!" Dave said convincingly.

"You? We were thinking your wife," Johns said.

"Is there anyone that you know of that would want your wife dead?" Lemons said.

"No," Dave said looking down at the table.

"You stand to lose a lot, your house, car, money in alimony, if your wife wins big in the divorce, Mr. Parker," detective Lemons said.

"And you would gain a lot if she were to die," detective Johns said. "A cheating wife is motive for murder, or should I say hiring someone to murder your wife."

"I have already told my attorney to let her have the house and the car. I was fired yesterday, so I don't think she is going to be able to get much alimony," Dave explained. "Plus, I realize that my wife never loved me. I just want to get this marriage behind me. I want to get on with my life. I've wasted too much of my life already. When you work hard to give your wife everything she wants, and you try your best to make her feel loved and appreciated and then you find out that she has been bringing another man into your house and having sex with him in your bed, it made me angry. Wouldn't you be? Then I realized that it was my fault. I thought I could make her love me. Now, I know. You can't make a person love you if they don't. She doesn't love me. She doesn't want me. In fact, she just might hate me. I just want to move on. I do not want my wife dead. I wish her the best." Dave looked them both in the eyes then he looked at his watch. "Look, gentlemen, I need to be across the street at the courthouse in ten minutes, to find out if my wife is going to accept my offer or if she is going to contest the divorce. So, am I being arrested?"

"No sir," Johns said. "Just because your neighbor thought she saw someone, doesn't mean they had anything to do with the death. All the evidence points toward a drug induced accidental death. Thank you for coming in and we are sorry for any inconvenience it may have caused."

"I was glad to help," Dave said as he rushed out of the office. He ran down the steps of the police station, dodged cars as he crossed the street, and ran up the stairs of the courthouse. Suddenly, Dave had an urge to pee. He rushed in the men's room and sang his "I Peed a River" song. When he went into the courtroom, everyone else was already there. His lawyer, Carol, Carol's lawyer, and the judge all watched as Dave came down the aisle.

"I thought we were going to have to conclude this procedure without you, Mr. Parker," the judge said.

"I'm sorry Your Honor," Dave said, "but the police kept me longer than I expected."

"Well, Mrs. Parker has agreed to your offer," the female judge said. "You will quit deed the house over to her, sign over the Mercedes to her, and pay her a lump sum of twenty-five thousand dollars. She has agreed not contest the divorce and forfeit all rights to alimony. All I need for you both to do is sign the papers, and Mr. Parker, your petition for divorce will be granted. Also, the restraining order has been rescinded. Congratulations to you both."

The clerk had Carol and Dave sign the paper, then he took them to the judge. The judge checked the signatures and struck the gavel. "Court dismissed."

Minutes later Dave, Carol, and the two attorneys walked out of the courtroom. To Dave's surprise, Calvin was waiting in the lobby. Dave smiled, held up his divorce papers and walked toward him. However, before he could speak, Carol ran into Calvin's arms. They embraced warmly and then kissed for a long time. Dave walked pass them and was about to walk out of the building when he looked back at them. Their lips separated and they both turned and looked at him. Calvin had an apologetic expression. Carol had an expression of contempt.

Dave walked out of the building and looked up into the sky. "Thank You, Jesus," he said loudly. Then he walked to the parking lot and got in the certified used car he had just bought with the money from his severance check. Subtracting the twenty-five thousand he had to pay Carol, and then the nine thousand he paid for the car, he only had six thousand left. "Thank You, Jesus," Dave said looking up again. "Lord, I am so glad I lied and told Calvin that I had received twenty-five thousand in my severance package. Carol thought she took it all. Lord, I thank You for getting me out of that marriage and I thank You for this car, which I like very much, and I pray that Jason and Rev. Zackery are safe. I hope that the people who killed the insurance man were not sent to kill me. In Jesus name, I'm outta here."

CHAPTER 22
KEEPING THE FAITH

(Thursday 2:30 PM)

Walt knocked on the hotel door, in the rhythm, one two, one one two three. Rev. Zackery opened the door. Joy flooded Rev. Zackery's heart when he saw Jason. Walt pushed the hugging men into the room and closed the door.

"I am so glad to see you, Jason," Rev. Zackery said. "The Lord has answered my prayer."

"I'm glad to see you, reverend. Sibal sent some men to kill me, so I was worried that she would try to kill you, too."

"Yeah, she did, and she almost succeeded. If it hadn't been for Walt and the Lord, I would not be here today," Rev. Zackery said. "I just hope Dave is okay." Walt and Jason looked at each other. "What is it? You heard something about Dave."

"Rev. Zackery, when we were at the house, we had a shootout with Sibal and her men. We killed all of them, however, Sibal got away, but she called us on a radio we had taken from one of her men, and she said that she had Pam trapped in the crystal ball," Walt explained.

"Pam is alive," Rev. Zackery said in relief. "Praise God."

"Sibal also said the men she sent to kill Dave were successful. She said he was dead," Jason said.

"I've been praying for Dave, just like I have been praying for you," Rev. Zackery said defiantly. "I just don't believe he's dead. Maybe, he's just injured. Maybe he's in the hospital. I can't accept that. The Lord told me He would protect all of us. The Lord said it, I believe it, and that settles it."

"I'm with you Rev. Zackery," Walt said. "I don't believe anything that comes out of Sibal's mouth."

"There is another reason I don't believe Dave is dead," Rev. Zackery said.

"What's the reason?" Jason asked.

"I had this vision of the future," Rev. Zackery said. "In it I saw all of us in us in my church at Miss Mammie's funeral. Me, you, Pam, Dave, and Walt, we were all there."

"So, you had a dream," Jason said.

"Well, actually, the demon showed me this vision."

"And you believe it is really going to happen," Jason said incredulously. "If there is one religious thing I know, it is this, demons are not prophets," Jason said,

"I know that demons are not prophets, but I also know that God uses demons to achieve His will. You act like you have forgotten that a demon showed me the burning barn before it happened and that same demon showed you that same barn and how to get to it," Rev. Zackery countered.

"I need to rest," Jason said. "Digging a grave for six people was hard work. Plus, I haven't had but about two hours of sleep in the last twenty-four hours."

"Yeah, you better get some rest, cause we need to leave this motel today," Walt said. "I'm sure Sibal has somebody looking for us. I just don't know where we can go."

"While I was praying the Lord revealed a place where we would be safe," Rev. Zackery said.

"Okay," Jason said as he laid across the bed. "Wake me up when it's time to go."

Chapter 23
A New Alliance

(Thursday, 4:00 PM)

Sibal had been to her home. She had showered, changed clothes, and had come to her office building. She drove up to her reserved parking space on the side of a strip mall where her business was located. Three large letters, SPS were on the wall above the door. She walked to the door with a silver-colored metal briefcase in her hand and saw the sign inside the door had been flipped to 'closed.' She unlocked the door, walked into the building, and then went back to her office. When she opened her office door, she saw her assistant, Howard, at her desk, arranging his pictures and desk paraphernalia.

"You didn't waste any time, I see," Sibal said.

"Boss!" he said as he froze. "They told me you were," he paused, "had been killed in the fire."

"Is that my stuff in that box," Sibal snapped.

"I'll put everything back exactly as you had it."

"I'm sure you will, but there is something I want you to do first," Sibal said.

"What do you want, boss?"

"I have a debt to repay," Sibal said rubbing the stitches below her ear. "I need to blow somebody up. Get me enough dynamite so that the explosion won't leave any body parts, not even a finger." Sibal walked to a large combination safe in the corner of her office, sat the briefcase on top it. She opened the safe, and then the briefcase. She surprised Tamera and Pam when the light hit the crystal. Before they had a chance to react, Sibal picked up the crystal, lifted it up to her face to make sure Tamera and Pam were still there, placed it in the safe, and closed the door.

"Okay, boss," Howard said looking down not wanting Sibal to know he had seen the two figures inside the crystal. "Anything else?"

"Get a metal case a little bigger than mine. It needs to be soundproof. Hide the dynamite in that metal, soundproof, case, leaving a space in the middle for something the size of a softball. I want a remote-control detonator, and I'm going to need a location where I can safely detonate the dynamite that is not far from the blast site, a place that has a wall I can hide behind or a place near a cliff I can throw the case over and blow it up."

"Okay, boss. I'm on it," Howard said as he pushed everything on Sibal's desk into an empty box and quickly walked out.

Sibal went to her phone and dialed.

"Hello," the voice answered.

"Richard?"

"Yeah Sibal, what's up."

"I've got some bad news," she said.

"What is it?" he said anxiously.

Those guards you let me borrow," she said softly, "they are dead."

"All of them?" Richard screamed.

"Yes," Sibal said

"How in hell did that happen?"

"We were ambushed."

"Ambushed? Who ambushed you?" Richard asked. "Those were some of my best guards."

"It was a drug gang," she said. "It seems that one of the members of our coven got a large amount of cocaine from a local drug dealer and failed to pay for them. That member was killed in the fire. The car I was driving belonged to him. Remember I told you, I thought I had seen someone following me, yesterday. Anyway, it turned out to be the drug dealers. They ambushed us, believing I was him. I'm so sorry."

"How did you get away?"

"Your guards sacrificed themselves so I could escape."

"Like I said they were good men," Richard said. "Where are their bodies?"

"They are gone," Sibal said sadly. "The drug dealers must have taken them."

Richard took a deep breath and blew it out in the phone. "I should have buried you with the others. Goodbye, Sibal."

"Bye," Sibal said to a dial tone.

Inside the crystal, in the safe, Pam clicked her lighter. She and Tamera could see vaguely some of the things around them on the shelf where the crystal was. There were stacks of money on one side and a pistol on the other. Pam flipped the cover on the lighter and they were in the dark again.

"Okay, this is what we know, Pam said. "This person…"

"It's Sibal."

"What?" Pam said.

"We are in Sibal's safe, in Sibal's office," Tamera said. "It has to be her. So why isn't she talking to me?"

"Maybe, she's afraid you are going to kill her when you get out," Pam said. "You know you don't have the sweetest disposition in town."

"I wasn't going to kill her before," Tamera said. "But now she is toast."

"See what I mean," Pam said. "You and Jason are just alike. You both need anger management therapy."

"I'm not like him," Tamera shouted.

"Right now, we don't know what Sibal is planning. So, Jason may be our only hope to get out of this crystal," Pam said, "and you are planning to kill him as soon as you get out. He is risking his life. It's very probable that Sibal is going to try to kill him even before he gets us out. She hates him as much as you do. Maybe you should show a little gratitude. Cut him some slack, Jack."

"I'll cut him some slack all right," Tamera snarled

"We need to come to an agreement, now," Pam demanded.

"Or else what?"

"Or else, one of us dies right now," Pam said clicking the lighter and letting it fall to the bottom of the crystal. They faced each other, their noses only inches apart. The light from below cast eerie shadows on their faces. "Go ahead, make your move." Pam waited. "What are you waiting on?" Pam waited again. "Okay, I'll count down from five, then I'll make my move. Five, four, three…"

"If you are dead, then Jason will never try to get me out," Tamera said, "and if I am dead, Sibal will kill Jason and bury you. I lose either way. Okay, I'm willing to come to an agreement. What do you want, as if I didn't already know?"

"We get out, you and your people go your way and me and my people go ours. You leave us alone and we leave you alone, forever," Pam said. "That the agreement."

"All right, I agree," Tamera.

"Good, now let's get ready to get out of here," Pam said picking up the lighter and closing it.

"Aren't you forgetting something sister dear," Tamera said.

"What?"

"Pinky swear," Tamera said.

Pam clicked the lighter and stuck out her pinky finger and hooked Tamera's. "Picky swear?" Pam asked.

"Pinky swear," Tamera answered. "Okay what do we need to do."

"Jason will have to break into the crystal. When he does, he will have to be anchored to something that can pull him and us back out. My guess is he will be tied to something. Once he comes in, we need to move fast. He may just be halfway in, so we need to catch hold of him tightly and climb out as quickly as possible and if he is not already out, we need to pull him out. Then you will have to make sure Sibal doesn't do anything crazy."

"And you make sure Jason doesn't do anything crazy," Tamera said.

"I'll take care of..." Pam stopped speaking as the light appeared through the opening safe door. Tamera and Pam could see a man's image. He grabbed the crystal and lifted it up to his face. Pam raised one of her hands to cover her face. Tamera stood facing the man.

"Howard, I'm Tamera. I'm your queen. You must make sure I'm safe. I'm trapped in this crystal. You must..." Tamera stopped speaking because Howard had suddenly put the crystal back in the safe and picked up a stack of money.

"What are you doing in that safe," Tamera and Pam heard Sibal say just before the door closed.

Howard closed the safe and turned around. "I knew that we were going to need some guards, so I took the liberty of hiring some," Howard said. "I got you ten, trained, military contractors who will be here tomorrow morning. I have got to wire them their down payment. That's why I was getting the money."

"Good work," Sibal said. "But don't go in the safe again, unless you get my permission."

"Okay, boss," Howard said as he left the room with his eyes bulging.

Chapter 24
An Empty Home

(Thursday 4:20 PM)

Dave turned into the driveway and drove slowly toward Rev. Zackery's brother's house. He stopped his car almost at the porch, got out, and quickly and went to the door. He noticed that there were more bullet holes in the door and walls than he had remembered. The door frame was busted from a kick-in and there were blood stains on the door sill. He pulled the long-barrowed pistol from the back of his pants and pushed the door open slowly fearing what he might find. He searched the house and was glad that he did not find any bodies, even though he did find several spots of blood. He picked up the telephone. There was no dial tone. He expected that because he had tried to call Rev. Zackery many times.

He walked around house to check for bodies. That's when he noticed the cut telephone wire. He reconnected the wires and went back to check the phone for a dial tone. However, before he could get inside, the phone rang.

"Hello," Dave said.

"Hey, is this Rev. Zackery?" the voice said.

"No. He's not here at the moment," Dave said. "Can I take a message?"

"This is J. Jones, the contractor at the church. I am calling because Rev. Zackery was supposed to meet me at the church this afternoon. Do you know if he is still coming? I have been calling all day and this is the first time I was able to get through. All the other times, I got a temporarily out of service message."

"There was a wiring problem," Dave said.

"Do you know if he is coming?"

"As far as I know, he hasn't changed his mind. My name is Dave. I'm a close friend of his. I can meet you at the church just in case he is delayed and if you want, I can relay any information to him."

"Well okay, but he was supposed to inspect the work and let me know if anything else was needed."

"It has only been a couple of minutes before you called, that the phone line was repaired, so Rev. Zackery could already be in route there, now," Dave said. "Either way, I'll be there shortly. By the way, what is the quickest way there from here?"

Chapter 25
A New Deal

(Thursday 4:45 PM)

Earlier, they had left the motel without checking out at the front desk. Walt knew that Pam had paid for her room till Monday morning. He wanted to be able to come back, if necessary, even though he felt it would be unsafe. Now they were driving down the highway on the way to their unrevealed destination.

"Where are we going, Reverend," Jason said from the back seat as he loaded bullets in the ammo clips for the M16 rifles and the Glock 9M.

"It's almost time for the call," Walt said. "We better pull over somewhere so we can hear and take notes."

"There's a road up there, it leads to a fishing pond. We can take the call there," Rev. Zackery said.

Walt turned down the road, stopped and backed into a grassy area between some trees. The shade was nice and there was a cool breeze.

"Y'all know that this is a trap that she is setting for me," Jason said. "Sibal doesn't care anything about Tamera. She only cares about herself. All she wants to do is kill me. She thinks both of you are dead already. So, this so-called trade is just a trick to get me and the crystal somewhere so she can get rid of me, Pam, and Tamera."

"You are right," Walt said. "Sibal was glad when she thought Tamera was dead. With Tamera being dead, she had become one of the most powerful persons in the coven. If Tamera comes back, Sibal will return to being

Tamera's servant, and if Tamera finds out that Sibal tried to kill her, Sibal's life will be over, two seconds later. So, you can believe this, if Sibal gets the chance, she will put the crystal in a place where nobody will ever be able to find it again. Pam will be trapped forever."

"I never thought I would say this, but her hate for you, Jason is a good thing for us," Rev. Zackery said. "It is the only reason she hasn't gotten rid of the crystal already."

"We have got to save Pam," Walt shouted. "The next time I see Sibal, I'm going to put a bullet in the middle of her head right between her eyes."

"We need to locate the crystal first," Jason said.

"We need to get Pam out first," Rev. Zackery.

"If Pam gets out, then Tamera will get out, too," Walt said.

"When Tamera gets out, she will be all mine," Jason said. "I've got something I want to stick in her heart. I'll tell her that Dave sent it." He put his hand over the cross Dave had carved from a piece of wood from the communion table that had been blown up at Rev. Zackery's church.

"What are you talking about," Walt asked.

Jason pulled the wooden cross from around his neck and pulled the bottom end off, revealing a sharp tip. "The wood from Rev. Zackery's communion table burns Tamera when it touches her," Jason said. "Whenever we meet again, I'm going to stick this cross into her heart and burn her heart out."

"If you can get close enough to her," Walt said. "Look! Our best option is to make sure Sibal has the crystal, I kill her and anyone with her and then we can worry about opening the crystal. Tamera is in there with Pam now. We may have to make a deal with Tamera. Let's not be too quick to kill her."

"You can't make a deal with the devil. Tamera is responsible for my grandmother's death," Jason said angrily. "She is not going to get away with that. She is going to pay with her life."

"So, you can't make a deal with Tamera, but you are perfectly okay with making a deal with Sibal," Walt said.

"I'm not really making a deal with Sibal. I'm gambling my life that I will be able to outsmart Sibal and trick her before she tricks me."

"Let me say one thing, please," Rev. Zackery interrupted. Neither Jason nor Walt responded. They just waited for Rev. Zackery to continue. "We need to trust in the Lord. He will come to our rescue."

"Tell that to Dave," Jason said sarcastically.

"We need to wait on a word from the Lord," Rev. Zackery pleaded. "I'm sure He…"

"Are you there," the voice in the radio said interrupting Rev. Zackery.

Jason picked up the radio lying on the back seat. "Yeah, I'm here," Jason said. "So, what's the deal? Where do you want me to meet you?"

"Where are you now?" Sibal asked.

"I'm within radio distance," Jason answered.

"Can you be at the barn, you burned down, in ten minutes?" Sibal asked.

"I can be there in thirty minutes, but how do I know this isn't just a trick to get me out in the open so you can try to kill me again?" Jason asked.

"Jason! Don't you trust me?" she asked.

"Cut the crap, Sibal," Jason interrupted. "You know you don't want Tamera released from the crystal. Beside killing me what is it that you really want?"

"I know things didn't exactly work out the way we had planned, last time. I didn't take you to Tamera so you could kill her like you asked me to, but I did bring her to you. So, in a way I did keep my end of deal, the last time we had an agreement. You, on the other hand, did not keep your end of the deal. You didn't kill Tamera. You only trapped her in the crystal, and I guess, put it somewhere you thought nobody would find it. However, it seems, getting rid of Tamera and the crystal doesn't work very well. Somehow, she keeps coming back. Now your friend Pam knows that I tried to blow up Tamera in the church."

"Yeah Sibal, but you knew all of us were in the church. You wanted to kill Tamera, Pam, Dave, Rev. Zackery, your fellow assassin Dutchman, and me," Jason yelled.

"I know, but Tamera was the only one I really wanted dead. So, I took my opportunity," Sibal said. "The rest of you were collateral damage."

"Collateral damage!" Jason yelled.

"I'm sure you understand the term very well, since you murdered over three hundred innocent people in the barn," Sibal replied. "Could you hear them screaming as they were being burned alive in the fire set by you and your deceased friend David Parker. Your wanted to kill the head council because they were responsible for the death of your grandmother. Maybe they deserved to die. You took your opportunity to kill them. The rest of the people in the barn, I guess you thought they were collateral damage. Didn't you?"

Jason was quiet for a moment. He looked up, traded stares with Rev. Zackery and Walt, and then looked down again. "What do you want, Sibal?" he sneered.

"Pam has been in the crystal with Tamera for two days now. If Pam told Tamera that I tried to blow Tamera up, then it's over for me when Tamera gets out. So, this is the deal. You get Pam and Tamera out of the crystal. You kill Tamera, like you said you would do, and in exchange for that, I won't bother you or your friends again. If you don't take the deal, I just might send another team to Chicago to visit your mother."

"My mother!" Jason shouted angrily.

"Yes, your mother," Sibal sneered. "You did not care anything about my mother when you burned down the barn."

There was a pause. "Your mother was in the barn?" Jason said.

"No, but she would have been if she hadn't died five years ago." There was another pause. "Look, you want Tamera dead. I want Tamera dead. Kill her. That's the deal," Sibal shouted. "Take it or leave it." Sibal paused and waited for several seconds for a response. Jason said nothing. "Now, if you don't take the deal, I'll bury the crystal so deep it will take years for someone else to find it. Maybe by then Tamera and Pam will die in the crystal. Who knows? What do you say?"

"I say, I'll pick the time and the place," Jason said calmly. "I'll call you at ten A. M. in the morning with the location. You come alone, and I'll come alone. You bring the crystal and I'll bring what I need to get them out. No guns or weapons of any kind," he paused, "except for one. I'm going to need a knife to cut my rope, so you can bring one knife, too. Is that acceptable to you?"

"Yes," she said. "But there is something I think you should know."

"What now?" Jason said.

"Tamera has the ability to change forms. She can turn herself into animals, like birds."

"I already know that."

"Well, did you know that once she changes, for about five seconds, she is very weak, almost helpless," Sibal said.

"How do you know this."

"Dutchman told me," Sibal said, "you know, my friend, the one you killed. He witnessed it first-hand."

"That good to know," Jason said. "Thanks."

"We killed some of your people, and you and your friends killed many more of us. I'm willing to put an end to the killing, that is, after you kill Tamera. I will be waiting for your call."

The radio went silent. Jason laid back on his seat and looked at the interior roof of the car.

"I know a place where you can meet her," Walt said. "We can go check it out now. There is a cave off Kingston Rd. There are lanterns inside to provide light, and I should be able to find good place where I can get a clear shot. You and Sibal can go in the cave, you can release Pam, from the crystal, you can kill Tamera, and then when Sibal comes out I will put a bullet in between her eyes," Walt said. "Or, better yet, I could put a bullet in the back of her head before she goes in. Then you can get the crystal, get Pam and Tamera out, and I will help you kill Tamera."

"I thought you agreed to put all the killing behind you," Rev. Zackery said. "She sounded very sincere to me. What do you think Jason?"

"Maybe she was sincere, Rev. Zackery," Jason answered. "I don't know about that, but there is one thing that I do know. I know I don't want to get my mother involved in this and put her life in danger. All I want to do is avenge my grandmother. When I kill Tamera, and when we get Pam back, then I will be able to put all this stuff behind me. If Sibal is being truthful, this whole ordeal would finally be over."

"What's wrong with the two of you," Walt shouted indignantly. "Right now, Sibal is making plans to kill you, Jason. She already has Tamera and Pam. She can just bury them. She wants to lore you out into the open so she can kill you and get rid of Pam and Tamera at the same time. You killed all her associates, all her guards. She has no organization to run, and nobody to follow her orders. She has nothing now, because of you. As soon as you kill Tamera, if you can kill her, she will kill you. If you don't kill Tamera, she will still kill you, and bury the crystal. I can't allow that. Once I see her and I am sure she has the crystal, she's dead."

"You would deny me the chance to kill Tamera," Jason said angrily.

"You would deny me the chance to kill Sibal, knowing that she is lying about everything she said," Walt said. "Anyway, you can't kill Tamera by yourself. She's too powerful. You are going to need my help."

"And you can't be sure Sibal has the crystal unless I verify it," Jason shouted. "If you kill her and she doesn't have the crystal, neither one of us gets what we want. And another thing, what if Sibal and Tamera are working together? Killing Sibal before I get them out could backfire on you."

"If Sibal and Tamera are working together, you and Pam are as good as dead, and after they kill you, then Tamera will be coming after us. I need to kill Sibal ASAP, then we can bargain with Tamera. She won't kill Pam, at least until she gets out."

Jason and Walt stared angrily at each other through the rearview mirror.

"My church is not far from here. Could we stop by my church, just for a minute. I need to touch home plate and speak to the Lord. I promise not to be long," Rev. Zackery said calmly.

"All right reverend," Walt said, "but we need to go by the cave first so we can get it ready for tomorrow, and so I can pick me out a good location. We will be at the cave in five minutes."

"This is a strange time to be praying, Rev. Zackery," Jason said. "You think God is going to bless us, knowing what we are planning. What exactly are you going to ask God for?"

"I'm going to ask him for direction, Jason," Rev. Zackery said solemnly. "He always tells me what to do, even when He knows I'm not going to obey."

"I think that's a great idea, sir," Walt said as he turned on Kingston Rd. A minute later he turned on a lightly graveled dirt road. The road quickly turned into a car path, consisting of two lightly graveled tire tracks going through the woods. Walt drove down the lightly graveled car path about five hundred feet until he reached a large lightly graveled area at the end of the car path. The side of cave entrance could be seen straight ahead.

"Is that it?" Jason asked.

"Yeah. It's a good spot," Walt said. "I could setup on that hill and anywhere in this area will be my kill zone. Let me show you the cave?"

They walked into the cave and there were lanterns hanging on the walls just inside the entrance. They lit one and moved cautiously deeper into the cave. The cave was only about forty feet long and clear of any growth. There were support beams every five feet. At the back of the cave, was a wider area. Sitting in the middle of this area, there was a large section of wood cut from a tree. It was about three feet in diameter and two feet high.

"See, this is perfect, and you can use that, for a table," Walt said pointing to the section of tree sitting on the floor of the cave. He hung the lantern on a hook, on a nearby beam.

"Yeah, this will work," Jason said. "I can tie my rope to that beam and pull them out. I like it. The lanterns are less than half full. We may need to bring some more kerosene with us tomorrow," Jason said, as he led them out of the cave. Jason stopped and turned toward Walt.

"When we get here tomorrow, I will try to get her to show me the crystal before we go in the cave. If I see Pam inside the crystal, and if she has not been hurt by Tamera, I will rub my head, like this, then you can kill her, but don't do it until the crystal is covered up. I don't want Tamera to see you kill Sibal."

"Thank you," Walt said to Jason. "You will see that this is the safest way to get Pam out."

"Okay can we go to the church, now," Rev. Zackery said impatiently.

CHAPTER 26
BLASTS FROM THE PAST

(Thursday 6:00 PM)

Dave drove his car across the newly repaired bridge as he approached Rev. Zackery's church. He remembered the last time he had tried to cross that bridge. He could see it clearly in his mind.

Dave looked at the bridge, their only way of escape. Then he got into the back seat of the car and laid down on the floor behind Jason who was driving. Pam was peeping over the back seat.

"Get down," Dave yelled at Pam as pulled her arm down toward him. She would not move. Instead, she jerked her arm away, and began struggling with Jason for control of the car.

"Stop," she screamed at Jason. "There's dynamite on the bridge."

Dave felt the car swerve. Then he heard an explosion, a force hit the car, it rolled over, and all of them fell to the roof of the car as it lay with its wheels up in the air.

The images of the experience of the past disappeared, and Dave came back into the present. There was a pickup truck parked in front of the church. Dave parked beside it. He got out and saw only a brick chimney in the middle of a cleared area, where Rev. Zackery's house once stood. He remembered the last time he was in the house. The images appeared in his mind.

    Rev. Zackery was leading him across the sandy broom-swept yard to the front door of his wood frame house. Then, suddenly Dave was inside the house. He, Pam, and Jason were standing in Rev. Zackery's living room talking, when a stick of dynamite with a foot-long fuse, broke through a window and landed on the floor behind Jason. Jason ran toward the dynamite and was reaching for it. However, before he could pick it up, two more sticks of dynamite with shorter fuses, broke through two other windows. Hearing the noise, Rev. Zackery opened the door from the back room. Seeing the dynamite on the floor, he immediately closed the door. Jason picked up a chair, rammed it through a nearby window, and followed it through the window. At the same time, Dave followed Pam, who ran out the front door. Moments later, there was the deafening sound of an explosion that sent Pam and Dave flying. When Dave landed on the ground, he looked back. The house had been transformed into a thousand pieces of broken wood and debris flying up into the air. Dave fell to the ground and covered his head as the falling debris rained down, on and around him. There was pain as his body took blow after blow from the objects falling from above. There was a loud ringing noise in both his ears. When the objects stopped falling, Dave felt his leg. There was a wet spot. He looked back where the house had been and saw only a pile of rubble with a chimney stack in the middle.

    The images disappeared as he walked up the stairs to the front door of the church. When he reached for doorknob of this new door, he remembered the first time that he had opened the old door of this church. He looks behind him and more images from the past appeared.

    Dave was at the door. He looked back and saw a large she-wolf charging up the stairs of the church at him. Her fiery red eyes were filled with hate, and her fangs were fully exposed.

    "Please God! If you're there, please, let the door open," Dave said to God. Then he turned the knob, and the door was unlocked. He pushed the door open, just enough for him to slide in, which he did. However, before he could close the door, the wolf's head came through the opening. The door slammed on her head, but she continued her attempt to force her way in. Then Dave began kicking the growling and snapping wolf's mouth. Finally, the wolf pulled her head back out of the door.

The images disappeared when he opened the church door. He heard a voice.

"You must be Dave," a medium height, middle-aged man said with a southern accent said, "I'm J. Jones. We talked earlier."

"Yes sir," Dave said walking up and extending his hand. "Glad to meet you. I'm David Parker."

"Did you hear from Rev. Zackery," he asked.

"No," Dave replied, "but if you don't mind, why don't we give him a few more minutes. Then, if he doesn't come, you can tell me anything that you want me to tell him."

Dave looked at the repairs. "I must say that you have done an excellent job. You have made so many improvements. The pulpit has been totally redone."

"Yeah, we had to, "J. Jones said. "I don't know what hit that wall, but it did as much damage as a wrecking ball. We had to replace several wall studs, and we couldn't find any of the old paneling, so we went with this new woodgrain style. He told me to do whatever I wanted as long as I kept it under budget. That communion table took quite a bit of the insurance money. Do you think Rev. Zackery will like what we've done?"

"He will love everything," Dave said smiling from ear to ear, "especially this communion table. It is so beautiful. It makes the whole church shine."

"Yes, it does," J. Jones said. "I designed everything I did around it. It's so strange. The material that I bought should have cost so much more, but every time I went to buy something cheaper, I would find something better than I had planned to buy on sale. It was like God was guiding my steps. My workers did excellent work, and we finished a day ahead of schedule. It was…"

"A miracle," Dave said finishing the contractor's sentence and placing his hand on the communion table.

"Yep, it was one miracle after another."

"Thank You Jesus," Dave said.

"Are you a preacher?" J. Jones asked.

"No sir, but I have discovered recently that every time I say, 'thank You Jesus,' I see a miracle, and every time I see a miracle, I say, 'thank You Jesus.' I have been saying, 'thank You Jesus' all day."

They both looked at the door at the same time because they heard car doors closing. Moments later, Rev. Zackery came through the door followed by Jason and Walt.

"Thank You Jesus," J. Jones said.

"Amen," Dave said. They smiled at each other.

"Dave!" Rev. Zackery yelled. "They told me you were dead, but I told them that you were under the protection of God." The three men encircled Dave, hugging him tightly.

"Rev. Zackery!" J. Jones said. "It's good to see you. I'm glad you could make it."

"That's right, we had an appointment," Rev. Zackery. "With all that has been going on, I totally forgot. However, God remembered. He brought me here right on schedule."

"What do you think about the job we did?" J. Jones asked.

"The Lord blessed," Rev. Zackery said as he walked down the aisle toward the communion table as Walt followed protectively. "It's beautiful. Everything matches the Lord's table." He rubbed his hand across the front of the table.

Jason was glad Rev. Zackery and Walt had gone to the front of the church because he wanted to talk to Dave alone.

"Man, I thought you were a goner," Jason said relieved.

"Do you guys know something that I don't know?" Dave said after finally being released by Jason.

"Where do you want me to start?" Jason said. "Do you want the good news or the bad news first?

"Well since all of you are okay, give me the bad news first," Dave said concerned.

"Sibal is alive. She escaped the fire," Jason said.

"How in the world did she get out?" Dave said.

"I don't know," Jason said, "but somehow, Sibal escaped, and she sent men to your home and mine, to kill us. She knows I got away, but she said you were killed."

"You spoke to her?" Dave asked.

"Yeah. Me and Walt killed all her guards that she had brought to Rev. Zackery's brother's house when she tried to kill Rev. Zackery, but she got away and called us on the radio of one of the dead guards. That's when she told us that the men, she sent to kill you, had pumped you full of drugs, broke your neck, and threw you down some stairs."

"They thought the insurance man was me. They killed the wrong man. They killed the man who was having an affair with my wife. So, Sibal thinks I'm dead." Dave looked down and thought about Chuck. "I'm sorry the home wrecker got killed, but overall, that was not so bad cause I'm still alive. What's the good news?"

"Pam is alive." Walt said.

"Are you serious," Dave said. "I thought you said she fell in a pit of spikes. What happened?"

"There's more bad news," Jason said.

"Maybe I should sit down," Dave said, sitting on the one of the pews in the middle of the church.

"Pam wasn't killed when she fell in the pit, somehow the crystal opened up and now she is trapped inside the crystal with Tamera," Jason said.

"Tamera didn't kill her?" Dave asked.

"No, not yet anyway," Jason replied.

"So, what's the plan," Dave said, "we have got to get Pam."

"We made a deal with Sibal. I am to get Pam and Tamera, out. Then, Sibal wants me to kill Tamera, and when I do, she promises to leave us alone," Jason said.

"Do you believe her?" Dave asked.

"No. We believe that she wants to kill me, so the plan is to kill her first," Jason said. "There is just one problem."

"What's that?"

"Walt." Jason said.

"Walt?" Dave said louder than he had intended. They both looked at Walt to see if he had heard his name called. He had not, but he had noticed when he saw them both looking at him.

"See how good the church look," Jason said pointing to the pulpit, hoping Walt wouldn't realize that they were talking about him.

Dave nodded. "Yeah, it looks great," Dave said.

"Walt wants to kill Sibal first, get Pam and Tamera out of the crystal and then kill Tamera. I want to get in the crystal, kill Tamera, get Pam out and then kill Sibal."

"I don't get it," Dave said. "Both plans sound good to me."

"The problem with killing Sibal first is she may not have the crystal with her. I need to be able to verify that she has the crystal before he can shoot her. Also, if Tamera knows that Sibal is dead, she may kill Pam. That's why I need to kill Tamera first. That way Sibal will think everything is going as planned. Then Pam and I will have the upper hand on Sibal, and we will be able to kill her. Did I tell you, Sibal threatened to send someone to kill my mother if I didn't take this deal?"

"Okay, so what are you saying? Walt doesn't agree with you," Dave said.

"He's trigger-happy. I can't trust him. He is going to kill Sibal the first chance he gets. It could ruin everything. Then Pam would be trapped in the crystal forever or worse, killed."

"What are you going to do?" Dave said.

"I'm going to get Pam out, kill Tamera, and if Sibal tries anything kill her, too," Jason said.

"So, you think Sibal is not going to try to kill you?" Dave asked.

"No. I'm almost sure she will. I'm counting on it," Jason said. "That will give me an excuse to kill her. Then I can tell Rev. Zackery I did it in self-defense." Jason paused. "But I'm going to need your help."

"What do you want me to do?" Dave said.

"Take me to buy a rope," Jason said. "I'll tell you on the way."

"All right," Dave said.

"Hey Walt, Rev. Zackery!" Jason shouted. "Dave is going to take me to get a rope and some kerosene for tomorrow." They walked out without waiting for a response.

"Is there anything else that you want us to do in here, reverend?" J. Jones said.

"No, the church looks great," Rev. Zackery said. "How much is my bill?"

"I quoted you a price of $12,300, but the materials were a lot less than I thought they would be. So, it came to $10,000 even," J. Jones said. "And as you see we went ahead and sanded and stained the whole floor. Oh yeah, I cut up all the pieces I could find of the old communion table. The sawdust and some small pieces are in that five-gallon bucket by the door."

"That price sounds good J. J. and thanks for the sawdust," Rev. Zackery said. "When can you start on the house?"

"We'll start first thing Monday morning," J. Jones said. He waved and walked out the door.

"Now, we are almost ready for the funeral Saturday," Rev. Zackery said thoughtfully looking at Walt.

"Is there something wrong, pastor?" Walt said concerned by Rev. Zackery's expression.

"There is a reason I knew Dave had not been killed and there is a reason I am going to ask you to trust me and do what I say, even if you think it is unreasonable or downright crazy," Rev. Zackery said as he looked meticulously at Walt's reaction.

"I trust you Rev. Zackery, but what is this crazy thing that you want me to do?" Walt asked.

"You do remember I told you and Jason that this demon showed me a vision of the funeral, right?" Rev. Zackery asked.

"Yeah, I didn't really understand what you were talking about, but I remember," Walt replied.

"The reason I knew Dave was alive, is because he was in the vision of the funeral. Jason was in the vision. Pam, Tamera, me and even though I didn't realize it before, you were in the vision, too. None of us were hurt in any way, at least we weren't when the vision started." Rev. Zackery turned and walked toward the communion table.

"I was in the vision?" Walt said in amazement.

"Yeah, didn't recognize you before, because of what you were wearing," Rev. Zackery said.

"What was I wearing?" Walt asked.

"One of my preacher's robes," Rev. Zackery said. "You even had on my African Kufi hat. The reason I didn't recognize you before is because you were wearing my clothes, I thought you were me. I'm sure now, you were there in the vision."

"Is something bad going to happen at the funeral?" Walt asked.

"I believe so, but there is a possibility that we can alter the final events."

"What was this vision you were shown?" Walt asked.

"In the vision, I was standing in the pulpit, but I could not see my face. It was as if the view of the person showing the vision was standing behind me. I could see my back from the waist up. The church was half full of people. There was a coffin here in front of the communion table."

"Was the communion in the vision like this one or did it look different," Walt interrupted.

"It was the exact same communion table," Rev. Zackery said. "However, I admit when I was looking for a communion table in the catalog, I chose this one because it looked exactly like the beautiful communion table I had seen in the vision," Rev. Zackery explained.

"You are making the vision come true?" Walt asked.

"It may seem that way, but why was the exact same communion table in the catalog in the first place?" Rev. Zackery said. "Can I go on with my story, please?"

"Sorry," Walt said.

Rev. Zackery sees his back as he is facing the congregation at the funeral as he explains the vision to Walt.

"Anyway, there, standing in the center aisle was Tamera. She was dressed in her black hooded robe, and she was pointing at me. She said, 'You have been weighted and found unworthy. You are not a man of God. You are a liar and a deceiver. Your God has turned you over to my god for punishment. You stand condemned.' Then she orders two of her men to bring me to her. When I am placed in front of her in the aisle, she tells me to kneel. I refuse but her men who are holding my arms, kick the backs of my knees. I fall to the floor on my knees before her. Then she says, 'Your God has condemned you. Swear allegiance to me and you can live out the rest of your life in comfort and luxury, or you can watch your friends die and then be killed yourself.' Then she pointed behind me. When I looked, that's when I saw someone who looked like you, Walt. I hadn't met you when the demon showed me the vision, so I'm not sure, however, every time I think of the vision, I believe more and more that it is you. You were sitting in the pulpit with one of my preacher's robes on. Then, I saw several men bring in two large crosses from the back. Tied to the crosses were Dave and Jason. The men stood the crosses up in front of the communion table by dropping them into holes in the floor."

The images in Rev. Zackery's mind stop. Rev. Zackery looked down but did not see any holes. Rev. Zackery went on with his story.

The images in his mind reappear as he continues to explain what is happening.

"The men pushed the coffin back against the crosses and then she says, 'Swear allegiance to me.' I refuse again. Then she nods to the men who brought the crosses in. They begin to pour gasoline on Jason, Dave, and the coffin. Everyone sitting on the first three pews move to the back. Then one of the men opens the coffin. Instantly, Pam sits up in the coffin. Her arms are tied to her body, and she is gasping for air. Immediately, gasoline is poured over her head. Then Tamera says to me, 'this is your last chance. Swear allegiance to me.' A man walks up to Jason with a flaming torch and then Pam cries out, 'Rev. Zackery! Help us!' The vision end with me crying out, 'Wait, I swear.'"

The images in Rev. Zackery's mind disappeared. He was facing Walt feeling overwhelmed.

"Rev. Zackery, do you really believe that this vision is going to happen?" Walt asked.

"Unfortunately, I do," Rev. Zackery said sadly as he sat on one of the pews and put his head in his hands. "I know that I shouldn't swear allegiance to Tamera, but I can't let her burn them up."

"Don't talk stupid, reverend," Walt said. "You are smarter than that. Even if your crazy vision were to happen, swearing allegiance to Tamera wouldn't save nobody. Tamera would burn them up anyway and she would be laughing at you while she did it. Then she would think up some horrible way to kill you. Come on, Rev. Zackery? You know that."

"You are probably right, Walt."

"Probably? I can't believe you would be that stupid, reverend."

"Maybe I can convince her to let them go first, before I swear alliance to her," Rev. Zackery pleaded.

"Pastor, can't you see that this is not about saving Dave, or Jason, or even Pam, it is not even about Tamera, it's about you and you wife. If you do this, you will never see your wife again. She will be in heaven, and you will be in hell."

"I can't just let them die," Rev. Zackery said in anguish.

"Excuse me, for a minute, Rev. Zackery," Walt said dejectedly. "This is very disappointing. I need to go outside and get some air." Walt walked slowly down the aisle and out the door.

As he walked to his car, Walt noticed that the setting sun was casting a hill shadow in front of the church. He looked in the back seat and noticed the radio and one of the M16's, Dave had been loading was gone. He immediately opened the trunk and looked in his duffle bag. He pulled one of the other radios he had taken from Sibal's dead guards and turned it on. He heard Sibal's voice.

"…the grave site. Over," Sibal said.

"I'm going to say it one more time," Jason shouted. "Be here in ten minutes."

"Okay, I'm leaving right now," Sibal said, "but it may take me fifteen minutes. Over and out."

Walt took his long-range rifle from the duffle bag and made sure it was loaded. He got in the car and sped across the bridge headed for the mass grave site. It took him fifteen minutes to get to the gate leading to the grave site. He was turning off the highway when he heard the radio again.

"You should have been here by now," Walt heard Jason say.

"I'll be there in ten minutes. I'm about five miles away," Walt heard Sibal say. Walt sped down the road and backed his car into the trees at his familiar hiding place. In three minutes, he was in a good location to see the grave site area. There was only one problem. Nobody was there.

Chapter 27
Double-cross the Double-cross

(Thursday 7:30 PM)

Sibal stood by her car that had been parked on the car path off Kingston Rd. for the last ten minutes. She had been watching Dave who was standing in the clearing near the mouth of the cave.

"Okay, I'm turning off the highway now. I'll be there in three minutes," Sibal said. She watched Jason, who was standing next to his car, wave to someone on the hill, to get down and out of site. Then he got back in his car. Sibal got into her car and continued driving down the car path until she reached the large clearing near the opening of the cave. She stopped her car directly in front of the car Jason was in, but she turned it so that when she got out, her car would be between her and the person Jason had been waving to. They both got out at the same time. When Jason raised his hands and turned around to show he was not carrying a weapon, Sibal did likewise. She scanned the hill as she turned.

"Where is the crystal?" Jason called to her.

"Come and see," she called back.

Jason walked quickly and cautiously up to her. She looked on the back seat.

"It's right there, get it, and open it. See for yourself," she said. She moved away from him as he slid the metal case off the seat, sat it down on the ground between them. They both knelt as he opened it. They were both out of Dave's sight behind Sibal's car. There in the middle of a grey foam rubber lining of the case was the crystal. Pam and Tamera were standing side by side inside the crystal, looking up at Sibal and Jason.

"Satisfied," Sibal said.

"Yes," Jason said.

"Let me show you something else," she said lifting the corner of the foam rubber in the case, so Jason could see that the case was also lined with dynamite. Then she reached in her shirt pocket and removed a detonator. "If I press this button, we will all go boom."

"What are you trying to prove, Sibal," Jason said. "I thought we had a deal."

"We do," she said confidently, "but I see you trust me about as much as I trust you."

"What do you mean?" Jason said.

"I mean you need to tell whoever you were waving to earlier to get down here now."

Jason didn't try to explain, he just stood up and waved for Dave to come forward. Dave did not move. "She knows you are up there," Jason yelled. "Come on down."

Dave moved out of the trees with the M16 in his hands.

"Tell him to put the weapon on the ground," Sibal said while still crouching.

"Leave the gun there," Jason said loudly. Dave complied and then walked up to Jason.

"Mr. Parker," Sibal said in total surprise. "You are supposed to be deceased."

"So are you, officer Smith," Dave replied. "Twice."

"She has explosives in the case and a detonator in her hand. She saw me when I waved to you. That's why I told you to come out," Jason said.

"Hopefully, we can all get what we want. We just need to fulfill all the terms of our agreement," Sibal said. "Now let's go."

"I need my rope," Jason said.

"Get it," Sibal ordered.

When they reached the entrance of the cave, Jason stopped. "Take the crystal out of the case and leave the explosives here at the entrance. I wouldn't want your finger to slip," Jason said. "Put it over there, on the side of the opening, that way an accidental blast won't kill us, it will just bury us alive."

"All right," Sibal said as she opened the case. Jason took the crystal and walked into the cave.

Minutes later everything was set. The crystal was sitting on the tree trunk table, Jason and Dave had the ends of a rope tied around their waist with the middle tied to a nearby beam. Jason had cut a third of the rope for Sibal. She had tied it around her waist with the other end tied to a different beam. Jason stood next to the tree table. He had a big rock in his hand, that he had raised high over the crystal.

"Okay Sibal, turn off that detonator and put it in your pocket," Jason commanded and Sibal obeyed. "Now, when I bring this rock down on the crystal, it will expand into a large image, and it will pull me in. When I go into the image, I will grab Tamera. Dave, you go in and grab Pam. We will pull them out of the expanded image and then the crystal will close back up. Then, I will do what I'm supposed to do, and then we will go our separate ways. Right, Sibal?"

"That's right. We will go our separate ways. You leave me alone and we will leave you alone, forever," Sibal said.

"All right get ready," Jason said as he raised the rock higher over his head. "Go." He took a step back with one foot and brought the rock down, throwing it at the crystal as hard as he could. However, just before the rock touched the crystal, an image encompassed the tree table. The image created a dome on the floor with a radius of three feet all around it. Inside the image Pam and Tamera had quickly separated as the rock and most of Jason's body came into the image toward them. The bodies of Pam, Tamera, and the portion of

Jason's body that was inside the image was half their normal size. Only Jason's lower leg and his foot which were still outside the image, were their normal size. The rock that Jason had released against the crystal hit the floor between Pam and Tamera. Its size had been reduced by one half. However, it bounced against the floor and rolled out of the image, returning immediately to its original size. The tree table was no longer visible.

Dave quickly moved into the image toward Pam with arms outstretched. Pam seeing Dave reaching for her, raised her arms to catch hold of Dave. At the same time, Jason pulled the cross from his neck and then stretched his arms toward Tamera. Dave and Pam caught hold of each other.

"Hold my waist while I pull us out," Dave said to Pam as he reached one arm behind him for the rope. Dave turned as Pam clutched his waist. He then started pulling them out, arm over arm as quickly as possible. Unfortunately, as Dave pulled the image began to expand. It was now four feet in diameter. They were not getting out as fast as they had anticipated.

Tamera, seeing Jason coming into the image and his arms reaching toward her, put her left hand on Jason's shoulder, but instead grabbing him with the other hand, she hit Jason in his face with her right elbow. Jason saw the elbow coming toward his nose and turned his head just in time. The force of the blow hit Jason's jaw and almost knocked him unconscious. Dazed, he fell to the ground inside the crystal, dropping the cross from his hand. Immediately, Tamera untied the rope around Jason's waist and began to pull herself out of the image.

By now, Dave was almost completely out of the image with Pam's head, shoulders and one foot out as well. Dave reached his hand forward for another pull, but when he grabbed the rope, he saw a straight razor coming toward his hand. He jerked his hand back as the razor went down on the rope, cutting it completely. Sibal was standing in front of Dave, holding the other end of the rope she had just cut. He was now completely out of the image, however Pam, who was holding onto him, was being pulled back inside. To keep from pulling Dave back inside, Pam released Dave and she fell back into the image. Sibal raised the razor, looked into Dave's eyes, and then swung the razor toward Dave's throat. Dave pushed back to avoid the death cut and he fell to the ground inside the image, beside Jason, who had now become fully conscious.

Jason saw that Tamera was almost completely out of the image. Only her leg is inside the crystal. He crawled forward, picked up the cross from the floor, pulled off the end, exposing the sharp tip, then he grabbed Tamera's foot and stabbed the point of the cross into the calf of her leg. A flame appeared on her calf where the cross was stuck. Tamera screamed as she looked back at her lower leg. Then she turned and tried to free her leg with one strong pull on the rope. She pulled but the rope lost all its tension. Then Jason pulled her back into the image. Tamera looked up to see that her rope had been cut, and Sibal was standing there with the razor in her hand. As Tamera fell back, Jason removed the cross from Tamera's leg and stabbed her in her back behind her heart. A flame immediately began to shoot from Tamera's back. Everyone inside the image moved away from the flame. Tamera tried to reach the cross with her hands, but she couldn't. It was in a position that she couldn't reach. Eventually, Tamera fell forward on her knees moaning as the flame burned bigger and hotter. Suddenly the image disappeared, and the crystal was once again sitting on the tree trunk table.

Sibal looked closely at the crystal. Pam, Dave, Jason, and a burning Tamera were all inside. "He did it. He killed her," Sibal said to herself as she turned and ran out of the cave. Once outside she grabbed the case, she threw it into the cave, and she ran to the side of the cave. Then she took the remote from her pocket, covered her ears, and pressed the button on the remote-control detonator. The explosion she was expecting did not occur. She uncovered her ears and pressed the button several times.

Inside the crystal, there was a lot more space than before. Pam and Dave are lying feet apart on the floor of the crystal which was no longer rounded. The floor was now flat. After being sucked into the crystal everyone's energy had been drained. Jason walked in front of Tamera, who was sitting on her ankles with her head down. In anguish, she slowly raised her head. He grabbed her shoulders and pushed her roughly as Pam and Dave watched from the floor of the crystal. Tamera reacted to his push by slowly bringing her arms up inside of his and weakly grabbing his biceps.

"Look at me! I want to be the last thing you see before you die." Jason snarled with hate in his eyes, "and know it was me who killed you."

Tamera slowly raised her head and looked deeply into Jason vengeful eyes. Jason watched as Tamera's expression changed gradually from anguish to hate. As the hate grew, her grip on his biceps and her strength increased. Tamera pushed Jason back as she brought one of her knees up and put her foot on the crystal floor as she tried to get up. Jason pushed her back down.

"No, you don't," Jason said. "Die witch, die."

Dave and Pam sat up now.

"You first," Tamera shouted as she pushed herself up. Then she pushed him and waited for him to push back. When he did, she rotated her hips and using his force, she flipped him over her back and slammed him hard on his back to the floor. He was stunned. Immediately she puts her knee on his chest, pushed his chin up, exposing his larynx. She raised her pointed knuckles over his neck and drove her hand forward with all her might. Jason closed his eyes and waited for the pain, suffocation, and death he knew would follow. He waited but nothing happened, so he opened his eyes. There beside him was Pam. She had knocked Tamera off him and now had Tamera's head against her chest in a choke hold.

"I told you, you would have to go through me, first, sister dear," Pam said softly.

Tamera struggled for a moment and then stopped. Two tears rolled down her cheeks. However, just when Tamera's face was beginning to turn blue, Pam slowly released her hold on Tamera's neck, and she kissed Tamera on her forehead. Then Pam held her closed fist out in front of Tamera's face. Tamera could now feel the blood flowing into her brain. When Pam opened her hand, Tamera saw the cross that Jason had stabbed in her back.

"Our mother loved you," Pam whispered. "And I love you, too."

"Howard! Come in!" Sibal yelled, standing outside the cave. "Howard, this remote is not working. Howard!"

Walt, who was driving back to the church after nobody showed up at the grave site, heard Sibal on his radio. He listened carefully.

"This is Howard, come in Sibal. Come in," the voice in the radio said.

"Howard, the remote-control detonator is not working. I pressed the button, and nothing happens. What is the problem?" she said angrily.

"It could be the battery in the remote. It could be the explosives were wired incorrectly, or it could be a shortage," Howard said. "You need to be very careful because if it is a shortage the dynamite could explode at any time without warning. You need to cut the remote off, now."

"Okay," Sibal said switching the remote off. "It's off."

"Where are the explosives now?" Howard asked.

"I put them in the mine," she said. "You need to get over here now and fix this."

"Where are you?" Howard asked.

"I'm at the old silver mine, off Kingston Rd.," she said.

"I'll be there in ten minutes," Howard said. "Over and out."

"They are at the cave," Walt said to himself as he made a U-turn on the highway and headed for the cave.

Chapter 28
A Meditative Moment

(Thursday 8:15 PM)

Rev. Zackery opened the door to see if any cars were parked in the parking lot. There were none.

"What is going on Lord? Where are they?" Rev. Zackery said to the Lord. "Well, I have prayed for an hour that you will keep them safe, and I believe that you have answered my prayer. So, I can move on and use my time constructively. I can prepare my eulogy for Saturday, Lord."

He walked back in the church, went down the aisle and got behind the podium.

"Dearly beloved, we are gathered here together, in the sight of God and this congregation to unite. Woops, that the wrong ceremony. I still get weddings and funerals mixed up, Lord. So often people get married for the wrong reasons. They don't take the time to get marriage counseling. They don't take the time to get to know one another, either. As a result, two people, who are alive with hopes and dreams, get married and they kill each other's hopes and dreams. They die as a couple and their marriage ends up needing to be buried. The wedding then actually turns into a funeral"

Rev. Zackery examines his new podium.

"And then, on the other hand, when a person who has a personal relationship with You, dies, it should be a joyous occasion, because they will be going to meet the true bridegroom, where we will all sit at the banquet table, at that great celebration and reunion of the saints. I know I'll see my wife and I'll see my mother and my father, too. What a great day that will be, just to sit at Your feet. I can hardly wait to get there," Rev. Zackery shouted joyfully. Then he became more thoughtful. "I mean, when my time down here is done, when I have done all that You want me to do. I'm not saying that I want You to rush me to glory or anything like that, Lord. I am enjoying my work down here, and I would like to lead a few more souls to salvation, if You please."

Rev Zackery reached in one of the shelves on his new podium and got his old bible.

"Maybe I should get a new bible for my new podium." He looked up. "You're right Lord, the bible says don't put new wine in old wine skins. It doesn't say anything against putting old wine in new wine skins. So, my old bible will be just fine in this new podium, just like this old preacher will be fine in this new pulpit." Rev. Zackery began to chuckle. "I know Lord, Your word is a right now word, it is always fresh and new. Amen, amen, amen."

Rev. Zackery began flipping through the pages of the bible.

"Now, what can I preach about, for a converted fake fortune teller." He flipped more pages. "Miss Mammie was just like the rest of us, a pin cushion for the devil. She was caught up in this world of sin and led astray by the enemy, but praise be to You, Lord. You put love in her heart for a child that was not even her own. It was a love so great that she was willing to give her own life to save that child. As your word says, 'no greater love than this, that a man, or woman, would lay down his or her life for a friend.' Miss Mammie had that type of love, that great love. She sacrificed her life to save Pam.

I could preach that, but this eulogy, like all eulogies, should be preached for the benefit of those in attendance. In some way I've got to find the right scripture that will touch the hearts of the congregation and inspire them to live their lives so that when their time comes to be funeralized, something good will be said about them. I can't do this without Your guidance. Help me Lord. Give me the right words to say, in Jesus name, I pray."

Chapter 29
The Last Laugh

(Thursday 8:30 PM)

Sibal saw car lights coming through the trees toward her.

"Howard! Is that you?" Sibal said, speaking into her radio and aiming her pistol in the direction of the lights. "Speak now or forever hold your peace."

"It's me, boss," Howard said seeing Sibal pointing the pistol at him. "Don't shoot!"

"You better announce yourself, cause I will pronounce yourself, dead," Sibal said when he stopped the car beside her.

"Okay, sorry boss," Howard said getting out of the car. "Where is it?"

"I threw it in the mine," Sibal said pointing at the light shining out of the entrance.

"You threw it?" Howard said accusingly.

"Get in there and fix it," she ordered.

"I brought a new detonator and a new trigger. All I have to do is change the trigger in the case," Howard said. "I'll be back in a minute. You better get behind the car just in case."

"All right," Sibal said. "Go in, change the trigger, come out, and then get out of here. Don't touch anything else in there. Do you understand?"

"Loud and clear, boss." Howard said as he ran into the mine. Sibal hid behind her car. Five minutes later Howard ran out of the cave.

"It's done, boss. Here is the detonator," Howard said putting the detonator in her hand. Are you sure you don't want me to wait?"

"Leave!" Sibal ordered.

Howard did not say another word. He got in his car and drove down the car path toward Kingston Rd. He thought he saw something go across the car path in front of him. He stopped and turned on his high beams. He saw nothing. He continued driving. When he got to Kingston Rd., he turned and drove away.

It was Walt, who had darted across the car path that Howard had seen. Walt waited for a minute before he continued running down the car path. Then he saw the taillights of a car and a figure standing in the beam of the headlight which were pointed toward the cave.

"Sibal," Walt whispered to himself.

Walt saw Sibal raise her right hand. He stopped, took aim, and fired. Immediately, Sibal's wrist exploded. Her hand and the detonator fell at her feet as she screamed. Walt reloaded and tried to get off another shot, but Sibal had ducked in front of the car. Walt knew he had to stop her from pushing the button on the detonator, so he ran straight for the car.

Sibal had a choice. She could pick up the detonator, or she could get her pistol. She chose her pistol; however, she kept the detonator within reach. She dug a hole in the ground with the handle of her pistol and stuck her handless arm into the hole to slow the bleeding from her arm.

When Walt reached the back of the car, he kicked the trunk, and then threw his rifle over the roof of the car. When the rifle hit the hood, Sibal expected the shooter to be coming over the hood of the car. She fell flat and aimed at the front of the hood. However, Walt had pulled his pistol, duck down below the car and began firing at the body he saw lying in front of the car. Then he quickly ran around the car and saw Sibal, her hands were empty. Her pistol was lying beside her. Walt kicked the pistol out of her reach. She looked up at him as he aimed the pistol between her eyes.

"Walter," Sibal moaned.

"Sibal," Walt replied.

"You are too late. They are all in the mine," she moaned as she raised her finger and pointed to the cave. Walt looked at the cave and then looked back at her as her shoulder fell back. There was a loud explosion in the cave. When the dust settled, the cave had disappeared. The walls of the cave had been blown out, causing a landslide. Tons of earth from the hill above had filled the cave and completely covered the entrance. The headlights sadly revealed the newly formed marker-less tomb.

With tears rolling down his cheeks, Walt looked down at Sibal again. This time she had a little smirk on her face. She began to laugh. It didn't last long. Walt put his foot on her head, pushed it to the side, and shot Sibal's lips, teeth, and lower jaw off. Sibal was still alive when Walt drove past her in Dave's car.

Chapter 30
Blind Faith

(Thursday 9:00 PM)

Rev. Zackery was lying on a pew on the front row asleep when Walt opened the door. Rev. Zackery awoke and sat up and watched as a dejected Walt walked down the aisle. Rev. Zackery knew something terrible had happened. He got up and met Walt halfway, putting his arms around him. Walt said nothing as he laid his head on Rev. Zackery's shoulder and sobbed for several minutes. Finally, Walt spoke.

"They are dead," Walt said.

Rev. Zackery released Walt, pushed him back by his shoulders, and looked into his eyes. "Who is dead?" he asked.

"Jason, Dave, and Pam, all of them are dead," Walt said sadly.

"What happened? We were supposed to meet Sibal tomorrow." Rev. Zackery said as he turned away from Walt and walked toward the communion table.

"When I went outside earlier, I noticed that the radio and a M16 was missing from the back seat of my car. So, I got another radio from my trunk. When I turned it on, I heard Jason talking to Sibal. They were setting up a meeting for today. I heard them say something about the grave site, so I thought they were going to meet at the mass grave. I went there. That was not the meeting point. No one was there. Then later, I heard Sibal tell someone that the detonator did not work. She told him to come to the cave and fix the detonator. I knew then that she was trying to blowup Dave, Jason, and Pam.

So, I went to the cave. I got there in time to get off one shot. I saw her raise her hand. In it was the remote-control switch for the detonator. I had a choice, a head shot, or a wrist shot. I thought if I shot her in the head her reflexes might trigger the remote. I shot her hand off, but she was still able to detonate the explosives before I could stop her. If only I had taken the head shot," Walt said regretfully.

Rev. Zackery put his hands on the communion table. "Something is not right," he said. "They can't be dead. The vision was so clear. I prayed and I believe that the Lord spoke to my heart." He turned to Walt. "Did you actually see them die?"

"No. I saw Sibal blow up the cave. She said they were in it. She believed they were in it," Walt said.

"She could have been lying," Rev. Zackery said, "or, maybe they are just buried in the cave, but alive inside the crystal."

"Not even the crystal could withstand a blast like what I saw. The crystal was destroyed, Pastor," Walt explained. "They're gone."

"I don't know what you saw. All I know is, the Lord wants us to prepare for the funeral."

"Okay, Rev. Zackery," Walt said in an appeasing manner. "I'm with you. Whatever you say. I couldn't save her last time, and I couldn't save her this time either. I guess it was just meant to be."

Rev. Zackery walked up to Walt. "Sit down, Walt," Rev. Zackery said politely pointing to a spot on the pew next to them. Walt sat.

"What is it, Rev. Zackery," Walt said looking intently into his eyes.

"I know that you don't know much about God, and even less about Jesus and the Holy Spirit, however, I think you know me. I don't know how much you believe in God, Jesus, and the Holy Spirit, but I think you believe that I truly, with all my heart, believe in Them. I'm telling you that the Holy Spirit has spoken to my spirit and confirmed the vision, that was shown to me by the demon, is going to happen. Saturday, Pam, Jason, Dave, and Tamera are all going to be at the funeral. Pam, Jason, and Dave will be in Tamera's control, but they will be alive. We will have one last chance to save them. Walt, I am going to need your help."

"I saw the cave blow up, reverend," Walt said adamantly.

"I know you did, but they are not dead, and the only way you will be able to help is to believe that they are not dead, that God spoke to me, and that God wants us to save them."

"Believe what?" Walt said. "That your God got a demon to tell you what was going to happen in the future. Why didn't God give you the vision himself, reverend? Tell me that."

"Remember what I told you about my wife?" Rev. Zackery said. "Maybe God knew that I wouldn't believe the vision if He had shown it to me. So, He used a demon, that I had dealt with before, and who had shown me a vision before, a vision that came true."

"You really believe that they are alive, they are going to be here Saturday, and we can save them," Walt said.

"Don't you want another chance to save Pam?" Rev. Zackery said.

"More than anything in the world," Walt said.

"What do you have to lose by believing me?" Rev. Zackery said.

"Nothing," Walt said realizing the truth of his answer. "If you are right, I have everything to gain. I would get another chance to save Pam."

"Walt, God doesn't just want to give you another chance to save Pam. He wants you to save her," Rev. Zackery said. "He also wants you to understand He is doing this for you because He loves you. He wants you to love Him in return, to love Him first, even before Pam, and to accept his plan of salvation. He gave you Pam, even if it was just for one day. He showed you though your love for her, the type of love and devotion that He wants you to have for Him. The intensity and self-sacrifice of the love you have for Pam is the same type of intensity and self-sacrifice He wants in your love for Him. Pam was His gift to you. Her love for you, doesn't even compare to the love He has for you. You should love the giver of the gift more than you love the gift. Can you understand that?"

"Yes, sir," Walt said. "I understand that part but there is so much more that I don't understand."

"Leave that to the Lord. Just know that God has a responsibility to you. He will fulfill His responsibilities," Rev. Zackery said. "For now, we need to fulfill our responsibilities to Him. We need to have faith in Him, to trust in Him, and to get ready for the funeral."

"What do you want me to do?" Walt said committedly.

"The first thing I want you to do is to get saved," Rev. Zackery said.

"What?" Walt said.

"You need to accept Jesus as your Lord and Savior," Rev. Zackery said. "Then, after that, you can ask the Father to give you the Holy Spirit." Rev. Zackery looked at Walt sympathetically. "I know that you have always depended on yourself and your skills. Well, your skills and abilities are no match for the devil. Satan will sift you like wheat unless you have the anointing of the Holy Spirit working on the inside of you."

"How can I save Pam? That's all I want to know," Walt shouted.

"You can save her by learning how to fight a new way," Rev. Zackery said. "We can learn that tomorrow. For now, let's get you saved. After that we will go to my friend's house and get some rest and some sleep."

Chapter 31
A Taste of Reality

(Thursday 9:30 PM)

Howard rushed from his car, opened the office door, and ran down the aisle to his office. He took the crystal from his jacket pocket and sat it on his desk. Dave and Jason who had been sitting previously, quickly stood up. Pam remained seated with Tamera lying almost lifelessly next to her. Tamera's head was in Pam's lap. They all looked up at Howard who was very nervous and fearful.

"What do you want me to do?" Howard said anxiously. "Sibal is going to kill me when she finds out what I've done unless you stop her. I got you here. Tell me what you want me to do?"

Tamera sat up slowly. She put her hands over both her ears and began to concentrate. Howard's expression changed. He grabbed the crystal from the desk, put it in his pocket, and walked out.

Pam, Tamera, Jason, and Dave, where in the dark again for fifteen minutes. When they saw light again, they were in a jail cell. The crystal was on the floor of the cell. Howard was on the other side of the bars with a Billy club in his hand. There was also a chain with one end lying next to the crystal and the other end handcuffed to the cell bars.

"Are you ready," Howard shouted.

Everyone looked at Tamera as she jumped to her feet with suspiciously renewed energy. "Yeah! Do it!" Tamera yelled.

Everyone looked back at Howard as he raised the Billy club. Then he brought the club down toward the crystal. Tamera quickly turned facing the chain. When they saw Tamera move everyone else moved as well. Howard brought the club down as hard as he could releasing it just before it hit the crystal and then he jumped back away from the bars. Instantly, the crystal disappeared, and a dome shaped image appeared with the four of them inside. Tamera grabbed the chain and began to pull herself out of the image. Jason jumped on Tamera's back. Dave grabbed one of Tamera's arms, and Pam grabbed the other. They all pulled themselves over her, and they each climbed on the cell bars away from the image. Then finally, Tamera pulled herself out of the image. The image disappeared, and the crystal returned to the floor just as it had been before.

"Yeah!" Jason yelled as he jumped down off the bars to the floor.

"All right," Pam yelled

"Thank You, Jesus," Dave shouted.

"Amen," Pam said turning to Dave and hugging him.

Howard reached inside his jacket and pulled a pistol out. "Move back away from the door," Howard ordered.

Everyone except Tamera moved back. Howard unlocked the door, letting Tamera out with the crystal in her hand. Then he relocked the door, imprisoning Pam, Dave, and Jason.

"Here," Tamera said to Howard, "keep this thing away from me. Lock it in the safe. It's too dangerous. We'll dispose of it later."

Tamera and Howard began to walk out of the room.

"Tamera," Pam shouted, "I thought we had a deal."

"We did have a deal, until you let him stab me in my back," Tamera said looking angrily at Jason.

"I stopped him from killing you," Pam argued.

"You stopped me from killing him," Tamera said.

"That too," Pam said. "You pinky swore that when we got out, we would go our separate ways and leave each other alone."

"Sister dear, I am going to leave you and your little men alone. But first, I want to visit the preacher. Then, I will say my final goodbyes to all of you," Tamera said and turned toward Howard. "Are there extra keys to the cell?"

"Yeah. There's one in the desk," Howard said

"Give it to me," Tamera said. "I don't want anyone else to be able to open that door."

"Yes ma'am," Howard said handing Tamera the key.

"Now, when was the last time you talked to Sibal?" Tamera snarled.

"It was about an hour ago at the mine. She was getting ready to blow up it up," Howard said.

"Yeah, with me in it," Tamera said angrily. "I need to put something on my back and then we need to find Sibal." Howard followed Tamera out of the room and the door slammed behind them.

"Why didn't you let her die," Jason said looking at Pam. "The fire would have burned her heart out."

"Before you start complaining, at least you ought to thank me for saving your ungrateful life," Pam said.

"Yeah, that's right Jason," Dave said. "If Pam hadn't acted, you and Tamera would both be dead now, and we would still be trapped in the crystal."

"Well, we are still trapped, and she is free," Jason said. "You think this is better?"

"You hate her so much that you would let yourself be killed in order to kill her and you would sacrifice our lives as well." Pam said.

"You need help, man," Dave said. "Your hatred is consuming you and it is dangerous to us."

"Because of her, my grandmother was set on fire while she was still alive and burned to death," Jason said angrily. "You saw her, Dave, when she came out of that house. She was totally covered in flames. Yeah, I want to kill Tamera and I will kill her." He walked over to Pam and looked her in her face. "I am going to kill your sister dear."

"If she doesn't kill you first. She could have had her man shoot you five minutes ago, before they left, but she didn't," Pam said. "You are not only homicidal, but you are also suicidal. Forget you."

"I'm warning you," Jason said threateningly. "Don't get in my way again, not even to save my life."

Pam instantly brought her hands up and seized Jason's head. Her left hand had the back of his head and three of her fingers on her right hand pressed against his face. Two of her fingernails were cutting into Jason's eyelids the other one was cutting into his forehead. Jason did not dare move.

"If I were Walt, you would be dead now. He kills anyone who threatens him," Pam said softly. "However, since we use to be friends, I'm just going to give you a warning. The next time you threaten me will be your last time." She released the back of his head, and then pushed him back. Jason began rubbing his eyelids. "There are two beds" she said to Jason. "I'll take one, Dave can have the other one, and since you don't care if you live or die, you can sleep on the floor," she said to Jason.

"Okay, thank you for saving my life," Jason finally said to Pam. "But you act like it's a big deal. How many times have I saved your life? Five, ten, fifteen, twenty, it feels like that many. Every time I turn around, I'm saving your life, but I don't ask for thanks. No, I just do it because that's what friends do for each other. They save each other's lives, no hesitation, no questions asked." Jason paused. "And another thing, I may be homicidal and suicidal, but at least, I don't have a serious case of stupid. You saw in the cave; your sister was going to leave us in the crystal just like she left us in this cell. Your sister killed my Gramma, the woman who loved you and raised you. Your sister is going to kill me, Dave, and Rev. Zackery, if I don't kill her first. Then what? You think she's going to let you go. That is the 'most stupidest' thing I have ever heard." Jason walked to the cell door and looked toward the desk. "Anyway, you are the reason all of this happened. All these people are dead because your sister wanted you dead." Jason turned around and faced

Pam. "Gramma was burned up alive because Tamera was trying to find you. So now, are you going to let her kill us, too. You know she is lying. Whatever deal you think you have with her, she will break it. She wants you dead."

Pam stood there beside the bed in contemplation. "Did I ever thank you for coming back to get me when I was shot in the woods," she said sincerely.

"You didn't need to," Jason said.

"You have saved my behind a bunch of times," she said smiling. She walked over to Jason and gave him a tender hug. He responded in kind. "You are right."

"Hey," Dave said. "I have saved your life a couple of times myself," Dave said looking at Pam. "Come to think of it, I have saved yours a couple of times, too," he said looking at Jason.

They each held out an arm for him to join the hug.

"I was hoping I wouldn't have to kill my own sister," Pam said sadly.

"Don't worry, I'll take that burden off your shoulders," Jason said smiling. "That's what friends do."

"I knew you would say that," Pam said smiling back and shaking her head from side to side.

CHAPTER 32
ANOTHER ONE BITES THE DUST

(Thursday 10:30 PM)

From high above, a Red-tailed hawk could see Howard's car moving down the highway, through the woods. Inside the car, Howard and Tamera sat in the front seats. They had left Sibal's doctor's house ten minutes earlier.

"Call Sibal on your radio," Tamera said. "Find out where she is."

Howard did not respond. He turned the volume up on his car radio, put the speaker up to his lips, and spoke. "Ms. Sibal, come in. This is Howard." He waited for a response. There was none. "Sibal, come in, please. This is Howard. Come in!"

"You said she was at the old mine the last time you saw her, right?" Tamera asked.

"Yes, ma'am."

"Let's go by there first, since it's on the way to her house," Tamera said. "I want to see the grave she planned for me. Try her one more time."

"Boss, come in. This is Howard. Come in boss. Just checking to see if everything went okay," Howard said. There was no response.

Miles away in the living room of a farmhouse, Walt listened to the radio sitting next to him on the sofa, as he rubbed the head of a large German Shepherd.

"Lady," Walt said to the dog next to him. Lady turned her head toward him. "I don't think everything went okay for Ms. Sibal. In fact, I know things went very bad for her," he said rubbing Lady's head vigorously. "You are such a good girl. How dare they interrupt my bible time." He picked up the bible from the lamp table and continued to read. Then he heard something that shook him to his core.

"Sibal! You can't hide from me. This is Tamera and I'm coming for you. You tried to bury me in that mine. Your plan failed. When I find you, I'm going to rip you heart out and let you watch it beat it's last beat."

The radio went silent. Walt was in shock. "Rev. Zackery was right. They are alive. If God had spoken to me, and told me that they were alive, I would not have believed my ears. I would have thought it was just my imagination. So, God let me hear it from someone he knew I would believe, an evil witch." Walt fell back on the back of the sofa and looked up at the ceiling. "Thank You God, thank You Jesus, and thank You Holy Spirit for letting me see and feel your love for me."

Howard turned off Kingston Rd. and went down the car path toward the old mine. He and Tamera could see the back of a car whose dim headlight were shining on an area where the old mine had been.

"She blew it up. That scheming witch tried to bury me alive in that crystal ball," Tamera said disgustedly.

"No ma'am," Howard said. "Her plan was to blow up the crystal ball with you in it."

"I guess that makes you my second in command," she said.

"I'm pretty much all you have to command," Howard said. "Everyone else is either dead or they left."

"What about our businesses."

"After you went missing, our creditors got nervous. Then when the fire at the barn happened, accounts were frozen. The banks started foreclosure proceedings. We had a little over seventy-six thousand dollars in the safe yesterday, until Sibal had me to hire ten guards. I took five thousand out yesterday, because I had to pay each one of them five hundred down. I will owe them five hundred more when the work is done, next Friday. That will be another five thousand. I should be able to sell some of the businesses and properties before the foreclosures can be finalized."

"I'll stop the foreclosures," Tamera said confidently. "Let's go to Sibal's house. Maybe she's still there."

"I don't think she's there, ma'am," Howard said. "That's Sibal's car."

They both got out and walk up to Sibal car, Howard on the left and Tamera on the right. They looked in the car as they slowly walked toward the front of the car. When they got to the front of the car, Tamera saw Sibal's head and Howard saw Sibal's feet. They met in front of the car, standing over Sibal's body. Her hand was lying about three feet beyond Sibal's feet, and a pistol was lying about four feet beyond her head.

"It looks like someone beat me to the punch," Tamera said. "Somebody shot her mouth off and left her here, maybe for us to see. What do you think it means?"

"Maybe, it's saying she told one to many lies," Howard said.

"Do you know anyone who would want to kill Sibal."

"Yeah!" Howard said.

"Okay, who has she done something to, recently?"

"There are too many to count, ma'am," Howard said.

"Name the last one you know of," Tamera demanded.

"She took a girl's face last week," Howard said. "I think she had the girl killed afterwards. I'm sure that didn't make her any friends."

"Maybe, it was the preacher," Tamera said. "He shot me once."

"May be," Howard said.

"We blew his house up. Do you know where he is living now?"

"No," Howard said, "but his church is being repaired, so I can go to his church and I'm sure the contractor will tell me where he is living now."

"At least we know where he will be Saturday."

"Where?" Howard asked.

"He's got a funeral service planned at his church for the woman that raised my dear sister, Pamela," Tamera said.

"Maybe I should verify that the service is still going to take place on Saturday," Howard said.

"You can check it out in the morning, after you get rid of this body," Tamera said frowning.

Howard looked down at Sibal's partial face. "I should put the body in the trunk now, so the animals won't get to it," he said as he walked to see if the keys were in the ignition. They were. So, after putting on his gloves, he popped the trunk top from the inside. He walked around, picked up Sibal's hand and threw it in the trunk. Then he turned her over on her stomach and grabbed the back of her belt, lifted her up to the edge of the trunk, and rolled her over into the large trunk. She landed on her back. He picked up the pistol by the barrel and laid it on her stomach. The light in the top of the trunk revealed that Sibal's eyes were open. Howard was about to close them with his hand when the eyes turned and looked at him. Howard slowly backed away from the trunk. "Ma'am?"

"What is it?" Tamera snapped.

"She, Sibal, is not dead," he said.

Tamera turned and looked in the trunk. Sibal's head turned, and she was looking directly at Tamera. Tamera pushed her robe sleeve back to her elbow, picked up the pistol by the barrel, pushed Sibal's head to the side, pushed the top of Sibal's ear down with her finger, and hit Sibal hard on her temple. Then she dropped the pistol in the trunk and slammed it shut.

"I want her stripped of her clothes, I want concrete blocks tied to her ankles, and I want the body dropped in the middle of Lake Norman, tomorrow," Tamera commanded. "I like the thought of catfish eating her eyeballs out of her face, what's left of it."

"It will cost forty-five hundred to hire a disposal unit to do that," Howard explained. "Why not bury her at the mass grave site. I could get that done for a hundred and fifty."

"Fine," Tamera said angrily. "Take me to my house. My back pain is getting unbearable. I've got to check the book to see if there is something in it, I can do to stop this pain."

"Yes ma'am."

Chapter 33
New Hope

(Thursday 11:30 PM)

Rev. Zackery walked into the living room of Mr. Carson's house, where Walt was lying on the sofa reading the bible. Lady was lying on a rug in front of the front door of the house. Her ears perked up, she raised her head, and turned it toward Rev. Zackery. When she recognized him, her tail wagged one time and then she resumed her position.

"Are you okay out here?" Rev. Zackery asked.

"I am, Pastor," Walt said, standing up, "and I have some wonderful news."

"Wonderful news," Rev. Zackery repeated. "What is it?"

"You were right, again. They are alive."

"What happened?" Rev. Zackery asked. "How do you know?"

"I heard Tamera on the radio. If she is alive, then Pam, Dave, and Jason are probably alive, too. At least, they were not blown up in the cave."

"Thank you, Jesus," Rev. Zackery shouted. He hugged Walt tightly.

"God did it again, Pastor."

"What did He do this time," Rev. Zackery asked.

"I didn't believe you, a preacher and a man of God, so He let me hear it from someone I would believe, Tamera, an evil witch."

"That's just the way He is. He looks beyond our faults, and He sees and supplies our needs," Rev. Zackery said.

"I think I'm beginning to see how He has been working in my life," Walt said. "Even though things, bad things were happening to me, Jesus was always there to pull me through every one of them."

"That's right, son, and the Lord is not through with you yet. He has a plan and a purpose for you," Rev. Zackery said. "Do you have the faith to believe that Jesus will bring you through what's coming?"

"I believe so, Pastor."

"Your faith must be steadfast and unmovable because it will be tested, by God," Rev. Zackery warned.

"What are you saying, Rev. Zackery? Why would God need to test my faith? Doesn't he already know if I have faith or not?"

"Yes, He knows," Rev. Zackery said. "He wants you to know the level of your faith. Do you have no faith, little faith, or great faith?"

"How can I have great faith?"

"You have to totally depend on the Lord," Rev. Zackery.

"How can I totally depend on the Lord, if the Lord doesn't tell me what I should do?"

"You have to have faith, that when the time comes, He will tell you, or show you what to do," Rev. Zackery said.

"What if I don't understand what he tells me or shows me? What do I do then?"

"Then you wait and have faith that He will give you the clarity you need. Then, when you feel a peace within that He is directing you, do what you believe He wants you to do. Don't wait. Don't hesitate. Act. He won't fail you." Rev. Zackery paused. "You may suffer. You may even get killed, but He won't fail you."

"You're so funny, Pastor," Walt said shaking his head.

"Hey, I'm still working on my own faith issues," Rev. Zackery said. "The things I'm telling you to do, I haven't mastered myself. Even with good intentions and thinking that I was doing the will of God, I have made many bad decisions. The good thing about that is God saw my heart and He intervened on my behalf and turned my failures into victories."

"So, you're saying that Saturday, the funeral is going to be a suicide mission, that I won't survive," Walt said.

"I'm saying that you may have to sacrifice your life to save Pam's," Rev. Zackery said.

"That's not a problem. I would give my life for hers in a second, without hesitation," Walt said smiling.

"What if you had to choose between saving Pam or saving me, and you felt the Lord wanted you to save me. This is just a hypothetical situation," Rev. Zackery said smiling.

"If that was the situation, Pastor, you would be hypothetically dead."

"Without hesitation," Rev. Zackery said.

"I love you, Pastor, but I would die for Pam," Walt was stunned that he had said love.

"That's the type of love, Jesus wants you to have for him," Rev. Zackery said. "That 'to die for' kind of love. Try to get some sleep, we have a lot to do tomorrow."

"Good night, Pastor."

"Good night, Walt."

Chapter 34
Destructive Thinking

(Friday 1:00 AM)

Tamera and Howard were sitting at a table in Tamera's house. In the middle of the table was a large black book with cuts across the front cover. The word "Witchcraft" was printed in large gold letters on the leather cover. Tamera opened the book to the table of contents. She ran her finger down the list of chapter topics.

"Potions," Tamera said as she began turning pages as she twisted her back because of her pain. "Holy Objects! Here it is!" she shouted. "One small scoop of wainsbreath, one forth scoop of echinacea powder, one half scoop of burdock root powder, and two ounces of mamba venom. Mix into a salve and apply to infected area," Tamera read. "Come on," she said to Howard.

They got up from the table and went into an exterior room that had been added to the house. The temperature in this room was very cold compared to the warm and cozy room they had just left. This room was filled with shelves. Some shelves were filled with jars of various types of herbs, powders, and chemicals. Other shelves were filled with cages containing animals, reptiles, and insects. Tamera began mixing the powders she had read from the book into a beaker. After that she took the beaker with the mixture and taped a cloth over the top. Then she took a cage from the shelve containing reptiles. She sat it on the table next to the beaker. There was a poisonous snake coiled inside. It was a Black Mamba.

"Get that broom over there," Tamera said. "Beat the top of cage with the handle."

Howard got the broom and began hitting to cage.

"Harder," Tamera yelled. "Get it angry. I need to get its juices flowing. I need two ounces of venom."

Howard beat the cage harder. The snake was going crazy inside the cage.

"Okay, that's good," Tamera said.

Howard stopped and the snake coiled into striking position. When Tamera leaned over the snake, unlatched and opened the top of the cage, Howard moved back toward the door. The snake wasted no time. With fangs showing, its head shot up and out of the top of the cage toward Tamera's face which was looking down at it. Tamera quickly pushed the top of the cage down on the snake, pinning it to the top of the cage. Tamera grabbed the snake below its head and lifted it out of the cage. It was almost five feet long and it quickly wrapped itself around Tamera's arm. Its mouth was open, and a drop of venom was growing on each of its fangs. Tamera stuck the fangs into the cloth covering the beaker. Immediately, venom began to flow down the side of the beaker toward the mixture. After a minute went by and the venom stopped flowing, Tamera unwound the snake from her arm, and holding the head with one hand and the end of the tail with the other, she handed it to Howard.

"Put it back in the cage while I mix this," Tamera ordered.

Howard had little time to react. He grabbed the snake just below Tamera's fingers near the snake's head with one hand, and he grabbed the tail near the end with the other as Tamera released it. Immediately, the snake started squirming and twisting. Howard could barely hold it.

"You're dead, if it bites you," Tamera said nonchalantly, as she moved away from him while she stirred the mixture.

"I can't hold it," Howard shouted as the snake's tail slipped from his hand. It took only seconds for the snake to twist itself out of Howard's hand and fall to the floor. Howard was cornered. The mamba moved quickly toward Howard, who jumped to his right to escape, however, he was not fast enough.

The mamba lunged. Howard watched in terror as the fangs moved toward his thigh. "Ahhhhhhh," he screamed as he fell to the floor.

To his utter relief he had not been bitten. At the last second before the snake reached his leg, Tamera had slapped the snakes head, knocking it to the floor. Then she picked up the stunned snake, dropped its limp body into the cage, and then closed the top, and she did all this while still holding the beaker in her left hand.

Howard laid on the floor shaking, still paralyzed with fear. Tamera walked up to him and handed him a root.

"Chew on this," she said noticing his distress.

He took it, put it in his mouth, and began chewing the hard root as he continued to sit there.

"Get up!" Tamera ordered. "I need for you to rub this on my back." She walked to her bedroom and Howard, realizing how close he had come to death, followed gladly.

When they got to the bedroom, Tamera handed Howard the beaker, pulled the black hooded robe with the big burn hole in the back, over her head, and threw it on the floor. Then she kicked her shoes off and walked her naked body into her closet. When she came out, she had a fluffy white bathrobe wrapped around her. She was holding it closed in the front with one hand. She went to the bed, pulled the bed covers back, lowered the robe, and tied the arms of the robe around her waist. Then she laid her half naked body face down on her bed tucking her pillow below her chin with her hands.

"Okay, rub it on my wound," she said tightening her back muscles, not knowing what to expect when the salve touched her back.

Howard carefully and gently rubbed the salve around the small burned-out hole in her back. Then rubbed the salve on the edges of the wound.

"That feels better," Tamera said untightening her back muscles. "Put some more on. Please."

Howard had not been around Tamera very much, but that was the first time he had ever heard her say 'please.' "Yes, ma'am," he said as he rubbed the salve over her wound.

"Oh Howard, that feels so good," she moaned. "The pain is going away. I have never felt pain like that before. This is such a relief. It's even better than the relief I felt when I got out of that crystal. I thought I was going to die in there. I would have died in there if you had not saved me. Howard, you saved me from Sibal, you got me out of the crystal, and now you have stopped that terrible pain that was killing me. It was hurting so bad, I couldn't even think straight." Tamera stopped talking and looked up at Howard. He could see that she was chewing on a root.

In the cold room, on the table the Black Mamba began to move around in the cage. Even though the light had been turned off, the door had not been completely closed so there was enough light for the snake to see its new destination. It moved its head to the top of the cage. When it hit the top, the top moved. The top had not been latched. The snake pushed its head up against the top and out of the cage. Its body quickly followed.

"The pain is gone, now," Tamera said, "but, don't stop rubbing. It is so soothing."

Howard did not respond, he just kept applying the salve.

"Did you know that my sister, Pamela, saved my life while I was in the crystal ball," Tamera said.

"No ma'am. I didn't know that."

"She pulled that wooden cross out of my back," Tamera said. "It would have killed me. She said she did it because we were sisters and because she loved me. You saved my life, too, Howard. You knew that Sibal was going to try to kill me. You knew that if she found out that you had saved me, she would kill you. Yet, you saved me anyway. Why did you do it, Howard? Did you do it because you fear me more than you feared Sibal, or did you do it because you love me, like my sister said she did when she pulled that cross from my back?"

"I do fear you, but I did what I did because you are my queen. It is my duty to serve you," Howard said tactfully.

"So, you don't love me, you were just being loyal to me," she said.

"Ms. Tamera, I do not understand the meaning of the word love. It is used in too many ways to explain too many emotions and actions so that it becomes ambiguous and contradictory. I understand loyalty, obedience, duty, and commitment. These are the things I pledge to you. I will be loyal to you. I will obey your commands. I will fulfill all my duties and commitments to you and the coven. And, if you tell me to love you, I will, to the best of my ability."

"You are so right. Love is just a word to use conveniently when trying to get what you want. Pamela told me that she loved me just because I was her sister. Yet, she and her friends dropped me into a river, to be trapped forever in a crystal ball prison. What kind of love is that?" Tamera shouted angrily. Her anger was causing Howard to be fearful.

"You have her now," Howard said trying to calm Tamera. "She won't be causing you anymore problems. In fact, I can go back to the office and kill all of them right now, if you want me to."

"No," she said calmly. "I am planning something special for all of them, including that preacher who shot me. Go in the bathroom and get something to bandage up my back. Then I want you to lay here beside me and guard me while I sleep."

"Yes ma'am," Howard said getting up to go to the bathroom.

"I feel a cold breeze," Tamera said pulling the bed covers over her body up to her wound. "You didn't close the lab room door when we left. Go close it, now."

In the lab room, the snake was hanging halfway off the table. As Howard's footstep got closer to the door, the snake's tongue flickered out sensing Howard's body approaching. It dropped to the floor loudly causing Howard to freeze mid-step. Howard listened intently, however, there was no way he could have heard the Mamba move to within inches of the door opening and then coiled for a strike. With one foot still off the floor, Howard used that foot to kick the door. Then he quickly turned and walked away. Howard heard the door shut, but he did not see it bounce back open. There was a gap in the door about an inch wide, wide enough for the Mamba to get through.

When Howard returned to the bedroom, Tamera was still lying as he had left her, however, her white robe was on a chair in the corner of the room. He went in the bathroom and got tape, scissors, and a package of gauze. He taped a piece of gauze over her wound and pulled the covers up to her neck. Then he put the medical supplies back in the bathroom and tossed the wrapping paper and the root he had been sucking in the trash. He walked back into the room and laid down on the bed on top of the covers beside her.

Tamera turned her head toward him. She had a root sticking out of the corner of her mouth. "Take off your clothes and get under the covers with me," Tamera said calmly. Howard obeyed. Then, Tamera took the root from her mouth and gave it to Howard. "Suck on this."

"Are you sure you want to do this ma'am," Howard asked fearfully.

"While I was stuck in that crystal, I realized all the things I had never done. I have never been to Niagara Falls and I have never had sexual intercourse. I don't want to die without doing both," she said sternly, "and I came very close to dying yesterday."

"You are safe now, ma'am," Howard replied.

"Since I asked you to get in bed with me, I think you should call me baby, not ma'am," she said. "If you do a good job, maybe you can call me baby all the time."

"What happens if I don't do a good job?" Howard asked.

"I think you should get rid of anything that doesn't work," she said ominously.

"Ma'am, since it's your first time, wouldn't you rather do it with someone younger, who is stronger and has more stamina," Howard pleaded.

"What's wrong with you," Tamera asked angrily. "I thought all you had to do is have a penis. You do have one, don't you?"

"Yes ma'am, I mean baby, but I am very nervous," Howard said.

"What are you so nervous about," she said angrily.

He swallowed. "I don't think I'll be able to get an erection," he said.

She reached under her pillow, pulled out a straight razor, rolled on top of him, opened it so he could see the shiny blade, and looked down at him with a look of rage, "You'll either get an erection or I'll cut it off."

"Please, Ms. Tamera," Howard pleaded. "Give me a few minutes to calm myself down. Do you have any potions I can take to make me hard? Do you have any pornographic magazines? Please, Ms. Tamera, don't cut it off."

Tamera slid partially off Howard. While still lying on his right arm, she lowered the blade of the razor slowly down his chest to his navel where the covers were, removing all the hair the blade touched in the process. She did not stop. She continued lowering the blade against his skin as she pushed the covers down with her hand. The sharp edge of the razor shaved off every hair that it touched as it moved toward Howard's crouch. Howard's expression became more terrified the lower the blade went.

"What am I doing?" Tamera said meditatively. "She is stronger than I thought. She put these thoughts in my head. I don't want to see Niagara Falls." Tamera closed the razor and rolled off Howard. "Get out of my bed," she snapped. "I don't want to have sex!"

"Yes ma'am," he said jumping to his feet beside the bed.

"Put you clothes on and get back to the office and watch our prisoners," she ordered.

"Yes, ma'am. Thank you, ma'am," Howard said as he dressed quicky.

"Don't go back in the cell room with her without me. If she can push thoughts in my head, she will push thoughts in yours and make you release them. Do you still have the other key to the cell with you?" Tamera asked.

"Yes ma'am," Howard said pulling several keys from his pocket. "Here it is."

"Put it on the nightstand," Tamera said. When Howard came around the bed to put the key on the nightstand, Tamera stood and pulled his forehead up to hers. Her nakedness caused him to shake with fear. "If Pam pushes you and makes you go in the cell room, or if you have to go in there for any reason, and she tries to make you do anything, I want you to tell her that I instructed you to put her on punishment, and as a result of her actions they are to get no food or water. Tell her that you can't even come back in the room anymore. Do you understand me?"

Yes ma'am, I understand," Howard said.

"When you get back, make sure that the camera in the cell room is working and recording. I want to be able to see and hear everything that is happening in the room. I know they are going to plan either an escape or an attack. Call me if you see or hear anything strange. Also, see if you can locate that wooden cross that Jason stabbed in my back."

"Yes, ma'am. I'll call if I hear anything," Howard said as he rushed out of the room closing the door behind him leaving a naked Tamera standing by the bed. As he went through the living room, he noticed the door to the supply room was not completely closed. He took a step toward it, then he turned and walked out of the house. It was a good decision not to close the supply room door, because as he walked to the front door, he was being followed. The Black Mamba got to the door a few seconds after he had closed the door behind him. It turned at the door, raised its head a foot in the air and shot its tongue out, sensing the area. Then it lowered its head to the floor and moved under the sofa near a floor register, where warm air was blowing.

Chapter 35
The Key Is Not in the Mind

(Friday 6:30 AM)

Even though there were no windows in the room where the jail cell was, Dave, who had taken the second watch, could see daylight coming under the door leading to the next room.

"Hey," he said as he walked back from the cell bars and shook Pam, who was sleeping peacefully on one of the beds, "it's morning."

"Good morning," Pam said cheerfully.

"You sure did sleep good, last night," Jason said sitting up on his bed. "You slept the whole time I was on watch. Are you sure you never spent time in jail before?"

"No, I have never been in jail before," Pam explained. "However, after sleeping on the floor in that crystal for the last three days, this bunk was like sleeping on a cloud. It was heavenly." She smiled joyfully. Her smile was so bright that Dave and Jason smiled, also.

"I hate to be the one to spoil the mood, but we need a plan if we are going to survive this," Jason said.

"You mean you don't already have a plan?" Dave said.

"Well, actually, I have been thinking and…" Jason said before being interrupted.

"I knew it. The plan master always has a plan," Dave said with a smirk.

"He who fails to plan, plans to fail, my dubious inmate," Jason said.

"What's your plan?" Pam said.

"Okay, the way I see it," Jason began enthusiastically. "Tamera doesn't have anyone but that dude Howard. It's two against three. I'll take those odds any day. When they come to move us or feed us, whenever they open the door, me and Dave will jump Howard and Pam will take Tamera. Tamera is still weak and hurt from her back wound. Pam, you should be able to take her easy. The only problem is one of us, either me or Dave may be shot, before we can get control of Howard's gun."

"I liked everything about your plan except the part that came after, 'Okay, the way I see it.' We don't know if any of what you say is true. We need more information." Dave argued.

"I like it," Pam said. "But only if the situation presents itself. I also agree with you, Dave," she said turning to Dave. "We need more information. So, the next time Howard comes in the room, I will push a thought in his mind. If he reacts, I will know that I can distract him long enough for you two to take his gun."

"What about Tamera?" Dave asked. "Can you take her?"

"Without a doubt. She's weaker, I'm stronger, and I have this," Pam said reaching down into her pants and panties and pulled out the cross Jason had stabbed in Tamera's back.

"How will we know when to attack Howard," Dave asked.

"If I find out that I can push thoughts into Howard's mind, I will say 'Mammie' in a sentence. Once I say that get ready for the signal. I may not say it in a few seconds, I may not say it in a few hours, but whenever I say the words, 'so beautiful' that's when you should attack," Pam concluded.

"See Dave," Jason said smiling. "If you start a plan, your plans have a way of just working themselves out."

"That may be true, but true or not, I like my chances of not getting shot much better now," Dave said.

"Truthfully speaking, I don't understand why they haven't shot all of us by now," Jason said. "And please don't say that your sister is going keep the deal you made with her," Jason said looking at Pam.

"Why do you have to say, 'your sister' like it's the nastiest thing in the world," Pam said.

"I'm sorry," Jason said. "The truth is, when I was growing up, I would have given anything to have a brother or a sister. It's not Tamera's fault that she was put in this situation. It's not Tamera's fault she was born first. I apologize." Jason reached out his arms to hug Pam.

"Don't hug me," Pam shouted, causing Jason to step back. "I have got to pee, real bad. If you hug me, I'm going to pee on myself."

"Did you have to mention pee?" Dave said. "Now, I've got to go. Hey, Mr. Howard!" Dave shouted. "We need to use the restroom, bad. Hey! If you don't come, we are going to pee on the floor."

Only seconds later, Howard opened the door and rushed in. He had three portable male urinals which he threw one by one between the bars. Pam picked up one of the urinals and then took a blanket from the bed. She gave the blanket to Dave.

"Would you gentlemen hold this up for me, please?" Pam said.

Jason and Dave held the blanket as Pam pulled her pants down, squatted behind the blanket, and peed in the urinal. "Oh, man," she said in relief, "that was close."

"My turn," Dave said handing his end of the blanket to Pam and picking up one of the urinals from the floor. He went behind the blanket. The sound of his urine hitting the urinal was extremely loud. "Thank You, Jesus," Dave shouted, "and thank you, too, Mr. Howard." He peed a long time. The pitch of the sound, the urine made in the urinal began to get higher as the urine began to reach the top. "I don't think it's gone hold it all."

Quickly, Jason reached down, picked up the last urinal, and held it back to Dave. Dave pinched off his urine, sat the full urinal on the floor, took the other one from Jason and continued peeing. When he was done, he handed the one-third full urinal to Jason.

"There's a little room left," Dave said.

"Are you serious," Jason said, refusing to take the urinal. "I'm not peeing in your pee."

"Give it to me," Pam said, taking the urinal from Dave. She sat it on the floor and poured her urine into the one she had taken from Dave. That left hers empty. She handed that to Jason and snapped the tops of the full urinals closed. Jason peed. When he was done, he turned to Howard. Pam picked up the other two urinals and walked toward the cell door.

"Sit them outside the bars and move back to the wall," Howard ordered.

Jason sat his urinal outside the bars and moved back. Pam sat the two she had between the bars, but she did not move back. She pushed a thought 'Put the urinals on the desk' at Howard.

Howard picked up the three urinals and put them on the desk. Then he wrote something on a piece of paper that was on the desk.

'What is Tamera planning on doing with us,' Pam pushed into Howard's mind.

"She is going to take all of you to the preacher's church tomorrow. We found out about the funeral that he is having for the woman who raised you, the one who died in the fire," Howard said.

Dave and Jason were surprised that Howard was answering a question that he had not been asked. Then, they realized what Pam was doing.

"What is she going to do at the funeral," Pam said aloud.

"It's a surprise," he said.

"Open the cell door," Pam said.

"I don't have the key," Howard said.

"Where is the key?" Pam asked.

"Tamera has it," Howard said. "She said, you would try to make me release you. She was right. She also told me, if you did try to make me release you, then I should punish you."

"Punish me how?" Pam asked.

"You get no food or water, and I am not to come back in this room without Tamera. Goodbye," Howard said. He picked up the urinals and walked toward the door.

"Howard, stop!" Pam ordered.

Howard walked out the door, closing it behind him.

"I guess we need a plan B," Dave said.

"I need that piece of paper on the desk," Pam said while trying to see what was written on it.

"Why?" Dave said. "What's on it."

"Did you make him write on that paper?" Jason asked.

"It was a test," Pam said. I just wanted to see if he would do what I told him to do."

"Take off your pants, Jason," Dave said. "We can use our pants to get it."

"How do you know I have on underwear," Jason said.

"That doesn't matter, I won't look, that long," Pam said with a giggle.

"Don't worry Dave, I have underwear on," Jason said.

"Boxers or briefs?" Dave asked smiling.

"Depends," Jason said laughing.

They both removed their pants, tied the legs together and then tied a knot at the end of one of the legs. Dave held the pants outside the bars, swung the knotted leg toward the desk, and released it. The knot landed on the desk.

"You're good," Jason said surprised.

Dave slowly pulled the pants and the piece of paper moved to the edge of the desk. Dave gave the pants a little jerk and knot fell to the floor. The piece of paper floated down and landed on top of the knot.

"Do you believe this man," Jason said in amazement.

"That's incredible," Pam said.

"When you got the touch, you just got it," Dave said smiling widely. Dave dropped to one knee and looked up at Jason as he slid the pants back toward the cell. Unfortunately, when he pulled, the front side of the paper tilted up and it slid back off the knot and under the desk.

Dave was still looking at Jason while he continued pulling the pants, so he had not seen the paper fall off the knot as Pam and Jason had.

"When I was younger, I could juggle four balls at one time. I was the best juggler in," Dave stopped speaking when he saw Jason frown, turn around and sit down on one of the beds. Dave looked around and saw the paper under the desk

"Mr. Juggler, can I have my pants back, please," Jason said.

"That's okay Dave," Pam said patting him on the back. "You almost got it."

In the next room Howard was talking on his radio to Tamera who was sitting on the side of her bed. "Pam tried to get me to release them, but I told her that you had the key. Over," Howard said shouting into the radio.

"What time are the guards going to get to Sibal's office," Tamera asked.

"In about an hour, at eight A. M. Over.," Howard answered very loudly..

"Turn the volume on your radio down," Tamera shouted. "it's too early in the morning for you to be screaming in my ear."

"Sorry ma'am. Is this okay?" he whispered without adjusting the volume controls at all.

"No. Turn it up a little higher," she said.

"What about that?" Howard said in his normal volume without touching the volume knob.

"Yeah, that's better. Now, as soon as the two guards arrive, I want Pam taken care of," Tamera snarled. "Don't take any chances. Shoot her with a tranquilizer, get a casket, and put her body in it, alive. I want her to wake up suffocating. We will take her in her casket to the funeral tomorrow."

"Yes, ma'am," Howard said. "I'll take care of it." Howard said. "Over and out."

Walt had heard the whole conversation, as he sat on the sofa at Mr. Carson's house. He rushed to put on his shoes and his coat. Then he pulled his long-range rifle from beneath the sofa, and he went out the door.

Howard had turned off the radio and he put the telephone to his ear. "What's going on?" Howard asked. "Why did you want me to call you on the radio, when I was already talking to you on the telephone?"

"The last time I talked on the radio, I could hear a radio being adjusted," Tamera said. "I thought it was Sibal, but it was not Sibal, because she had been lying in front of her car for at least an hour when we found her, and her radio was in her car. I heard that same sound of somebody adjusting a radio, when our conversation started, and then again each time I told you to adjust your volume."

"Was somebody listening to the conversation we just had?" Howard asked.

"I'm almost sure of it," Tamera said.

"So, that's why you told me not to do anything to the volume control on my radio, but instead just speak louder and quieter into the radio when you told me to adjust the volume."

"I wanted whoever was listening to have to adjust his volume both times. That way, I would have two chances to hear if they adjusted the volume. I heard him change the volume on his radio when you were speaking loudly. Then he adjusted it again, when you were whispering."

"Who do you think it was?" Howard said.

"They are probably the ones who shot Sibal. If it is the preacher, he has someone helping him and now that they know where their friends are. They are going to come to save our prisoners. Tell the guard to get ready. If possible, capture them alive. I would like the pleasure of killing them softly."

"Ma'am, yesterday, I heard Sibal tell Mr. Reeves from the regional office that the guards he had loaned her had been killed. She told him that drug dealers ambushed them thinking she was someone else because she was in someone else's car. She told Mr. Reeves that all six of the guards were killed. Only she was able to escape."

"She had six guards?" Tamera said. "They were all killed?"

"Yes, ma'am," Howard said, "but I don't believe it was drug dealers. I think it was Pam's people. If the preacher is involved, he is most definitely, not alone. I don't think we will be able to take them alive."

"All right," Tamera said. "Tell the guards to shoot to kill. However, if they see someone in a preacher's collar, tell them to try not to kill him if possible. I want to see him take his last breath."

"Yes ma'am," Howard said. "I'll go and talk to them now. They all arrived early, they have been paid, and they are ready to start work. Is there anything else?"

"Yes. Go ahead and tranquilize Pam. Separate her from the other two. Tell one of the guards to take her to Leo's funeral home."

"Do you want her killed and put her in a casket?" Howard asked.

"No, tape her up good, put her in a casket, but don't close it down all the way. Let her get some air. I don't want to kill her, yet. We may need her," Tamera said. "Tell the guard to lock her in one of the back rooms at the funeral home. I don't want him to stay in the room with her. Tell him to not to go in the room unless he hears from me or you. I know that Pam will play tricks with his mind. Tell him emphatically, that he is to guard the door with his life."

"Will do. I'll see you when you get here." Howard hung up the phone and went to talk with the guards. They were in the office reception area drinking coffee and talking.

There was a group of five by the coffee maker, a group of four near the front door, and one sitting alone in the corner of the room rubbing his silver 38 caliber revolver with a white handkerchief. He was the only one wearing gloves, a flak jacket, and a shoulder holster. The other men had waist holstered Glocks, some on the side and some on the back. Howard walked to the door, stopped, and turned around facing them.

"Let me have your attention, please," Howard said and waited until all noise had ceased and all eyes were on him. "You have been hired to protect Ms. Tamera. There will probably be an attempt on her life. You will be required to use lethal force. I have read all your resumes and each of you have had at least one confirmed kill. We will be in combat against a group of very hostile individuals. They are not associated with any police or military authorities, but they are highly trained. These men ambushed and killed at least six of our guards. When you were hired, you did not know how dangerous this job would be, so I want to give you one last chance to back out. Just return the five-hundred-dollar deposit and leave now." Howard waited but nobody moved. "Okay, these are the rules. You are being paid for one week of service. On next Friday, you will receive the remaining funds due you, five hundred dollars, provided Ms. Tamera is alive and unharmed. If she is killed or seriously injured, consider yourselves fired, immediately, and you will forfeit any additional payment. If you agree to these rules raise your hand," Howard said and watched while each man raised a hand. "The armory is in that room over to my right. Each man should get a vest with ammo clips, and a M16. There's one more thing. We have three prisoners locked up behind bars in the back room. They are leaders of the group that killed our guards. Ms. Tamera will be here soon. She told me to expect our office to be attacked by their men within the next hour. I want three of you outside with semi-automatic rifles, I want two on the roof, and I want four inside with me."

"How many men are we expecting?" said the largest man in the group of five.

"What's your name sir?" Howard asked.

"I'm Turk. This is my team," Turk said.

"As far as we know, there are two, maybe three," Howard said.

"Why are they coming here? That doesn't make sense," Turk said. "That's suicide."

"The three prisoners are very important to these men," Howard said. "They are coming because they believe that there will only be three men guarding them here, not ten. They don't know that we are waiting for them. They think they will take us by surprise. If we defeat them here and now, most of our work will be over, and you will be able to get paid and leave Monday."

"My team can take the roof and the outside perimeter, if that's okay with you," Turk said.

"Okay," Howard said. "The radios are on the table over there."

"We have our own communications," Turk said touching his earpiece.

"Okay, you get one, so I can communicate with you, and then get in position as soon as possible."

Turk gathered his men together and gave them instructions, while Howard addressed the remaining men.

"I want you four to set up inside," Howard said to the group of four.

"I'm King One, and these are my brothers, King Two, King Three, and King Four," the oldest of four men said. "We got this. You can go do what you do. Nobody is getting passed us."

"You, come with me," Howard said to the man sitting alone.

"My name is Ashton, Ash for short," he said.

"Okay Ash, I have a special job for you," Howard said as he took Ash's arm and pulled him toward the back rooms. "I want you to transport one of the prisoners to a nearby funeral home, tape her up, including her mouth, and put her in a casket. Don't kill her. Leave the top of the casket up. Lock her in a room, go outside the room, and lock the door. Don't go in the room with her unless I tell you to. Don't talk to her. Don't listen to her. She is a hypnotist. She is very dangerous. She is a liar. She will get inside your head, so don't go in the room."

"If she is so dangerous, how am I going to get her to the funeral home," Ash asked as they entered a room with monitors, computers, and electronic equipment on a long table.

"I'm going to open the door to the room where she is, just enough for you to see her and the two men behind the bars. I want you to shoot her with this tranquilizer gun to knock her out," Howard said, handing him a short rifle from the table. "Then, when the men go to help her, I'll open the door completely and you can shoot the two men as well." He handed Ash two tranquilizer darts. "Then you will be able to transport her to the funeral home, tape her up, get her in the casket and lock her in one of the rooms before she comes to."

"Okay," Ash said pulling back the bolt on the rifle halfway so he could see the dart in the cylinder. "It loads one at a time?"

"That's right. Are you ready?"

"Whenever you are," Ash said.

Let's go," Howard said as he turned the doorknob and pushed the door open just enough for Ash to push the tip of the rifle barrel through.

The dart hit Pam in the side of her neck as she was sitting on one of the beds. She raised her hand to her neck and began to fall forward. Dave, who was sitting directly in front of her caught her shoulders and laid her over on the bed, while Jason stood up and faced the door. Jason could see movement behind the opening of the door. Then he saw something appear in the crack, however, before he realized what it was, he also was hit in the neck.

Dave had little time to react, as he saw Jason begin to lose his balance. He caught Jason and lowered him down on the other bed as the door was opened completely and he looked back and saw two men come in. A dart hit him in the buttock, causing him to fall on top of Jason.

Chapter 36
Search and Rescue

(Friday 7:45 AM)

Walt was driving toward Sibal's office, trying to think of the best way to rescue Pam. He could not come up with a plan that would work.

"Okay, I'm on my way, but what am I going to do when I get there?"

Walt rubbed his hair back. "What do I know? What did they say?" He turned right on the next road. "There are two guards coming at eight. I could get there and kill them before they get inside. But then what? They could kill Pam in retaliation. That won't work."

Walt looked at the speedometer. He was going too fast. He didn't want to be stopped by the police, but he was running out of time. In fact, he knew he would never make it there before eight.

"I won't be able to get there by eight," he said in anguish. "I could intercept the delivery of the casket. No casket, no casket to suffocate Pam in. Maybe that would buy me more time. What if the casket is already there, then what?" Walt pulled the car over to the side of the road. He put both hands on the top of the stirring wheel and rested his forehead on his hands. "I should have asked Rev. Zackery about this. But I already know what he would say. He would tell me to 'wait on the Lord,'" Walt said imitating Rev. Zackery. "He would say, 'just have faith that the Lord will tell me what to do just when I needed Him to.'"

Walt put his hands together and began to pray more to himself than to God. "Lord, I don't know what to do, I need for You to tell me what to do, please." Walt looked at the clock on the dashboard of the car. It showed eight o'clock. "I guess I waited too long to pray," Walt said as he laid his head back on the car seat. He closed his eyes as tears rolled down both sides of his face. In his mind he could see Pam locked into a casket with her hands clawing at the inside top of the casket. A panicked expression is on her face as she tries to scream but can't because she has no air.

"Maybe I should just go back and get ready for tomorrow. Rev. Zackery did say that Pam was going to be there, that she was going to be alive, and that I was going to have a chance to save her. He truly believes that his vision is really going to happen. Things seem to be developing. Tamera said she was going to bring a casket with Pam inside to the funeral, just like in the vision. How could that happen?" Walt thought for a minute. "Maybe Pam told Tamera about the vision, and now Tamera is going to make it happen exactly like Rev. Zackery described it. That's how it could happen."

After sitting in the car for five minutes, Walt looked around, took his rifle from the front passenger seat, got out of the car, and walked to the trunk. After opening it, he opened the duffle bag and put his rifle in. When he did, a stick of dynamite fell out. He looked in the duffle bag and found three more sticks of dynamite, a detonator and a remote trigger.

"Thank you, Rev. Zackery. If I gotta go out, I might as well go out with a big bang," Walt said with a slight smiled. "If Pam is dead, I'll make them pay."

Just at that moment a car approached him. It was a black Lincoln Continental. Walt recognized the tag on the front of the car. The tag had an eye in the center of two triangles. One triangle was pointing up, and the other was pointing down. It was a witchcraft symbol. He had seen this car at Sibal's office before. When it was there, only certain people were allowed to be in the building. He pulled his duffle bag from the trunk and placed it on his shoulder. The bag and his arm hid his face from the driver of the car. As the car got closer, he could discern the driver's facial features. Walt turned his body as the car went by. He got a very good look at the driver. Walt was in a trance for a moment because the driver looked so much like Pam.

"Miss Tamera, how do you do." Walt said smiling. "He dropped the duffle bag and quickly pulled his rifle from it. He aimed at the darkly tinted back glass at a location that he felt would hit the driver in the head. However, before he could shoot, the car turned right. As the car was beginning to disappear behind some trees, he aimed at the back tire and fired. He did not know if he had hit the tire or not. There was only one way to find out. He got in his car and drove down the road. When he reached the street where Tamera had turned, he kept straight and then stopped, because he had looked down the street and saw the black Lincoln parked beside the road.

"You are mine now," Walt said to himself as he reached for his rifle. He walked to a tree where he could see the car and aimed at the back glass again. Then he heard her voice on the radio in his car.

"Howard! Come in," Tamera said.

"This is Howard ma'am, go ahead."

"Has anything happened?" Tamera asked.

"No ma'am everything is quiet," Howard said. "Are you still in route? Over."

"I have a flat tire. Send two guards out to get me, immediately," she said. "I'm on Church St. near Norwood Rd."

"I'll have someone there in ten minutes, over and out," Howard said.

Walt put the sites of his rifle on the back glass again. "Wait," he said aloud. "I've got to make sure she is still sitting behind the steering wheel."

Walt walked back to his car, got two of the sticks of dynamite, taped them together, attached the detonator, and put the remote trigger in his jacket pocket. Then he drove down the street where Tamera's car was parked. When he reached the car, he slowed down. Tamera was inside the car with her radio still in her hand. She looked at him and waved for him to keep going. Walt was glad he had not tried to shoot her, because at the bottom of the window he saw the words, "Bulletproof Glass." Walt parked his car in front of hers, got out of his car, and began to walk toward her holding the dynamite behind him. To his surprise, she lifted an Uzi pistol up so he could see it and then she pointed it at him. Knowing that he was protected by the bullet-proof glass, Walt continued to walk confidently until he was next to her window.

"Do you have a death wish?" Tamera yelled. "I do not need any assistance. Now get the hell outta here, before I shoot your dumb…" Tamera stopped speaking when she saw Walt hold up the dynamite and detonator in one hand and the remote trigger in the other. "What do you want?" Tamera said putting the Uzi on the seat beside her.

"You had my," Walt hesitated, "soon to be wife, killed. I want you and me to join her in death."

"Wait. I have no idea what you are talking about," Tamera yelled. "I don't know your fiancé. Why would I have her killed?"

"You know who she is, because she is your twin sister, Pam," Walt said.

"Pam is not dead," Tamera shouted.

"I heard you order your men to kill her," Walt said.

"You are the one who was listening on the other radio. I knew you were listening, so I said that because I thought if you felt that Pam was going to be killed you would try to rescue her," Tamera explained. "She is not dead!"

"Take me to her then," Walt ordered.

"Okay. Let's go in your car. As you can see, and probably because of you, mine is out of service," Tamera said.

"Get in the back," Walt ordered. "I know your people are coming to get you. So, when they arrive, tell them that I am your personal guard sent by Richard at the regional office."

"You know Richard?" Tamera asked as she opened the door.

"Leave the Uzi right where it is. Get in the back." Walt said again. "When your men arrive, tell your men to fix the flat and that we will follow them back to the office," Walt said. "Don't be foolish. I'll be happy to take your men to hell with us. The more the merrier, they say."

"What's your name?" Tamera asked. "At least, tell me that."

"It's Walt."

"Okay Walt," Tamera said warmly. "What is it that you really want?"

"I wanted for you and your people to leave me and Pam alone, I wanted to live a normal life with Pam, but you wouldn't let us. Even now, I believe you are lying. I believe you had her killed. I'm pretty sure of that, but I've got to make sure."

"You love her so much that you don't care if you die avenging her," Tamera said. "She told me about you. When we were trapped inside the crystal ball together, she told me how much she loved you. She will be very glad to see you again."

A black sedan sped down the road and stopped beside the Lincoln. Tamera let the window down and spoke to the driver whose window was down across from Tamera. Walt felt the urge to give the remote trigger to Tamera.

"Push me one more time, witch, and I will see how many pieces of you I can scatter across this road," Walt said softly.

"Who are you?" Tamera asked the driver of the sedan.

"I'm K3, and this is my brother K4," the driver said. "Mr. Howard sent us to pick you up."

"I'm Miss Tamera, your client, and this is my personal guard, Walt."

"We were told to pick you up, and bring you back to the office," K3 said. "Howard didn't say nothing about no guard."

"Fix my tire. Then me and my personal guard will follow you back to the office," Tamera ordered.

"Fix you tire?" K4 said disgustedly. "We were hired to protect you, not change your freaking tires."

"You're K3, right?" Tamera asked, looking at the person sitting on the passenger side.

"Yeah," K3 said cautiously.

"Take out you pistol and put it to K4's head," Tamera said.

K3 pulled his pistol and put it against his brother's head.

"What are you doing," K4 yelled at K3.

"Tell him that he has ten minutes to change the tire," Tamera said. "If he is not done in ten minutes shoot him in the head."

"You have ten minutes to change the tire," K3 said to K4.

Walt popped the trunk and K4 hurriedly changed the tire. The job was completed in eight and a half minutes. The two men returned to their car. K3 put his pistol back in his holster and acted as if nothing unusual had happened.

"K4?" Tamera said.

"Yeah," K4 replied angrily.

"Am I going to have any more problems with you?" Tamera asked.

"No," K4 answered, still angrily.

"That's no ma'am," Tamera snapped.

"No ma'am," K4 said, submissively.

"We will follow you back to the office."

K3 turned the car around and drove away. Walt followed. Walt looked in the rearview mirror at Tamera and was amazed how much alike she and Pam were.

"You said that Pam told you how much she loved me?" Walt asked.

"Yeah, my little sister and I had plenty of time to talk and get to know each other while we were trapped. She said that you and she had the most wonderful day together. You don't know this, but while we were inside the crystal ball, we made an agreement. We agreed that if we ever got out of the crystal ball, we would go our separate ways and we would leave each other alone. She said she would keep her people from bothering me and mine, and I said I would keep my people from bothering her or hers. That was the deal, however, as soon as we were about to get out of the crystal, one of her people, Jason, tried to kill me. He stabbed me in my back with a wooden stake. He broke the agreement. Pam cannot control him. He is determined to kill me or die trying. Now, I'm willing to abide by the agreement I had with Pam in the future. I will leave you and Pam and all your people alone, except for Jason.

It is Jason who is disrupting everything. Jason is standing between you and a life of happiness with Pam. He has to die."

Tamera stopped so Walt could absorb everything she had said. Then she continued.

"This is the deal I will make with you. If you will kill Jason, then all this will be over. You and Pam can have your normal life together. You can have children and live a life together filled with love and happiness. If I kill him, the agreement will be broken completely and irrevocably. But, if you kill him, the agreement will remain intact. Either way, he is going to die. Either you kill him, or I will. We're here, what do you say?"

"I say, take me to Pam."

Walt got out of the car with dynamite in his inside jacket pocket, the remote trigger in his left hand, and the Uzi in his right. He opened the door for Tamera. K3 and K4 lead the way and Walt followed closely behind. When they had all entered the building, Howard was shocked to see Walt. Howard looked at the all the other guards in the room and then pointed at Walt. They immediately pulled out their weapons and pointed them toward Walt.

"What is Walt doing here," Howard asked as he watched the Uzi in Walt's hand being raised toward him.

"Walt is my personal guard," Tamera said loudly.

"What? Walt was Pam's personal bodyguard," Howard yelled. "He killed at least twenty of Sibal's elite guards, and how many times has Pam tried to kill you?"

"Did you know that Howard was Sibal's personal assistant, that is until I shot her mouth off and left her to bleed out in the woods. How many times did Sibal try to kill you with his assistance?"

Tamera looked at Howard and frowned. All the guards turned their weapons toward Howard and then looked at Tamera as if they were waiting for a kill order.

"I never tried to kill you. Sibal told everybody you were dead. I only found out differently when I saw you inside the crystal ball. I saved you. If I hadn't tricked Sibal, she would have succeeded in blowing you up," Howard said frantically.

"Calm down!" Tamera shouted. "You saved my life. I owe you and you will be handsomely rewarded." Tamera could see the relief on Howard's face as she looked sternly into his eyes. However, when Tamera looked back at Walt, instantly her expression became almost joyful.

"You did that to Sibal?" Tamera asked.

"I thought, and she thought that she had blown up the crystal with you and Pam inside," Walt said.

"We got there before she died," Tamera said smiling. "Finishing her off was one of the most satisfying experiences I have ever had. Thank you, Walt."

"The pleasure was all mine," Walt said.

"Should we be expecting any more company today," Tamera asked Walt.

"You already have everybody here except Rev. Zackery," Walt said, "and he is expecting to see you tomorrow at the funeral."

"Really now. I wouldn't have it any other way," Tamera said.

"Now, where is Pam?" Walt said.

"Let's go see the love of your life," Tamera said as she turned and walked toward the back of the building.

Howard waited for Walt to follow but he didn't.

"After you," Walt said. "I wouldn't want you to get any crazy ideas. I know how close you and Sibal were."

"Gentlemen," Tamera said. She had stopped when she heard what Walt had said. "Walt, you should really be more appreciative of Howard. When he saved me, he also saved Pam. And Howard, Walt is my guest. Treat him that way." Tamera opened a door to a room where Walt saw some electronic equipment on shelves, a sofa, and some chairs in front of a long table with a computer and a large monitor on it. Straight ahead beside the table was a window. On the wall on the right side of the room at the back, was a door.

Howard went to the computer and hit some keys and the monitor came on. On the screen of the monitor was a still frame of Pam, Dave, and Jason behind bars.

"What is this?" Walt said angrily.

"It's a recording of this morning, when they were planning their escape," Howard said and then he hit another key. Immediately the video began to play. On the video, Dave was talking. Howard fast forwarded the video and then stopped it. "Ma'am, you should be interested in this." Howard hit the play key.

On the monitor Jason was speaking.

"Why didn't you let her die," Jason said looking at Pam. "The fire would have burned her heart out."

"Before you start complaining, at least you ought to thank me for saving your ungrateful life," Pam said.

"Yeah, that's right Jason," Dave said. "If Pam hadn't acted, you and Tamera would both be dead now, and we would still be trapped in the crystal."

"Well, we are still trapped, and she is free," Jason said. "You think this is better?"

"You hate her so much that would let yourself be killed in order to kill her, and you would sacrifice me and Dave as well." Pam said.

"You need help, man," Dave said. "Your hatred is consuming you and it is dangerous to us."

"Because of her, my grandmother was set on fire while she was still alive. My grandmother was burned to death," Jason said angrily. "You saw her, Dave, when she came out of that house. She was totally covered in flames. Yeah, I want to kill Tamera and I will kill her." He walked over to Pam and looked her in her face. "I am going to kill your sister dear."

Howard stopped the video and looked at Tamera. Tamera looked at Walt.

"Just like I told you, when I was in the crystal, Pam and I made a deal. We agreed that when we got out, I and my people would leave Pam and her people alone, and Pam and her people would leave me and my people alone. But before we could get out, Jason attacked me. He would have killed me if Pam hadn't stopped him. Jason won't abide by the terms of the agreement. Because of him, nobody can have what they want," Tamera argued.

Walt looked at the door at the back of the room. "Are they in there?"

"Yeah," Howard said.

"Let's go," Walt demanded. "You two go first."

Howard opened the door, and they all entered the room.

When Jason and Dave saw Walt, they froze. Neither of them said anything.

"Where's Pam?" Walt said to everyone in the room.

"Where is she?" Tamera said to Howard.

"You told me to separate her, so I had her moved," Howard said to Tamera.

"Take me to her now," Walt shouted.

"We need to talk in the other room," Tamera said calmly. "Do you need any time alone with these two?"

"No, let's talk, just me and you," Walt said turning and walking out of the room. Tamera followed. However, before she could leave the room, Dave yelled out.

"Miss Tamera? Could you ask Mr. Howard to give us the urinals, please," Dave asked.

"Give them the urinals," Tamera said to Howard.

Howard hurried through the video room and Tamera walked to the desk and sat in one of the seats.

"Sit down, Walt," Tamera said. "We need to talk about our deal."

"I need to see Pam before we talk about anything," Walt said ominously. "And I need to see her now."

Howard rushed back through the room and was about to go into the cell room when Tamera stopped him.

"What is the name of the guard holding Pam?" Tamera asked.

"Ash, his name is Ash," Howard said.

"Get him on the radio," she said.

Howard took the radio from his belt and began speaking. "Ash, come in. This is Howard. Come in."

"This is Ash, over," Ash said.

"Your boss Miss Tamera wants to speak with you. You are to follow her instruction to the letter. Over," Howard said.

"Roger that, over" Ash replied.

Howard handed Tamera the radio.

"Ash, take the radio to your prisoner. Tell her that someone wants to speak with her," Tamera said.

"Yes ma'am," Ash said as he unlocked the door. He walked over to Pam who was lying in a casket with her upper arms taped to her body and tape over her mouth. "Somebody wants to talk to you," Ash said to Pam as he pulled the tape from her mouth. "Go ahead, ma'am." Ash held the radio in front of Pam's face.

Tamera gave Walt the radio.

"Pam. Are you there?" Walt said excitedly.

"Walt, it's so good to hear your voice," Pam said with equal excitement. "You're alive. Are you safe?"

"Yes, I'm safe," Walt said. "Did they hurt you? Are you injured?"

"No, just uncomfortable," Pam said. "They have me taped up too tight."

Walt looked at Tamera. "Tell him to take the tape off her," Walt yelled.

Tamera took the radio. "Ash, loosen the tape on her."

"Yes, ma'am," Ash responded. "I will as soon as the conversation is over, ma'am."

Walt took the radio. "I'm going to get you out of this. Hold on for a little while longer. Don't worry."

Tamera took the radio. "Ash if you don't hear from me in one hour, shoot Pam in the head."

"Yes ma'am," Ash said.

"Over and out," Tamera said and turned off the radio and turned toward Howard. "Go and watch our prisoners." Then she turned to Walt. "Now, let's talk about our deal."

Chapter 37
Dealing with Demons

(Friday 9:00 AM)

Howard had been sitting at the desk in the cell room for several minutes when Dave spoke.

"Mr. Howard we really appreciate you getting those urinals for us," Dave said politely and waited for a response. There was none. "Two of them need to be emptied please, when you get a chance. I'll just sit them outside the bars." Dave waited for a response again. Howard only looked up at him, frowned, and looked back down.

"Where is your boss, Sibal," Jason said nastily, "I haven't seen her in a while. She's not in trouble with Tamera, is she?"

"Not anymore," Howard said without looking up. "She's dead."

Jason was shocked. "What happened to her?"

"For one thing your buddy shot up her pretty good," Howard said.

"Who? Walt?" Jason said loudly.

"Yeah. He shot her in her lungs, her kidney, her leg, and her face. Then he left her to die," Howard said standing up. "He didn't even have the decency to put her out of her misery. When we found her, she was still bleeding to death. The whole bottom of her face was gone. Tamera put her out of her misery."

"It wasn't her face anyway," Jason said. "She probably killed some poor innocent child to get it. So, if you are looking for sympathy, you will get none here."

"Yeah, Sibal wasn't the sweetest girl in town. She may have had it coming," Howard said. "She really got off much easier, than she would have if Tamera had found her first," Howard said.

"What do you mean?" Jason asked.

"Tamera found out that Sibal had tried to kill her. We were looking for her and if Tamera had found her before your buddy did, it would have been so much worse. Tamera is," Howard paused, "sadistic in the worse way. But you'll find out soon enough."

"What are we going to find out?" Dave said.

"Didn't you try to kill Tamera?" Howard asked.

"Yeah, more than once," Jason replied.

"Not me. I have never tried to kill her," Dave said.

"No, you gave her that bald spot in the back of her head when you set her hair on fire," Howard said. "She was very angry when she told me about that."

"Oh, I had forgotten about that." Dave said sadly.

"Well, she hasn't. She is reminded of it every time she looks in the mirror and combs her hair," Howard said pulling the desk draw open and taking out some folders. "She has asked to read your files." Howard dropped the folders on desk. He spread them apart and opened them both. "Hmmm. David Parker. Looks like you have a wife, and Jason Scott doesn't have a wife, but you have a mother."

Suddenly a smiling Tamera opened the door. Walt was standing behind her. She had an old five-gallon paint bucket with a lid on it. She handed it to Howard.

"Put this in the cell and let's go," Tamera said handing Howard a key. "We need to get ready for tomorrow." Then she looked at Jason and Dave. "Hopefully we can all let bygones be bygones, and we can move on."

Howard quickly opened the cell door and sat the bucket inside. Just as quickly Jason rushed out the door toward Tamera. Jason stopped five feet in front of her. He was surprised that she had remained calm. She slowly pivoted to her right so that her left side was now facing him. She raised her palms and quickly pushed them toward him. Jason could see a visual distortion moving toward him as he quickly dived to the floor beside the desk. He could feel a force hit his foot as he dove to the floor. Howard, Walt, and Dave watched as Jason scrambled back to his feet, ran back into the cell, and sat on the bed as if nothing had happened. Howard locked the cell door and gave the key back to Tamera. Tamera was staring at Jason.

"Are you ready, ma'am?" Howard asked.

"I'll see you tomorrow, at the funeral," Tamera said looking at Jason. She turned and walked out. Howard followed. Jason and Dave could hear the door being locked.

"Are you trying to get yourself killed," Dave shouted.

"No, I just wanted to find out what was on that piece of paper," Jason said pulling from his pocket, the yellow piece of paper that they had tried to get off the desk earlier.

"Well, you risked your life to get it, what does it say?" Dave asked.

"R17, 26, 35, 44," Jason read.

"What does it mean?" Dave asked.

"I don't know, but at least it's easy to remember," Jason said. "I'm just wondering why Howard was talking about your wife and my mother."

"Do you think they are in danger," Dave said.

"It feels like it," Jason said. "Whatever is going to happen, it's going down tomorrow at the funeral"

"What have they done with Pam?" Dave said. "Do you think she's still alive?"

"They haven't killed us, so they probably haven't killed her either," Jason said. "I wonder why they moved her away from us?"

"Do you think they knew about our plan? Do you think this place is bugged?" Dave said.

"If it's not, it should be. So, lets act like it is. Anything that we don't want them to hear we will whisper in each other's ear."

"It looks like we need to prepare our souls to meet the Lord," Dave said.

"All is not lost, my friend," Jason said with a smile. "I have one more ace up my sleeve. Come closer let me whisper in your ear."

Dave sat down beside Jason and Jason began whispering in his ear.

"You remember how those demons used to take control of Billy, don't you?" Jason whispered.

"How could I forget that?" Dave said loudly.

"Last week after you left, Billy got out of Rev. Zackery's house and ran in the woods. I went looking for him, but when I found him, a demon had taken control of him. The demon told me that Pam was going to double-cross us. He told me that Pam had made a deal with Sibal. Pam was planning to take over the coven. He showed me a vision of Pam and Sibal making the deal while they were both in ICU. As you know, that is exactly what happened. Pam would have double-crossed us if Sibal hadn't double-crossed her first."

"So, why are you telling me this?" Dave asked.

"After this demon told me about Pam, he offered to help me," Jason said.

"Help you do what?" Dave asked.

"Help me kill the witches, warn me whenever trouble was near, and help get out of trouble."

"And why was he going to help you?" Dave asked.

"He said, if all those witches died, he would get credit for their souls when they got to hell," Jason answered.

"I know there has to be some strings attached. What did the demon say you had to do to get his help?" Dave asked.

"He said all I had to do was to give him permission to help me," Jason said.

"You believed that?" Dave said. "I know you didn't fall for that lie, did you?

"I told him I didn't want his help," Jason said.

"Okay," Dave said. "You had me going there for a while."

"Then, he told me that he would give me one free request before I made my final decision," Jason said. "That way I would know what I was getting. After that he let Billy come back. Billy pulled a gun on me and took me prisoner."

"Did you ever use your free request," Dave asked.

"I wasn't going to use it, but Billy was about to nail my hands to this chair," Jason said. "Look, after Billy captured me, he took me to his barn where he had the crystal with Tamera inside. Tamera made him tie me up. She told me to get her out of the crystal. When I didn't, she told Billy to nail my hands to the chair. As Jason told what happened, he could see the past in his mind.

Billy got a hammer and two long nails from a box on the floor. He held Jason's right hand and positioned the nail in the middle of the back of it. He raised the hammer. Jason closed his eyes and tightened all his muscles in anticipation of the pain, but nothing happened. He opened his eyes and Billy was still holding the hammer up.

"What are you waiting on? Do it!" Tamera screamed from inside the crystal.

Billy raised the hammer higher and began to bring it down.

"Bailtron," Jason shouted.

Billy froze, the hammer only inches away from the nail. Bailtron's demon head covered Billy's.

"You like to cut things pretty close, I see," Bailtron said as he put his head down close to the nail. Then he looked at Jason, their faces only three inches apart. "You rang. What can I do for you, Jason my boy? Are you ready to make a deal?"

"You said I had one free request," Jason said.

"Did I say that? You know for yourself nothing in this life is free. However, I guess I did say that. What is your request?"

"Make Billy release his grip on that nail," Jason said.

"Okay."

The nail being held by Billy's fingers, fell over and slid off Jason's hand to the floor.

"I never thought I'd say this but, thank you demon."

"Oh, it was Bailtron when you needed me, but now that I have got you out of your mess, it's demon. Well, your mama is a demon, and your grandmama was, too."

"I'm sorry," Jason pleaded. "Thank you, Bailtron."

"Look, I really didn't mean that about your grandmother," Bailtron said apologetically. "Have you considered my offer? Are you ready to make a deal?"

"I have been pretty busy. Can I sleep on it and tell you in the morning?"

"I'll give you till sun-up. Then I will need an answer," Bailtron said. "Remember we want the same thing, all those witches dead. I'm the only one that can really help you."

"Okay, Bailtron."

"Get some rest," Bailtron said. "Here's Billy."

The demon head disappeared, and Billy brought the hammer down full force on his thumb and forefinger.

"Got to be more careful," Billy yelled, dropping the hammer, and grabbing his hurt fingers.

Inside the crystal, Tamera stood in a state of shock, her mouth open, wondering what she had just seen. Her shock was interrupted when Billy quickly took the crystal off the table, threw it in the safe, and closed the top. Billy made his way to the door while rubbing his fingers.

Billy cut off the light and walked out of the barn.

Jason paused to give his story time to sink into Dave's mind as they sat on the bed in the jail cell.

"Did Tamera see Bailtron?" Dave asked.

"I don't know," Jason answered.

"It appears that Bailtron is more powerful than Tamera," Dave said.

"Yeah, at least powerful enough to get me out of any situation she may put me in, if I use him."

"If you make a deal with this demon, it may cost you your soul," Dave said.

"If I don't make a deal, it may cost all of us our lives."

Dave stood up and faced Jason.

"Don't make a deal with the demon to save my life. I don't want to be the excuse you make for choosing the devil over the Lord. I know Rev. Zackery would feel the same way. And believe me, Pam can take care of herself," Dave said loudly disregarding the possibility of being over-heard. "If you do this, it's on you. You will be doing it because you choose to, for your own hateful reasons, and I know what the main reason is. You want to kill Tamera."

"We killed hundreds of people. We burned them alive, and now you want to act like a holier than thou saint," Jason said. "When I go to hell, you are going to have a seat right beside me, with the rest of the murderers, buddy."

"Those witches were enemies of God," Dave said.

"So is Tamera," Jason shouted.

Dave thought for a minute. "Didn't the demon say you had to let him know the following morning if you were going to accept his deal?"

"Yeah," Jason said.

"That was over three days ago," Dave said. "Your deadline has already passed. How do you know that he will still come to your rescue?"

"He'll come," Jason said confidently.

"How can you be so sure?" Dave said.

"He wants credit for my soul," Jason said.

"Think about it," Dave said. "That demon only spoke to you through Billy. Billy is dead now. How is he going to speak to you?"

"I didn't think about that," Jason said. "He said he was a supervisor. Supervisors are put in charge of more than one person, so he is probably over more than one demon. Maybe someone else, who has demons that he is in charge of, will be at the funeral."

"Maybe you should forget about making deals with demons," Dave said. "Your soul could end up in a burning hell for eternity. Nothing is worth that."

CHAPTER 38
JUST A THOUGHT

(Friday 10:00 AM)

Pam was sitting up in the casket. Her wrists were tied to the handles of the casket as Ash cut and removed the tape from around her upper body. She was still groggy from the tranquilizer, but she was beginning to think more clearly.

"Did you put all this tape on me?" Pam said. "She called you Ash, right?"

Ash did not reply. He kept carefully cutting and removing tape.

"Did she tell you why she wants you to put a bullet in my head?" Pam said. "Oh, by the way, my name is Pam."

Again, he did not reply. He was almost done.

"She wants to kill me because I had sex with her husband. I did not know he was married. We had been dating for a month. He told me he loved me and that he wanted to marry me. "He bought me this ring." Pam said raising her left hand as high as she could.

This time Ash reacted. He looked at to the brass compression washer on her pinky finger and sadly shook his head.

"We had sex one-time, last week. It was the second time in my life that I have ever had sex. I didn't want to have sex. I told him that I didn't want to, but he would not stop. After constantly begging me and telling me how great it would be to make love with him, I finally agreed to do it. It only lasted five minutes. I didn't even have a climax. I have never had a climax." Pam stopped and pushed the thought, 'rub your nose' at him. He rubbed his nose. "It's bad enough to be killed because I had sex with a married man who told me he was not married, but it is even worse to die without ever having a climax."

Ash pulled the last bit of tape from her fatigue shirt. "You have never masturbated before," Ash asked incredulously.

"What's that?" Pam asked.

"That when you play with your sex organ with your hand or fingers until you reach an orgasm," Ash said.

"How do you, masturbate?" Pam asked. "Show me. My hands are tied. Masturbate me."

"What?" Ash said in astonishment.

"You are going to kill me, at least you could give me a little pleasure before you do it."

Ash thought for a moment and then he put his hand on her breast and began to squeeze it and rub it. "Does that feel good?" Ash asked.

"No," Pam answered.

Ash put his fingers between Pam's legs and rubbed. "What about that? Does that feel good?"

"No," Pam replied.

"You know, there is a possibility that you might be frigid," Ash said.

"I'm not frigid," Pam said. "What's frigid?"

"That when you are numb in the places where you should be very sensitive," Ash said, "and it makes it almost impossible for you to reach an orgasm."

"Take my clothes off. Maybe that would help."

"I don't know about that, Pam," Ash said. "You're supposed to be my prisoner."

"Prisoners on death row get one last request, don't they?"

"Yes, they do," Ash said, "but I'm not going to rape you. I'm not a rapist."

"You are not a rapist, but you're a killer." Pam paused. "You are very young to be a killer. How many people have you killed?" Pam asked.

"I've killed five," Ash replied boldly.

"You have killed five times?" Pam asked incredulously.

"No. I killed all five at once, with a grenade launcher, when I was in the Marines in the in war with Grenada," Ash replied.

"That wasn't a war," Pam sneered. "Y'all were fighting against some untrained islanders. That was a joke."

"You don't know," Ash said angrily. "You weren't there."

"You had grenade launchers, bazookas and machine guns and all they had were old rifles," Pam said. "You call that a fair fight?"

"That just goes to show how stupid you sound. War is not supposed to be fair," Ash said.

"It wasn't a war. The gigantic United States invaded the tiny little island of Grenada," Pam said, "and you took your grenade launcher and killed some men who were hundreds of feet away. You probably couldn't even see their faces, and they were probably just lowly soldiers, following orders."

"And I was a just lowly soldier, following orders, too," Ash said angrily.

"So, I will be your first murder victim," Pam said. "How much are you getting paid to kill me?"

"Look, I'm not going to murder you. I was paid to protect this Tamera lady," Ash said. "You have nothing to worry about from me unless you try to harm Ms. Tamera. Anyway, the job will be finished come Friday. I will collect the other five hundred I'm supposed to get, and I'm gone, lady."

"You are not going to put a bullet in my head if Ms. Tamera doesn't call you in an hour?" Pam asked.

"No! I am not a murderer, and I am not a rapist," Ash said still angry about her Grenada comment.

"Then let me go," Pam pleaded. She pushed a thought, 'untie her,' at him.

"You don't know nothing about fighting a war, just like you don't know nothing about guarding a prisoner. I'm not going to let you go."

"Where are we?" Pam asked.

"We're at a funeral home."

"Well, at least let me get a bath. I smell myself. And please, get somebody to wash my stinking clothes," Pam said. She pushed another thought 'She smells bad.' "They have got to have a washing machine in this place."

"Is that you?" Ash said. "I thought I was smelling a dead rat."

"You got jokes, I see," Pam said while she pushed the thought, 'let her get a bath' At him.

"You smell so bad, I'm embarrassed for you. You smell so bad, you make onions cry. You smell so bad, you ain't number one, you ain't number two, you are number five," Ash said laughing.

Pam pushed the thought 'I'm going to help her. "If you are finished with the jokes, can I get a bath, please," Pam begged. Then she pushed the thought 'help her get a bath.'

"I'll see what I can do about that," Ash said. "I'll be back in a minute." He turned and walked toward the door. Then he stopped and looked back at her.

"Why did the chicken cross the road?" he asked and waited for an answer. When she didn't respond, he answered for her. "He had to get away from your smelly behind." Ash chuckled as he turned to leave the room.

Pam pushed the thought, 'I can't stand the smell.' "Hurry back," Pam yelled. "I got to pee."

"First, you want a bath, then you want to pee. I guess next, you'll be wanting breakfast in casket." Ash laughed again as he closed and locked the door behind him.

Chapter 39
A Good Resort

(Friday 10:30 AM)

Lady and Mr. Carson walked out of his front door and across the front porch toward Rev. Zackery. Lady, with tail wagging, reached Rev. Zackery first. Rev. Zackery rubbed Lady's head affectionately.

"Hey Lady," he said softly.

"He's not back yet?" Mr. Carson asked.

"No," Rev. Zackery said concerned. "The last time he left like this, bad things happened."

"He seems to be a very troubled young man," Mr. Carson said.

"Yes. He has seen more hardship and disappointment than most his age. He was abandoned by his mother at birth, raised in a harsh orphanage, falsely imprisoned for several years, and all this before his seventeenth birthday. Then he went into the military where he had to kill or be killed. He became ruthless. When I met him a couple of days ago, he wanted to commit suicide. However, something finally happened to him, Carson. Something that turned his life around."

"What was that Pastor?" Mr. Carson asked.

"It was the Lord. The Lord Jesus brought love into his life. It was so amazing how through his love for Pam, the woman that he fell deeply in love with, the Lord showed Walt in the most perfect way, how much he was loved by Jesus. The Lord allowed me to show Walt how similar his love for Pam was, to the love Jesus had for him. Then, he was able to see how Jesus was loving him and protecting him through all of the bad things that happened to him in his life. Our God is so amazing."

"Amen Pastor," Mr. Carson said smiling. "So, you think he's going to be okay."

"I pray that he will," Rev. Zackery said. "However, Walt has a big test coming. The results of the test may determine the destination of his soul."

"He's not saved?" Mr. Carson asked.

"I led him to salvation. He repeated the words I said, however, I don't know if he believed them in his heart. I don't know if he really has faith in God."

"I remember when I first got saved. I was pretty shaky. The Lord had to test my faith, many times. Give him time, Pastor," Mr. Carson said.

"You are so right, Carson. It is only through the tests that we are able to see our shortcomings. I have failed many tests in my Christian life, but in each failure, I grew closer to the Lord. Eventually, I discovered that I can't even pass one of God's tests without His help.

"I think we should lift Walt up in prayer now, Pastor," Mr. Carson said.

"Good idea. Why don't you pray?"

"Okay Pastor," Mr. Carson said as they joined hands. "Dear Heavenly Father, we come to You in the name of Your Son and our Lord and Savior, Jesus, asking that you would hear our prayer. We pray that Your will be done on earth as it is in heaven, knowing that Your will is to bless Your children. Therefore, we are lifting up Walt to You, right now Father. We ask that you give him the wisdom, the knowledge, and the will to do what You want him to do. Give him the faith to believe and trust completely in You. Help him to pass his test. And finally, bring him back here, safe and unharmed. This we ask in the precious name of Jesus. Amen."

They both opened their eyes and looked at each other. Then Rev. Zackery hugged Mr. Carson tightly. Mr. Carson responded in kind.

"That was a great prayer, Carson," Rev. Zackery said releasing him. "I felt it way down in my soul. I know the Lord is going to answer that pray."

"It looks like He already has," Mr. Carson said looking at the car coming down the driveway.

"Before you pray, I will answer you; While you are still speaking, I will hear you. Isaiah 65:24. The Lord is true to His word," Rev. Zackery said smiling.

"Yes, He is, Pastor," Mr. Carson agreed.

Walt got out of the car and ran up the steps to Rev. Zackery.

"I talked to Pam. Tamera has her, but she is not hurt," Walt said excitedly.

"Praise the Lord," Rev. Zackery said raising both hands to the sky.

"Come on in the house. The grits, gravy, and biscuits were ready an hour ago. We can eat while you fill us in on all the details."

"There's not that much to tell," Walt said as they went to the kitchen.

"Why did you leave without saying anything?" Rev. Zackery said as he began putting grits and gravy on his plate.

"I heard Tamera on the radio. She told this guy, Howard, to have Pam killed. They were going to lock her in a casket and slowly suffocate her. I had to leave immediately because every second counted," Walt said filling his plate.

"So, what did you do, then?" Mr. Carson said.

"I tied dynamite to myself, intercepted Tamera on her way to where Pam was, and then I force her to take me to Pam. Only Pam was not there. I did see Dave and Jason, though. They were locked up in a jail cell. They were okay. Then, I tried to get Tamera to take me to see Pam, but she refused, but she did let me talk to her. Like I said, Pam said she was not hurt."

"Let me get this straight," Mr. Carson said. "You forced this person Tamera to take you to where she thought Pam was, so why couldn't you force her to take you to where Pam really was?"

"Because after I finished talking to Pam, Tamera told the guard to put a bullet in Pam's head if he didn't hear from her in an hour," Walt said. "Since Tamera said that she is planning to come to the funeral tomorrow, and since she said she was going to bring Pam, Jason, and Dave, I asked her to take me back to my car."

"And they just let you leave?" Mr. Carson asked.

"My dynamite and I persuaded Tamera to drive me back to my car," Walt explained. "She knew that I would blow both of us up, if she didn't. Then I drove around for a while to make sure I wasn't being followed."

"So, nobody was following you?" Mr. Carson asked.

"There was a car following me," Walt said. "I had been with Tamera the whole time I was there, so I know she didn't tell anyone to follow me. It must have been Howard, her assistant. Anyway, I lead them around in circles and I should have lost them, however, I saw them following me again on highway 121. I remember that Howard had touched me on my shoulder, so he must have put a tracker me. So, I lead them to the mass grave site.

Walt could see himself in his mind, driving down the road to the mass grave site. He felt something hard in the seam between the arm and shoulder. He took off his jacket. He found the tracker as he passed the burned-up limousine that he had been in when he was ambushed earlier in the week.

"It was a miracle that I made it out of there," Walt said to himself. "I guess that was You once again showing me Your love," he said looking up.

Walt drove out into the middle of the field beside the mass grave, took his duffle bag from the back seat, and ran into the trees about fifty yards away. He worked his way through the trees toward the entrance road until he found a good shooting location and then he waited. His jacket with the tracker was still in the car. He didn't have to wait long. The car that had been following him came into view. It passed by him with three persons inside. The car turned and stopped thirty yards from Walt's car. The passenger side of the car was facing Walt's car. Immediately, three men exited the car on the driver's side. They each had semi-automatic rifles. One laid his weapon over the hood, and one laid his weapon over the trunk. They both aimed their weapons at Walt's car. The last man propped his weapon against the car, got down on one knee, and opened a bottle of water. Neither of them imagined that Walt was behind them. Neither of them imagined that death was only seconds away.

The man who had the bottle of water, casually raised it to take a drink. Walt put the crosshairs of his rifle on his head.

"This is for you, Rev. Zackery," Walt said. "Lord, please don't let me regret this," he said looking up for a second. When he looked back through the scope, he moved the crosshairs from the man's head to the plastic bottle of water and fired. The end of the plastic bottle exploded as the bullet went through it and into the side of the car door. All three men immediately turned and faced in Walt's direction, as Walt quickly chambered another round. The man in the middle held out his hands toward the other two for them not to move or return fire. Walt watched through his scope as the man in the middle stood and came to the position of attention. He then saluted in Marine style. After saluting, he brought his fingers to his lips and then extended his hand palm up, which was 'thank you' in sign language.

"You're welcome," Walt said softly.

Walt watched as the man signed other words.

"Become, calm, between, you and me," Walt said as he read the symbols. "Peace between us."

Then the man yelled out. "My men and I will be leaving as soon as I get back to the office. I was out of line. I'm sorry. Good luck, brother."

The men got back in the car as Walt moved through the tree so that he could watch the car leave the area. When Walt was in his new location, he watched the car move toward the highway.

"Thank you, Lord. I really didn't want to kill them," Walt said looking up.

He waited for ten minutes before going back to his car.

The images of the past faded as Walt ended his story.

"What a mighty God we serve," Rev. Zackery said in amazement.

They all ate in silence for a while. Then Rev. Zackery broke the silence.

"Was there anybody there in the building besides Tamera and these other men?" Rev. Zackery asked.

"The men that followed me were not at Sibal's office. However, I did see four different men plus the other man, Howard, and Tamera spoke to another one who was somewhere else guarding Pam."

"At least now we know what we're up against," Rev. Zackery said.

"We need to get to the church and prepare for tomorrow," Re. Zackery said. "Thank you for everything, Carson."

"You are very welcome, Pastor, but aren't you coming back to night?" Mr. Carson said.

"No, we can't take the chance that someone will follow us back here, so we will spend the night at the church," Rev. Zackery said. "It will be the safest place for us to be once we get it ready. However, I would like to borrow two pillows and two blankets if you don't mind."

"You sure can, Pastor," Mr. Carson said. He turned and went back into the house.

When he returned, he had two blankets, two pillows, and a brown paper bag. He handed everything to Walt. Then he shook Rev. Zackery's hand.

"What's in the bag?" Rev. Zackery asked.

"You're gonna need something to eat, so I put some cheese, a box of crackers, and a couple of can of sardines in there, you know your typical emergency food kit. Oh yeah, I put a little bag of instant coffee in there, too.

"Thank you," Rev. Zackery said.

"Anytime you need a hideout, you know where to come," Mr. Carson said.

"See you later, Lady," Rev Zackery said.

Lady wagged her tail goodbye.

"We need to stop and pick up my car on the way to the church," Walt said as they went to Walt's car. "I hid it in the woods near the cave."

"Okay."

Chapter 40
Food and Facilities

(Friday 11:30 AM)

Dave walked over to the five-gallon plastic paint bucket that Howard had put in the jail cell.

"I guess this is our new restroom facilities," Dave said. "I, for one, would not like to see me taking a crap on a video. Let's put a blanket up so we can have some privacy just in case there's a camera somewhere in here."

"Okay, why don't we put the new bathroom in that corner over there," Jason said.

"That's my side of the cell," Dave responded. "Why not put it on your side?"

"I figure that since you are going to be using it more than me, I would make it more convenient for you, but if that's going to be a problem, we can just put in the middle and hang the blanket on the door," Jason said sliding the paint bucket to the middle of the cell in front of the door. "Hey, there's something in it," Jason said grabbing the lid.

"Be careful," Dave warned.

Slowly Jason opened the can. "Okay!" Jason said as he reached in the can and pull out two large bottles of water, four wrapped sandwiches, and a roll of paper towels. "We hit the jackpot." He laid everything on his bed.

"Do you think Walt had anything to do with this," Dave asked.

"There's a good possibility," Jason said.

"So, you have been very quiet. Do you have a plan?" Dave asked.

"Yeah. I think we should both eat a sandwich now and save the other one for tonight. We should drink plenty of water and we should get as much rest as we can today because tomorrow, we may need all the strength we can muster up."

Dave jammed the ends of the blanket between the bars of the cell door and the cell bars. He picked up the bucket and lifted it up by the handle, thigh high, pushed the lid over a few inches, and facing the blanket, began to pee in the bucket.

"Thank you, Lord, for the food, and the water," Dave said. "Also, thank you for not letting me pee on them."

"Yes! Thank you, Jesus," Jason said just before taking a bite of his sandwich.

Chapter 41
A Clean Break

(Friday 1:30 PM)

Pam was taking a shower. On the other side of the shower curtain sitting on the commode was Ash.

"I really appreciate you allowing me to get this shower, Ash," Pam said as she rinsed the soap from her body.

"Believe me when I say that I was very glad to be of assistance," Ash said. "My nostrils had had as much as they could stand."

"You can stop it with the 'you stink' jokes. You are beginning to make me mad," Pam snarled.

"And you had the nerve to offer me sex, smelling like that. My mama told me that if you can smell it before you see it, don't touch it," Ash said. "I could smell you, as soon as I walked in the room."

"That's it," Pam said furiously. She raised her right hand up in a three-finger claw. She looked at her fingers, and then looked through the curtain at his image.

"Are you about done? You have been in there for almost an hour. I gave you extra time because you smelled so bad."

"Yeah, I'm done," Pam said relaxing her fingers and shutting off the water. "What am I going to wear while my clothes are being washed."

"This towel," Ash said as he suddenly pulled back the shower curtain and held out a large white towel. He had expected Pam to be shocked. He had expected her to quickly grab the towel and cover up. She didn't. She just stood there in front of him. She didn't even reach for the towel. At first, he was looking in her eyes, but then his eyes began to slowly move down her body. She turned her back to him.

"Would you mind drying off my back, please," Pam said with emphasis on the 'please.'

"That would be my pleasure, Ms. Pam," Ash said as he rubbed the towel with both hand from her shoulders down to the buttock. When he reached her buttock, he lingered. She turned her head around and smiled. Because he was mesmerized by the softness of her buttock, he never saw her elbow come around. She hit him on the side of his face so hard that it almost knocked him unconscious. She quickly stepped out of the bathtub and caught him after he hit bathroom door. She put her arm around his neck, and she put him in a choke hold. She slowly allowed his body to fall to the floor as she sat on the commode seat. When he was completely unconscious, she took off his shirt and put it on. Then she took off his shoes and pants. When she had put on his pants, she put her hands under his arm pits a drug him to the door. She opened the door without looking back and then she dragged him out of the bathroom into the bedroom. Then she felt something hit her in the right cheek of her buttock. She looked around and saw Tamera and Howard. Howard was holding a tranquilizer gun.

"Sister dear," Tamera said. "I see you're up to your old tricks again."

Pam fell over on Ash and rolled to the carpeted floor.

"Check to see if he is dead," Tamera said.

"He's not dead. He's breathing," Howard said.

"Well, wake him up, then," Tamera snapped. "He needs to help you get her to the dressing room. I want Leo to fix her up real pretty before we put her back in the casket. Tell him to keep her unconscious."

"Did Mr. Leo say how much his funeral services were going to cost?" Howard asked. "We are running low on funds."

"I told him I was going to get him some extra business to cover my bill," Tamera said casually. "Didn't Sibal have an insurance policy?"

"Yeah," Howard replied.

"Well, assign a portion of the policy over to him. I believe the company was her beneficiary. So, we should have about ninety thousand left after we pay Leo, right?" Tamera said.

"Yes, that's right," Howard said.

"If I'm not mistaken, the company has a one-hundred-thousand-dollar policy on you, too."

"Yes, ma'am," Howard said slowly.

"Keep that in mind next time you question me about spending money," Tamera warned.

Howard didn't respond. He slapped Ash's face until his eyes opened.

"What happened? What is she doing with you, Mr. Howard? And, what happened to her hair?" Ash asked.

"This is not Pam, the person you were supposed to be guarding. Pam is over there," Howard said pointing to the limp body lying on the carpet three feet to his left. Ash looked at Pam who was now wearing his clothes. "This is Ms. Tamera the person you were hired to protect.

Ash looked from Tamera to Pam and back in amazement.

"She is my twin sister, and you were supposed to keep her taped up in a casket, that was to be locked in a back room," Tamera. "Why did you let her out?"

"She smelled so bad, I had to let her get a shower. I couldn't stand the smell," Ash said.

"She's been playing with his mind," Tamera said to Howard.

"Do you want me to get rid of him?" Howard asked.

"Let me see what she put in his mind," Tamera said. Then she pushed the thought, 'I will repeat every thought that Pam put in my mind.'

"Untie me, she smells bad, let her get a bath, I am going to help her, help her get a bath, I can't stand the smell," Ash said and then waited to be released from his trance.

"He's okay," Tamera said. "She didn't put anything in his mind that will cause any problems. Leave him here to guard her. Since she is going to be kept unconscious, she can't cause any more problems. Bring her to the dressing room ASAP."

"Hey, get your clothes off her and put them back on," Howard ordered Ash. "I told you she was dangerous."

"I'm sorry sir," Ash said as he regained coherence and began removing his clothes from Pam. "Pam told me that Ms. Tamera wants Pam killed because she had sex with Ms. Tamera's husband. It that true? Cause I didn't come here to murder nobody. I'm not going to just shoot somebody in the head, especially a woman, because she had sex."

"Listen to me!" Howard said sternly. "The only reason you are alive right now, is because Ms. Tamera and I kept Pam from killing you. Can you put a bullet in somebody's head after they have tried to kill you, or do you have to wait for them to try it again?"

"She was about to kill me?" Ash asked.

"You were unconscious when we came in. She was about to twist your neck and break it. If we had come two seconds later, I would be taking you to the dressing room instead of her," Howard said. "Now, if I tell you to put a bullet in her head, are you going to do it, or not?"

"I'll go and put a bullet in her head right now, if you say so," Ash said angrily. "She was going to kill me."

"Help me get her to the embalming room. We need to get some more drugs in her before she wakes up," Howard said.

CHAPTER 42
FUNERAL PREPARATIONS

(Friday 4:45 PM)

Rev. Zackery was filling offering envelopes from a bucket of sawdust from the old communion table, when Walt walked in with several big bags. Walt brought the bags down the aisle to the new communion table and began taking the boxes out. He had three large size CO_2 fire extinguishers.

"Take them out of the boxes, please." Rev. Zackery said as he scooped another envelope into the bucket of sawdust. "Put one on each side of the communion table behind it, so they can't be seen. Put the last one behind the podium."

Walt did as he was asked. Then he went back outside and brought in some additional packages and a five-gallon bucket. In the packages there were two ten-foot runners, two six- foot runners, an electric drill, a long handle squeegee, and some drill bits. The five-gallon bucket was flame retardant.

"Are we expecting a fire tomorrow, in your newly repaired sanctuary, Pastor?" Walt asked.

"Unfortunately, I am, Walt," Rev. Zackery said. "I want to keep the damage to a minimum if possible."

"You saw a fire in the vision the demon showed you?" Walt asked.

"No, but remember, in the vision Tamera's men poured gasoline on Dave, Jason and Pam. I believe Tamera is going to set them on fire if I don't swear alliance to her. So, I want to fireproof that area as much as possible. Also, I want to be able to put out a fire if one is started."

"Yeah. You wouldn't want the church to be damaged again," Walt said.

"I love this church. However, I would rather see the whole church burn down than for someone to lose their soul."

"You included?" Walt said.

"Me included," Rev. Zackery said smiling.

"That's the Rev. Zackery I know and look up to," Walt said smiling back. "So, can I try on my robe now. I hope there is room for a M16 under it."

"There is room enough for two," Rev. Zackery said.

"In that case I will prepare some special bullets for the Homegoing Celebration," Walt said picking up the drill.

"Special bullets?"

"Yeah," Walt replied. "You have heard of hollow points, haven't you?"

"Yes."

"Well, these are going to be holy points, because the tips will contain holy wood from the old communion table," Walt said. "I'm going to set Tamera's world on fire. Between my bullets and your dust, she won't have a chance."

"Don't underestimate her. We are still going to have a fight on our hands. I believe Tamera is going to try to kill all of us, tomorrow," Rev. Zackery added. "Walt, this is a battle between good and evil. We will be fighting for God. She is fighting for Satan. If we put our faith in God, we will be victorious. I can't promise that all of us will survive, but I know God will prevail."

"The thing that matters to me the most is Pam," Walt said. "I'm going to do whatever I have to in order to save her, whatever it takes."

Walt began drilling holes in the tops of the bullets for his M16 weapon. Then he stuck small pieces of wood in the holes. Rev. Zackery went to get the robe that Walt was going to wear to the funeral. When Rev. Zackery returned, Walt had his M16 strapped over his shoulder. Rev. Zackery helped him get the robe over his head. There were openings on both sides of the robe where Walt could reach his hand through. Walt reached his hands through the robe, grabbed the M16 and then pointed it, from beneath the robe, straight ahead of him.

"Is this the robe you saw in the vision?" Walt asked.

"Yes, this is the one," Rev. Zackery answered.

"It is perfect," Walt said smiling. "Tamera's men don't stand a chance. Neither does Tamera with my new bullets."

"Once we get these mats down and then cover this whole area with fire retardant, we should be ready."

"Okay, let's do it," Walt said enthusiastically.

CHAPTER 43
THE LAST NIGHT

(Friday 745: PM)

Pam was lying on her back naked, underneath a white sheet on an embalming and dressing table in the funeral home. She had two IV drips attached to her hand, one bag contained saline, and the other bag had contained anesthesia. However, the anesthesia bag was now empty. The mortician was replacing the empty bag with a new bag containing anesthesia when Pam's eyes opened slightly. She could see the second bag being connected to the tube going into her hand. She closed her eyes and pretended to be asleep.

"I'll give this time to get in her system, before I do her make-up and dress her," Leo, the mortician, said to Ash. "Do you want a cup of coffee?"

"Yes sir, Mr. Leo," Ash said following Leo toward the door.

Pam pushed a thought, 'when she tells me to, I am going to help her escape' into Ash's mind. Then she pushed the thought 'cough' into his mind. Ash coughed as the men left the room. Pam tried to reach over to remove the needle, but the anesthesia had already begun to disable her. Her hand fell back down on the hard table with a loud thud. Her eyes closed and she was out.

Several miles away Dave was hungrily watching Jason eat his second sandwich as they sat across from each other on their beds. Jason ignored Dave's pleading looks.

"You're not even going to give me a little bite," Dave said.

"No! I told you to wait," Jason said, "but you just had to eat your other sandwich. You have no discipline."

"I'll buy a piece of your sandwich," Dave said.

"This could be my last meal," Jason said. "How much would you give me for that, a million dollars?"

"I thought you said your demon was going to save you," Dave said. "If he is going to save you, then this is not going to be your last meal."

Jason crammed the last part of his sandwich into his mouth. Dave picked up his bottle of water. It was almost empty. He drank some of it. Now, he was almost out of water, too.

"Now that you mention the demon, maybe I should find out if he will respond to my call."

"No, don't do it. That was just my hunger talking," Dave said. "You don't need to find out anything."

"Bailtron," Jason shouted. "Bailtron." Nothing happened.

"I guess he is not here," Dave said.

"You were right," Jason said. "Someone he possesses has to be near before he can respond."

"Or maybe he is here and he's just not responding because your time has expired," Dave said.

"That sounds creepy," Jason said.

"Well, if anyone has demons, you do, with your anger issues," Dave said. "Maybe, Bailtron doesn't have any authority over Chicago demons."

"Yeah, maybe he doesn't have any authority over South Carolina demons either," Jason said slurring the 'South Carolina.'

"What about Howard?" Dave asked. "He is from this area, I guess. Maybe your demon friend has authority over his demon."

"So, he's my demon 'friend' now," Jason smirked.

Jason was about to wash down the last bite of his sandwich with his water when Dave raised his bottle.

"Toast," Dave said.

"What are we toasting to?" Jason asked.

"Here's to the women that do, and here's to the women that don't, but to heck with the women who say they will and turn around and won't."

They both laughed and then drank all of their remaining water.

"For someone who might be dead in twenty hours, you sure are cheerful," Jason said.

"Cheerful? I'm ecstatic. I just got a divorce from a cheating wife who was using me and screwing the insurance man in my bed, even though I tried to give her everything she wanted. I cared for her. I was a good husband. I was faithful to that low down conniving huzzy. I wasted all those years with her." Dave was getting emotionally depressed. "She never loved me, man," Dave said as tears fell from his eyes.

"Don't cry for her. Like you said, you're free, now," Jason said. "All that is behind you now. I have to admit though, seeing you sitting over there crying over a woman who brought a man into your bed, had you locked up and almost sodomized, got you fired, took you house, your car and almost every penny you possessed, well, that is pathetic."

"Yeah, you're right. I'm pathetic," Dave said angrily. "I was pathetic for listening to you, and letting you get us trapped in the crystal, because of your hatred of Tamera. I knew you had lost control of your mind. I'm in this situation because of you. I'd be better off with Carol."

"So now, you want to blame this whole thing on me," Jason stood up. "I was minding my own business, too. I was just visiting my grandmother, who was burned alive because of you and Pam."

"Me? You ain't gone blame this on me. I was minding my own business, when Pam ran out in front of my car," Dave stood up and faced Jason. Then he sat back down quicky. "Man, I am really sleepy," Dave said as he laid down on his bed.

"Yeah, me too," Jason said as he fell back on his bed. "Too, sleepy."

Dave was out, as soon as he put his feet on his bed. Jason raised his water bottle close to his eyes. On the bottom of the bottle was a white substance.

"That dirty, sneaky, Howard. He poisoned us," Jason said as he put his feet on the bed.

He tried to fight the sleep, but numbness began to move from his feet up. It was only seconds before he felt it move up his arms.

"I guess I should have let Rev. Zackery save…" Jason was out.

At the church, Walt was putting the last of the fire retardant on the mats and the area of the floor inside the mats. Walt had on a pair of pants and a sweater Rev. Zackery had given him to wear while his clothes were being washed and dried in a small washer/dryer unit in Rev. Zackery's office. Rev. Zackery had finished putting envelopes filled with communion table dust in the envelope holders on the back of the pews near the center aisle, and he was carrying the remaining dust in the bucket to the podium.

"How's this, Pastor," Walt asked, pointing to the floor.

"That's great, Walt. It should dry in four hours," Rev. Zackery said sitting the bucket beside the fire extinguisher behind the podium. Rev. Zackery, standing behind the podium, smiled at how funny Walt looked in his pants with the hem well above the tops of Walt's combat boots, and the waist of the pants being squeezed several inches down to Walt's waistline. "Is there anything you need to tell me, Walt?"

"Anything like what?" Walt asked.

"Anything that you may have overlooked when you were telling me and Carson about your interactions with Tamera this morning." Rev. Zackery looked sternly at Walt.

"No sir. I can't think of anything else, except one thing," Walt said.

"What's that?" Rev. Zackery asked.

"Tamera said that while she and Pam were trapped in the crystal, they made a deal. Tamera promised to leave Pam and all of us alone, if we would leave her and her people alone." Walt said. "But then she said that Jason broke the agreement. She said that when they were about to be released from the crystal, Jason attacked her. He stabbed her in the back and tried to kill her."

"Hate and vengeance has corrupted Jason's mind," Rev. Zackery said sadly shaking his head.

"Pastor, Tamera seemed sincere about keeping the agreement she had with Pam, but I guess your vision proves that she was lying, doesn't it?"

"Yes. I guess it does, Walt," Rev. Zackery said. "Like you said, we can't believe anything she says. She'll break her promises and laugh in our faces while she's doing it."

"Yeah, but it seems like being trapped in the crystal has changed her. It seems like she is fearful of us, now." Walt looked seriously into Rev. Zackery's eyes. "If only Jason hadn't tried to kill her, maybe, we wouldn't be dealing with all this, now." Walt paused. "I'm tired, Pastor. I think I'm going to get a nap, so that I will be able to stand watch tonight" Walt said as he walked to a pew where two pillows and two blankets were lying.

"Okay. I need to prepare my eulogy, anyway," Rev. Zackery said. "Get some sleep. I'll wake you up in three hours, around midnight. I don't expect anything to happen tonight, but you can never be too careful."

"If you hear anything, wake me up," Walt said. "I put one of the Glocks in the podium in case you need it tonight or tomorrow. The magazines are filled with 'Holy Point' bullets. One more thing, you should probably sleep in your vest, just to be on the safe side."

"Thanks, Walt," Rev. Zackery said. "Between you and the Lord, everything should be covered. Oh, that's right, the Lord sent me you, so the Lord has everything covered."

"Yes sir, he does," Walt replied.

CHAPTER 44
MORNING GORY

(Saturday 7:00 AM)

When Walt opened his eyes, it was black dark, much darker than it was supposed to be in the church. Then he realized that his head had been covered. As the adrenaline flowed through his veins, he quickly pulled the black curtain that had been draped over the pew to block the light from his eyes and grabbed his M16 which was lying on the pew above his head. He looked to the front of the church and saw Rev. Zackery arranging a picture of Miss Mammie on a small table next to the communion table. Hearing Walt scrambling for his weapon, Rev. Zackery turned and faced Walt, who was already aiming the M16 at him.

"I know I said I was going to wake you, but it took longer to prepare my message than I figured, and you were sleeping so good," Rev. Zackery said as Walt laid his weapon on the pew.

"I slept very well, Pastor, but almost having a heart attack when I woke up completely cancelled out all of that good sleep," Walt said holding his heart with both hands.

"I'm sorry son," Rev. Zackery said. "Please, forgive me. Would you like a cup of coffee and some sardines and crackers."

"I should have gotten something to eat while I was out yesterday, but I can go get something now if you like," Walt said.

"No, it's too late," Rev. Zackery said. "After I finished my message, I spent an hour or so praying for a covering over this building. I asked God to sanctify it, fill it with His Spirit, and to send a legion of angels to surround this house. We need to stay inside, where we have the upper hand."

"Okay. I guess it's sardines, crackers, and coffee," Walt said smiling. "Pastor, in your vision you said the church was half filled. Did you announce the funeral?"

"No. I told J. Jones that I wanted him to finish his work by today, because I would be conducting a private funeral for only the family and friends of Miss Mammie. When I told him that, I was only expecting Pam, Jason, Dave, and whoever they brought with them. I really don't know who those people are. I couldn't see their faces that well in the vision," Rev. Zackery said.

"Do you think that Tamera is bringing that many of her people with her?" Walt asked. "I may need to add some more clips to my ammo belt."

"Walt, I would prefer that you would not shoot anybody inside this church, unless it is absolutely necessary," Rev. Zackery pleaded. "We need to stand still and let the Lord fight our battle."

"Okay Pastor," Walt said. "I'll stand still, until somebody messes with Pam. If that happens there will be hell to pay."

"Believe me, I understand," Rev. Zackery. "I tried to shoot Tamera last time she was here. She was trying to kill Pam, so I shot at her."

"What happened?" Walt asked.

"I missed. Then she made me put my pistol under my chin and pull the trigger," Rev. Zackery said. "If Pam had not used her powers to make me move the pistol before I fired, I would be dead now. Pam made me move the pistol and shoot into the ceiling, several times before Tamera realized that Pam had done it. Then, Tamera made Pam knock herself out. Tamera made me put the pistol under my chin again and she made me pull the trigger. The only reason I'm still here, is because I was out of bullets. I told you that because I wanted you to know, if you try to shoot her and miss, she will make you kill yourself."

"I won't miss, Pastor," Walt said.

"I didn't think I was going to miss either," Rev. Zackery said.

"What about you, Pastor? Do you want me to use lethal force to protect you?" Walt asked.

"No!" Rev. Zackery answered. "I am putting my total trust in the Lord that there will be no killing in this church."

"Okay," Walt said reluctantly. "But you need to pray real hard that they leave Pam alone."

"I have already prayed that the Lord would protect all of us, but I will also pray that no one would even threaten any harm to Pam," Rev. Zackery said even though he could see in his mind how in the vision Pam had been doused with gasoline as she sat in the casket.

"Pray for me too, Paster. Ask God to give me the strength to do what I need to do," Walt asked.

"I will," Rev. Zackery said.

Several miles away, at the funeral home Tamera, Leo, Howard, and Ash were gathered around the casket where Pam was lying. The color of the wooden casket was medium brown mahogany with gold hedges on the wood handles. The lining was light blue. Only the top half of Pam's body could be seen since the bottom of the casket was closed. Pam was dressed in a royal blue V-neck dress with no sleeves. A push up bra made her breasts seem larger than the were. Her hair was spread out on the pillow, away from her head. Her face was covered with white makeup, except for royal blue eye shadow and quarter sized circular royal blue spot on each of her cheeks. Her hands were folded over her chest, the IV anesthesia still attached to her hand.

"Leo, I love what you have done. My dear sister looks so, aah uniquely beautiful," Tamera said. "Don't you two agree?" she said to Howard and Ash.

"Yes ma'am," Ash said quickly.

"I agree completely," Howard said.

"How are you coming with our sacrificial lambs," Tamera asked.

"The crosses are done. We will mount them when we get to the church," Howard responded.

"Tell the guards to come here. We will all leave from here at twelve thirty," Tamera said. "I don't want to be late. It's going to be a grand celebration. The only thing missing will be that good old organ music."

"Is there an organ at the church?" Ash asked.

"Yes, the last time I was there, there was one. Why?" Tamera asked.

"I play piano and organ," Ash said smiling.

"I knew there was a reason why I didn't have you killed," Tamera said smiling, too.

Ash's smile quickly faded away.

"Ash, there is a Hamond B3 in the chapel. Why don't you play us some music while we get this coffin ready for the hearse?"

"Okay," Ash said enthusiastically. "What do you want me to play?"

"Play that funeral song," Tamera said. "Amazing…"

"Amazing Grace?" Ash asked.

"Yeah, that's it. Play that," Tamera said.

Ash went to the organ, turned it on and began playing. The sounds of the organ filled the entire building. The music was so touching that everybody stopped for a few seconds just to absorb the soothing cords.

"Amazing grace, how sweet the sound that saved a witch like me," Tamera said in rhythm. "I once was lost, but now I'm found cause Satin set me free. Ha, ha, ha, ha," Tamera laughed. Her laughter filled the entire building.

Chapter 45
The Homegoing Celebration

(Saturday 11:00 AM)

Walt heard cars coming across the new bridge leading to the church. He went to the door and looked out. There were cars coming toward the church.

"It's showtime, Pastor," Walt yelled to the back of the church. "They are coming. I see two cars."

"What? Why are they so early?" Rev. Zackery said. "Hurry up! Get your guns and your robe on."

Walt dressed in his fatigues and bulletproof vest, rushed to the back. When he returned, he had on Rev. Zackery's African robe, complete with the matching headdress.

"Hey!" Walt shouted. "I didn't see a hearse, Pastor. Something is not adding up."

"Miss Mammie said that she had invited, or more accurately, persuaded some folks to come to her funeral," Rev. Zackery said. "Go and greet them. Tell them that the family of the deceased has requested a private funeral for family and close friends only."

"Okay," Walt said as he went to the door of the sanctuary.

The door opened before he got to it, the henges struggling to handle the weight of the door.

"Who are you, and where is Rev. Zackery?" the stout man said as he led four men into the church.

"I'm minister Walt, and Rev. Zackery is in the back getting ready for the one PM funeral," Walt said.

"We came early because we wanted to view the body and to get a good seat. I'm Paul Crowder, by the way. I am a deacon of this church," the man said. "These men are all members of the deacon board of this church, and we want to know why Rev. Zackery is having a funeral for the local root lady, without getting approval from the deacon board."

Walt wanted to hit the deacon in his nose, however instead he looked behind him at the communion table and gathered his thoughts. When he had calmed himself, he spoke.

"Deacon Crowder, there will be no showing of the body, because Miss Mammie's body was burned severely and completely, when her house was set on fire," Walt explained. "It is my understanding that Miss Mammie joined this church before she was murdered. Also, my friend and the grandson of Miss Mammie requested that Rev. Zackery officiate the services here. That's why the funeral services are being held here, for the lady whom you so disrespectfully refer to as the local root lady." Walt paused. "Rev. Zackery wanted me to inform you that the family requested a private funeral, however, since you are deacons, I'm sure he would want you to help him serve the family in their time of bereavement. Go on down front and have a seat. I wouldn't want you to miss any of what is about to happen here today. The family will be on the left. You may sit anywhere on the right."

The five men walked down the aisle admiring the work that had been done to the church. They stood in front of the communion table and looked at the fairly young picture of Miss Mammie on the small table beside it. They were all surprised at how beautiful she been when she was young.

"What a beautiful picture," Deacon Brown said.

"That's the way God sees her now," Rev. Zackery said walking up behind them. "To Him she is still young and beautiful, and pure, because her sins have all been washed away when she confessed her faith in Jesus."

"How do you know she was sincere? Wasn't she still working roots right up until the time she died?" Deacon Crowder asked.

"You tell me. She said you came to see her two times last month," Rev. Zackery said. "Before and after you came to see me."

"Well, pastor," Crowder said, "I came and repented to you for going to see her but I went back to see her so she could undo what she had done."

"I know. She told me all about it," Rev. Zackery said. "When she came to see me to plan her funeral, she gave me a list of the people who were going give remarks. Three of you are on that list. Crowder, you are first on that list. Brown, you are on the list, too. You are fifth. Last but not least is your name Watts. Are you gentlemen ready?"

Without speaking, the three men shook their heads, 'yes.' Then they all went and sat down. Rev. Zackery walked back to the door where Walt was watching for cars.

"How did they find out about the funeral?" Walt asked.

"They knew about it before I even planned it. Miss Mammie told them when it was going to be, before she died," Rev. Zackery answered. "She even prepared remarks for them to say."

"Miss Mammie was something special," Walt said.

"Yes, she was," Rev. Zackery. "She served and loved and sacrificed. She was very special. Maybe, we should go ahead and get started. That way we can get these people out of here before Tamera arrives."

"I kinda wanted Deacon Crowder to be here when Tamera came," Walt said. "I don't like him very much."

"He is what most people become, when they get a little authority," Rev. Zackery said.

"What's that," Walt asked.

"A butthole," Rev. Zackery said shaking his head. "We might as well go ahead and start the service now. We can let them make remarks, and then let these people get out of here before one o'clock. I don't want anyone to get hurt needlessly."

"All right, Pastor, let's do this."

Rev. Zackery and Walt walked to the pulpit. Walt sat and Rev. Zackery went to the podium.

"May I have your attention, please," Rev. Zackery said and waited for all eyes to be on him. "Since the family has requested a private service and since some of you wanted to pay your respect to Miss Mammie, we are going to have two services. First, we will have a short memorial service where anyone may give three or four minutes of remarks of a positive nature, concerning Miss Mammie. Then, at one PM we will have a service exclusively for the family. Let us begin with prayer." Rev. Zackery turned and looked at Walt. "Minister Walt, would you come now and lead us in a word of prayer."

Walt's eyes opened as wide as possible as everyone turned their attention to him.

"Of course, Pastor," Walt said as he slowly made his way to the podium. When he was there, he cleared his throat. "Let us pray," he said testing the microphone for the right volume.

Everyone bowed their heads.

"Dear Heavenly Father," Walt began, "we are here to bury Miss Mammie Scott. That was her given name. However, she had many names. To my friend, Jason, she was gramma, to Pam, the child she raised as her own, she was auntie, to her friends and neighbors, she was Miss Mammie, and to her customers and some of the deacons, she was the root lady. However, the name that meant the most to You, Father, was my child, because You claimed her as Your child. She didn't live a perfect life. We know that Lord, nobody but Jesus did that. However, we know that it is not how you start out, but it is how you end up, that matters. Her ending was a good ending. Yes, she made some mistakes along the way. She did some bad things, well to tell the truth about it, she did a lot of things that were not pleasing in Your sight. However, Father, You didn't give up on her, just like You haven't given up on us, yet."

"That's right," one of the deacons shouted.

"Even when she was dibbling and dabbling in fortune telling and putting roots on folks," Walt continued, "You looked beyond all that fortune telling and root working and saw what her life would become. Lord, You had mercy on her."

"Yes You did, Lord," another deacon shouted.

Since he was being encouraged, Walt began to get louder.

"You had mercy, because You are a merciful God," Walt continued. "You reached down and touched her with Your finger of love. The first time You touched her, You caused her to take in a child that was not her own. She raised that child with a mother's love."

"Yes she did," Deacon Brown shouted.

"Then Father, your touch her again and caused her to accept Jesus as her Lord and Savior. Then finally Father, You touched her and caused her to sacrifice her life to save the child she raised."

"She did that?" Deacon Crowder shouted.

"Yes, she sacrificed her life. She did it because Your hand, Father, was upon her," Walt paused. "So, today we have come, not to say goodbye to Miss Mammie, but to say, see you later, when that roll is called up yonder. We will see you later. In the name of Jesus we pray, amen, amen, and amen." Walt turned, wiping imaginary tears from his cheeks, as he went to his seat.

Rev. Zackery, totally shocked at what he had heard, went to the podium. As he passed Walt he whispered, "Where did that come from?"

"I been listening to you praying when you thought I was asleep," Walt whispered back.

"Thank you for that heartfelt prayer, minister Walt," Rev. Zackery said from the podium.

"Yes sir, that wuz a goodun," one of the deacons shouted.

"Now, we will have comments, and since the prayer was a little longer than expected, please, no more than three minutes. Deacon Crowder, you come first since you are the first person Miss Mammie had requested to give remarks. Just stand down there in front of the communion table."

However, before Deacon Crowder could get in position, the door opened, and several people walked in. Walt reached through the slits in his robe and grabbed his M16. Deacon Crowder waited for some of the people to come down toward the front and sit down, while some sat in the back, then he started his remarks.

"Pastor and associates of Miss Mammie, I want to read a few prepared remarks," Deacon Crowder said. He then cleared his throat and holding up a piece of paper, he began to read. "Miss Mammie was a wonderful person. She lived a life of caring and giving to others. People in need would always go to Miss Mammie for help. She would never let them down. If you had a problem, she had a solution. If you were in trouble, she would help you get out. If you were sick, she would make you well. There was usually a small fee, but as she was known to say, 'a girl's got to make a living.'"

Some of the congregation laughed.

"I remember when my dear sweet mother-in-law got sick while she was staying with my wife and me. Miss Mammie gave me something to make her go, I mean, her sickness go away. I will always have fond memories of Miss Mammie, thank you."

The congregation applauded as Deacon Crowder went to his seat. Rev. Zackery, who was still standing at the podium called the next name for remarks. Deacon Brown went and stood in front of the communion table and pulled out a piece of paper.

"Miss Mammie," Deacon Brown started reading, but then he looked back at Rev. Zackery, balled up the paper, and looked back at the congregation. "I hope I don't get in no trouble with Miss Mammie, however, I don't want to read that note. I want to speak from my heart cause me and Miss Mammie, we loved each other, not like man and wife, but like sister and brother. She was my friend, and I was her friend. Sometimes we would talk on the phone for hours. If she needed something fixed at her house, she would always call on me. 'Brown, get yourself over here', she would always say, 'I got a busted pipe.' No matter what I had going on, I would drop what I was doing to go and help my friend. I remember when I was having trouble with my teenage boy. He wouldn't mine me. He was even talking back. He wouldn't do nothing that I would tell him to do, so I told Miss Mammie that I wanted her to put some roots on him. Y'all know getting roots put on somebody ain't cheap. Do you know what Miss Mammie told me? She said, 'You don't need to put no roots on that boy, he's just smelling himself. All you need to do is buy him a cheap car, then if he doesn't do what he's supposed to do, then take the keys until he starts acting right.' Now, I didn't think it was going to work, but show nuff, it worked. The boy is grown now. He even has a boy of his own."

"Tell the story, Brown," Deacon Watts said.

"Now, I could go on and on about all the happy times me and Miss Mammie had together," Deacon Brown said. "One time when my wife got sick, I sent her to see Miss Mammie."

"Brown!" Rev. Zackery shouted. "Your three minutes were up five minutes ago. Thank you."

"Sorry Pastor," Deacon Brown said turning to walk back to his seat. "I'm just saying, she was the best root lady that ever was."

"Deacon Watts." Rev. Zackery said, looking at the black man with the gray afro and matching beard.

Watts started speaking as soon as he stood up.

"Pastor, just like Brown, I took my wife to Miss Mammie when she got sick. The doctors couldn't do nothing for her, not a gosh dern thang, pardon my French. She was suffering so bad. But Miss Mammie, she gave her something to stop the pain. Then Miss Mammie told us that my, Betsy Mae, was going to die in six month, two weeks, and three days. That's exactly what happened. Betsy Mae died on the day that Miss Mammie said she would. On the day she died, she was not in any pain. She kissed me, said goodbye, closed her eyes, and she was gone. Because of Miss Mammie, me and Betsy Mae had the happiest six and a half months that we had ever had," Watts said as tears streamed down his face. He looked at Mammie's picture. "Thank you, Miss Mammie," he said and sat down.

"I think we will have time for one more person. As I said earlier, the family has planned a private ceremony to begin at one o'clock. Therefore, after these last remarks, please leave quickly and quietly," Rev. Zackery said. "Now, who would like to give the final remarks. Please make your remarks short, three minutes, please."

Several persons raised their hands. Then one person shouted out from group sitting in the back of the church.

"I would!" a female voice said.

"Okay ma'am, come on down front," Rev. Zackery said.

"Thank you," she said as she stood up and made her way to the aisle.

Rev. Zackery and Walt recognized her. It was Tamera. She had on a black leather coat. There was a black hood covering her head. An ominous atmosphere filled the room as all raised hands lowered.

"Rev. Zackery," the familiar voice said as she pulled her hood back and walked slowly down the aisle. "I never got to meet Miss Mammie. She was a friend of my mother. My mother met her before she became known as Miss Mammie, the root lady, before all the fortune telling and the roots and potions. My mother and Mammie became friends when Mammie was just a house cleaner and professional nanny." Tamera walked up to the small table where the picture of Mammie was. "You see, my mother needed someone to hide and keep one of her newborn babies just for a month or so. My mother trusted Mammie with her baby. However, my mother was killed and never came back to get the baby. Instead of giving the baby up to the state, Mammie kept that baby, my sister, and raised her and loved her as if she was her own child." Tamera turned and looked at the new communion table. She reached her hand toward it. She was about to touch it, but she stopped and looked at Rev. Zackery who was leaning over the podium, intensely watching to see what would happen when and if she touched the communion table. "I never knew that I had a sister until recently. It is because of Mammie that my sister, Pamela, and I have been reunited. I am eternally grateful to Mammie, my mother's cherished friend. Thank you, Miss Mammie, thank you," she said laying her hand on the communion table and winking at Rev. Zackery.

"Amen," said several people in the congregation.

"Now, if you don't mind," Rev. Zackery said from the podium, "I would like for all non-family members to leave, so that…"

"No!" Tamera shouted. "The family service as already started. Everyone, please remain seated for the family processional. Get on the organ," Tamera said to a man sitting on the end of the pew where she had been.

The man, Ash, got up, went quickly down the aisle, and sat at the organ. He immediately began to play, "Amazing Grace." The front double doors of the church opened. Two men, side by side, walked in. One had a chain saw. The other had a square block of wood. These men were followed by a coffin being rolled into the church by two other men, one in the front and one in the back. They all had on navy blue jackets with the letters LFH sown into the front pockets. The jackets were unbuttoned; therefore, the flax jackets and pistol belts were clearly visible. Nothing else about their attire was uniform.

Tamera pulled off her leather coat, tossed it on the first pew, and sat on the communion table as the man with the chainsaw cut two one-foot slits in the floor just inside the mat closest to the front door. Then when the man with the square block of wood found the floor joists, he laid the wood on the floor and marked a cut pattern to avoid hitting the joists. The man with the chain saw then cut two square holes in the floor.

Deacon Crowder stood up and was about to speak, however, the man with the block of wood, pulled out a pistol and aimed it at him.

"She said, remain seated," the man with the block and the Glock said.

Deacon Crowder sat down immediately. Walt recognized the men down front. They were K3 and K4, the men who had come to pick up Tamera after he shot out her tire. He looked carefully at the three men in the back of the church, who had been sitting on both sides of Tamera before she came down front. One was Howard and the other two were guards Walt had seen at Sibal's office.

"Zackery," Tamera shouted as she jumped from the table. "I was informed that today's service was supposed to be a joint service, for Miss Mammie and for my sister Pamela." Tamera walked down the aisle beside the casket and pushed open the top. "Here is our other guest of honor, Pamela."

Everyone stood up the see Pam's body in the coffin. She was lying motionless with her hands folded on her chest. Walt, in a state of shock, walked up to the podium beside Rev. Zackery.

Walt whispered in Rev. Zackery's ear, "Let me kill her, now. Let me kill all of them."

"No," Rev. Zackery whispered. "Don't do anything yet. Something is not right. Wait!"

"Bring in the family and friend," Tamera ordered her men.

The four Kings walk out the side sanctuary door beside the pulpit. A couple of minutes later, they returned carrying a man, tied to a cross. The man on the cross was Dave. They lifted the cross and the limp body up and dropped the cross down into one of the holes in the floor. The men left again. This time when they returned, they were carrying a cross with Jason's limp body tied to it. They dropped that cross into the other hole in the floor. Both Dave and Jason had on nothing, but a white cloth tied around their loins. There were ropes around their wrists and their arms near their shoulders, and ropes around their chests, and feet. Once they were in place, the four Kings closed the coffin, moved it forward out of the aisle, turned it sideways and pushed it back between the crosses. All of this took place as Ash, played a jazzed-up version of "Amazing Grace."

Tamera signaled for Ash to stop playing by sliding her straight hand across her neck. Then she pointed. Ash walked out of the side sanctuary door and returned with three plastic buckets and a five-gallon gas can. He filled each bucket. He sat the first one in front of Jason, the second one in front of Dave, and the last one in front of Pam's coffin.

"If you were wondering if our family and friend are dead, let me assure you," Tamera said, smiling. "They are not, yet." Tamera looked at Ash. "Revive them."

Ash picked up the bucket in front of Dave and swung it up as he moved back. About half of the liquid rose above Dave's face, and then fell down, covering the front of his entire body. Immediately Dave woke up with gasoline burning his eyes. Realizing his situation, he began struggling against his ropes. As he was pulling uselessly against the ropes, he felt another splash against his body. Dave stopped struggling. He could only watch as Ash walked up to Jason and dashed Jason's body with the liquid in the bucket at Jason's feet. The four Kings, who were standing near Jason, jumped back as some of the fluid landed close to them.

"Watch what you're doing?" K1 shouted as he smelled the gasoline on his hand.

"I would move back, if I were you, especially if you got some gasoline on you," Ash said arrogantly. "I'm sure you don't want to be a part of the show when the fireworks start."

K2 pulled K1 by his arm and the four Kings moved a little further back down the side aisle. Ash turned and faced Tamera, who was standing in the middle aisle, the hood of her black robe covering her head.

Jason woke in shock as the smell of the gasoline went up his nose. He began to spit out the gasoline that had gotten in his mouth. He looked a Tamera and hate filled his heart. His face confirmed it.

"Jason, welcome," Tamera said smiling. "If I recall, the last time I was here, Rev. Zackery shot me, and you trapped me inside a crystal ball. Now, I'm not an authority on the subject but I don't believe that is how Christians are supposed to act." Tamera looked at Walt and then back at Jason. "You, Rev. Zackery, Dave, over there, and my dear sweet sister, locked me in a safe and threw me in the river. That also was not very Christian. However, I am willing to forgive and forget all the evils you have done to me, if you will forgive and forget all that I have done to you. Can you do that? Can you swear right here, right now that you forgive me, and that you are going to forget everything that I have done to you?"

"Tamera," Jason said. "I swear before everybody here, that I will never forgive you, however, I will forget my foot up your butt next time I get an opportunity to put it there."

"Jason, Jason," Tamera said still smiling, "so much hate. That's proof positive that you can't be reasoned with. It is also proof that you are not a Christian either. In fact, you are an enemy of the God you claim to believe in."

"The only thing I claim to be is an enemy of yours," Jason said.

"I'll come back to you," Tamera said. "Now, I want to talk to your spiritual leader, Rev. Zackery, the one who taught you how to be a Christian." Tamera raised her arms and looked down. "Dark Lord empower me, empower me."

Immediately her hands and her face began to glow slightly and for a second, her face changed into a devilish likeness, with horns and a pointed chin. A second later her face and body were back to normal. It happened so fast that no one who saw it had a chance to get scared. No one even believed what their own eyes had seen, except Rev. Zackery and Walt, who were still standing together behind the podium. Walt immediately put his hand on the trigger of his M16 and pointed it in Tamera's direction. Since he was behind the podium, she could not see the barrel protruding under his robe. Tamera seemed to be concentrating intensely on the two of them.

"She is trying to read our minds. I can feel it," Rev. Zackery whispered to Walt. "Say 'Jesus' over and over in your mind. That will block her."

Walt began saying 'Jesus' over and over in his mind, and even though he was looking at Tamera, he was thinking about things that had happened in his past. He could see someone opening the door to the orphanage and picking him up and taking him inside to safety when as a baby he was left there by his mother. Walt continued saying 'Jesus' in his mind. He saw himself escaping from the burning orphanage when he was a boy. Then he saw in his mind, one of the soldiers in his squad get killed only ten feet from him when a mortar shell exploded near them in the Vietnamese jungle. He continued to say Jesus. Each time, he would see in his mind an event when Jesus had saved him.

"Leroy," Tamera shouted. "You have been weighted and found to be unworthy. You are not a true man of God. You are a liar and a deceiver. As a result, your God has turned you over to my god for punishment. You stand condemned." Then she cried out with an extremely loud voice, "Bring him to me."

Two men, Ash and Howard came to the pulpit from the left side of Rev. Zackery. Before they could reach him, Walt grabbed Rev. Zackery's hand.

"What should I do, Pastor?" Walt asked.

"Don't worry about me," Rev. Zackery said. "I'm in the hands of the Lord. Just remember what you told me. She cannot be trusted."

As Ash pulled Rev. Zackery by his arm, Walt released his hand. However, he put some communion dust in Rev. Zackery's hand when he did. The two men forced Rev. Zackery from the pulpit and stood him in front of Tamera.

"Kneel at my feet," she commanded.

"I will not," Rev. Zackery shouted defiantly.

Tamera nodded and the two men holding Rev. Zackery' s arms, kick the back of his knees simultaneously, and he went down to the kneeling position.

"Your God has condemned you. Swear allegiance to me and I will let your friends go, everybody but Jason. I will also let you live out the rest of your life in comfort and luxury. However, if you don't, you can watch your friends die and then be killed yourself."

Rev. Zackery said nothing. He just looked down at the floor until he felt Tamera grab his chin and pull his face up.

"Swear allegiance to me!" she screamed.

"Never," Rev. Zackery said calmly.

Tamera nodded again and Ash threw some more of the gasoline on Jason from the bucket in front of him. Howard, who was standing next to Dave, brushed against Dave's leg. Dave looked down at him. Then Dave heard words in his head. At first, he thought it was Howard speaking. However, Howard's mouth was not moving, and Howard was looking at Jason.

"I can't let him be killed. I need to tell Jason to swear that he will keep the agreement," the voice in his head said. "She is going to burn him alive, and then she is going to burn me alive. The pain will be the worst pain that I have ever felt."

Fear filled Dave's heart. The thought of being burned alive was horrifying.

"Jason," Dave yelled, "just tell her you will not try to kill her again. Tell her you will keep the agreement."

"I ain't telling that witch nothing," Jason shouted back angrily.

"Tell him to call Bailtron," the voice in Dave's head said.

"Then call Bailtron," Dave shouted.

In an instant, Howard was standing in front of the coffin.

"Call Bailtron," a voice in Jason's head said. "Sacrifice your soul for your friends."

Jason's anger disappeared. "Bailtron, Bailtron," he yelled. Nothing happened. "Bailtron, Bailtron," he yelled desperately.

Suddenly, everyone froze, except Deacon Crowder. Deacon Crowder's body stood up, however, the head on the body was the enlarged head of Bailtron.

"Why did you call me? What do you want? I can't do anything," Bailtron said.

"But you said you would help me," Jason said. "Just loosen these ropes so I can get off this cross."

"If I do that, what are you going to do then?" Bailtron asked.

"I'm going to kill Tamera, and end all of this," Jason snarled looking at Tamera who had heard everything he had said. "Then you can take my soul."

"The good deacon can't help you," Tamera shouted.

Jason was in shock because everyone had become unfrozen. In fact, they had never been frozen. They all had heard his conversation with Deacon Crowder, whom Jason had only imagined was Bailtron.

Howard walked over to Jason. He was holding a stick with a rag tied to the end of it. Walt could not decide whether to kill Tamera first, or Howard, or the guards. He turned his weapon toward the guards in the aisle to his right. He stepped out just far enough for the M16, protruding from beneath his robe, to clear the podium. He was about to shoot when a large flame appeared at the end of the stick Howard was holding. Walt was too late. If he were to shoot Howard, the torch would fall and set everything on fire, Pam included.

"Walter," Tamera shouted. "It's all up to you, now. You can end this, by eliminating the only real problem, Jason. None of us will be free until he is dead. Go down and take the torch from Howard."

Walt released his weapon, pulled his hands out into the open, and walked down to Howard. When Walt reached Howard, Howard handed him the burning torch. Walt walked up to Jason as Howard quickly moved back.

"Why can't you just stop," Walt whispered. "Why are you making me do this?"

"Don't feel bad," Jason said. "I deserve this and some. I can still here the cries of all those people we burned up. I don't believe God can forgive me for what I've done."

"Okay, I hear you," Walt said softly. "But she said she would let us go. All you need to do is just agree to end this."

"Come on, buddy," Jason whispered. "You know her better than I do. She is just lying. After you set me on fire, after Rev. Zackery swears allegiance to her, if he does, she is going to kill you, Pam, Rev. Zackery, and everybody in this building. Am I right?"

"Yeah, you're right," Walt said, shaking his head 'yes.' "You are right about Tamera, but you are not right about God. I read last night that everybody has sinned and come short of the glory of God, but the blood of Jesus cleanses us from all sin, even sins as big as yours and mine. Rev. Zackery was right."

"What did he say?" Jason asked.

"He said, that we were in God's hands. I know that now. He also said that today would be a battle between God and Satan. I have a M16 under my robe and as soon as Rev. Zackery makes his move, I'm ready to go to war." Walt turned around and faced Tamera.

"What are you waiting for," Tamera shouted. "Set him on fire."

"I don't think so," Walt said confidently.

Immediately Howard opened Pam's coffin. When Pam sat up gasping for air, Howard took the bucket near the coffin, and emptied it over her head and on the coffin. At the same time Ash, who was standing next to Dave, lit another torch and walked to the coffin.

"Get Walt and tie him to the bottom of Jason's cross," Tamera ordered.

"Walt!" Pam cried out blinking the liquid from her eyes. "Baby, is that really you?"

"Hey, babe," Walt said affectionately.

When the four King brothers, moved toward Walt, Walt turned to Jason, and he stuck the burning torch between Jason's legs.

"Hold this," Walt said.

Jason squeezed the handle of the torch between his thighs, while Walt reached down and grabbed the bucket, which still had some gasoline in it. He threw what was left in the bucket at the King brothers and showered them with it. Then he took the torch back from between Jason's legs and pointed it at them. They quickly moved back down the side aisle as they pulled out their pistols.

"Walt," Tamera shouted. "Set Jason on fire or I'll have your lover set on fire."

Walt looked at Pam who was looking back at him. "We are in God's hands, baby," Walt said to her.

"What?" she responded in utter disappointment. Then she turned toward Rev. Zackery. "Rev. Zackery, help us."

"That's right Leroy, help them," Tamera shouted. "Swear allegiance to me and I'll let them all live, all but Jason."

Rev. Zackery, who had been looking back at Pam, slowly turned his head and looked at Tamera.

"I swear," Rev. Zackery shouted, "that I will serve Jesus and no one else. My allegiance is to Jesus."

"Torch her," Tamera screamed.

When Ash lowered the torch toward the coffin, Walt pulled his pistol through the slit in his robe. However, since he had the torch in his right hand, he had to use his left hand to get the pistol from his back holster. Consequently, he had to grab the handle in the wrong direction and when he pulled it out, it was upside down.

"He's got a gun. Kill him!" Tamera shouted.

Before Walt could get his little finger on the trigger and point his pistol at Ash, he was hit by a barrage of bullets from the King brothers.

"No!" Pam screamed a scream so loud that it caused the windows in the church to vibrate. Her scream was so hard that it took her breath away. Finally, after five seconds which seemed like five minutes, she was able to inhale. She inhaled as much air as she could and then cried out again.

"Ahhhhhhh," she wailed.

Walt dropped his pistol, fell against the end of the coffin, and with his last bit of energy tried to swing the torch toward the King brothers, who had stopped firing. The torch did not go toward them, instead it went straight up six feet, spinning in the air. When Walt hit the floor, suddenly, Pam's last scream stopped. All eyes were on the torch as everyone anticipated what would happen when it hit the floor. Their anticipation turned to shock when the torch stopped spinning, suspended in midair for two seconds and then flew toward the Kings brothers. The touch hit K1 in the head, K2 on the shoulder, K4 on the hip, and K3 on the leg. Wherever the torch hit, a flame started. They all ran burning and screaming down the side aisle.

Tamera threw her palms out toward the King brothers, and they all were knocked against the wall, and the flames on their bodies were extinguished. The King brothers regained their footing, however, even though the flames were gone, the pain was severe, and they continued running. They went out the church doors moaning in pain from their burns. Tamera quickly jerked her head back toward the coffin. Her suspicion was confirmed. Even though Pam's upper arms were taped to her body, Pam was pointing her finger at the King brothers.

"Sister dear," Tamera snarled as she stared angrily into Pam's eyes. Pam returned her snare with one that was far more ominous.

Tamera pushed her palms forward and immediately the coffin closed down on Pam.

"Torch her!" Tamera screamed at Ash.

Ash touched the flaming torch to the coffin. The explosion of flames that everyone expected, didn't happen. The coffin did not catch on fire. Tamera was so confused that she couldn't react, that is until she saw Ash run toward the people in the congregation.

Ash took his torch and began waving it at the people, and they began running in fear.

"Get out of here," Ash screamed.

Everyone began to run from the flaming torch toward the door.

"Sit back down!" Tamera screamed.

With the flames coming at them, nobody even heard her scream. Tamera raised her palms in the direction of Ash. However, Rev. Zackery took this opportunity to throw the dust Walt had put in his hand. The communion table dust hit Tamera in her face and made a cloud around her head. Sparks appeared all over her face and hair. She inhaled the dust and immediately began exhaling smoke. She pointed her palms at Rev. Zackery, however, before she could push them forward, she started coughing continuously and severely. Howard rushed up to her.

"Come on Boss, let's get out of here," Howard said.

Howard turned her and was helping her toward the door when Tamera stopped and coughed so deeply that she almost fell over. Howard released her as she laid over the end of the pew closest to her. Then Howard looked furiously back at Rev. Zackery who was still kneeling in the aisle watching and praying and giving thanks to God. Howard turned and put his hand on his pistol. He was about to pull his pistol and shoot when he heard a weapon being cocked. Howard looked up and saw Walt, knelling next to the coffin, pointing his M16 at him. Walt had pulled off his hat and his robe, exposing the two highly damaged bulletproof vests, he was wearing. He also had a portion of the Kevlar vest material taped around his arms and legs. Howard moved his hand away from his pistol.

"I promised Rev. Zackery that I would try not to kill anyone in his sanctuary today. Don't make me break that promise," Walt said as he moved toward Howard and Tamera. "Put it on the floor. It's mine, now."

Howard slowly reached for his pistol.

"Left hand," Walt said.

Howard stopped moving his right hand, took the pistol from his holster with two fingers of his left hand, and laid it on the floor. Then he went back to Tamera and continued to help her.

"Open the coffin, and see if Pam is okay," Walt said to Ash.

"Okay," Ash said sticking the flaming torch into the bucket in front of the coffin.

Walt didn't have time to turn and shoot Ash. He could only watch in fear as the flame went out. Then Ash opened the coffin.

"Are you okay?" Ash said to Pam. There was no response. Pam just laid there looking up in despair.

"Is she okay?" Walt yelled.

"Walt!" Pam shouted as she sat up and looked at Walt. "Baby, are you okay?"

"Yeah, I'm good if you're good, and if you're good, I'm real good," Walt said with a quick smile. "Give me a minute, babe."

Walt rushed painfully to the open door. Howard and Tamera had already gone out of the church door. He watched as they went toward their car. Walt had Tamera's head in the sights of his M16, as Rev. Zackery walked up beside him.

"They are not in the sanctuary now, Pastor," Walt said. "I can put an end to all of this with two bullets. Should I do it?"

"Don't ask me. Ask the Lord," Rev. Zackery said and turned to go back down the aisle where Ash was removing the tape from Pam.

Walt watched Howard help Tamera in their car. Tamera was coughing smoke continuously and was in obvious severe pain. Walt put his sights on Howard's head as he walked around the car parked next to the hearse.

"Okay, Jesus," Walt said as he lowered his rifle and watched Howard and Tamera leave.

"We could use a little help down here, if you don't mind," Rev. Zackery said as he and Ash were trying to pull the cross, Jason was on, out of the hole in the floor. Pam climbed out of the coffin, turned toward Walt, and smiled. Walt immediately began moving painfully toward her, laying his M16 on the floor as he came. She ran to him. When they met, they embraced vigorously. They kissed for a long time as everyone else looked on. Eventually, when it seemed that they would never stop, Dave spoke.

"Hello, hello, up here on the cross," Dave said. "I would like to get down, please."

Walt released Pam and she swung around still holding Walt's waist with one arm.

"Okay! Okay! Keep your loin cloth on, we're coming," Pam said.

Moments later, Walt and Ash were standing in the open coffin which had been pushed behind Jason's cross. They lifted the cross up while Pam and Rev. Zackery pushed it away from the hole. Then they all lower it to the floor. Walt took his belt knife and cut Jason loose and then they moved the coffin and lowered Dave to the floor. Walt cut him loose, too.

"Pam, did you use your powers to stop the gasoline from burning when the torch hit it," Dave asked.

"No, not that I know of," Pam answered.

"What happened, then?" Dave asked. "Why didn't you catch fire?"

"I don't know," Pam said.

"It was the Lord," Rev. Zackery said. "He performed a miracle."

"Thank you, Jesus," Dave said.

"It wasn't gasoline," Ash said.

"What are you talking about," Dave shouted. "I know it was gasoline you poured on me."

"Me, too," Jason said. "My hair is still wet with it which is not good."

"I poured gasoline in the bucket in front of the two crosses, but I poured water in the bucket in front of the coffin," Ash said.

"I saw you fill all of the buckets from the same gasoline can," Rev. Zackery said.

"That's true, sir," Ash said, "but I filled the buckets in front of the crosses first."

"So, what's your point," Jason snapped.

"I had added water to the gas in the gas can," Ash said. "Since gasoline is lighter than water, I knew the gasoline would be on the top and the water would be on the bottom. So, by the time I filled the bucket in front of the coffin, I knew it would be almost all water."

"That was ingenious," Dave said.

"It was a miracle," Rev. Zackery said. "Only the Lord could have given him the wisdom to do that."

"Yeah, but why did you do it?" Jason asked.

"She told me to do it," Ash said looking at Pam.

Dave was free now.

"Oh yeah, I pushed a thought in his mind when I was in the funeral home. The thought was 'when she tells me, I will help her escape,' but with everything that was going on, I never told him to help me." Pam said.

"I heard you say, 'Help us,'" Ash said. "So, I did."

"I was talking to Rev. Zachery," Pam said. "But you thought I was giving you the signal."

"Like I said, it was a miracle," Rev. Zackery said.

"Amen, Pastor," Dave said. "Thank You Jesus!"

"Thank you, son," Rev. Zackery said to Ash.

"Yeah, thanks man," Jason said. "You're a life saver."

"You're a four-life saver," Dave said shaking Ash's hand.

"What are you going to do now," Rev. Zackery asked.

"If you will give me a hand with this coffin, I'm going to take it and the hearse back to Mr. Leo at the funeral home, get my car, and then go home."

"We can do that," Rev. Zackery said smiling.

"Excuse me," Jason said. "What are we going to do about Tamera? We need to track her down and kill her while she is weak." Jason turned to Walt. "Why didn't you kill her when you had the chance. What in God's name were you thinking?"

Everybody quietly and calmly looked at Jason for a minute. Then they turned and walked Ash to the door, pushing the coffin and leaving Jason standing alone.

Is he okay?" Walt said to Dave. "He almost got himself killed when he attacked Tamera at Sibal's office. That was really a dumb move."

"It was even dumber than you think," Dave said. "He wasn't attacking Tamera. He faked like he was going at her so he could get this piece of paper under the desk."

"Why did he want the paper?" Walt asked.

"Pam had made Howard write something on the paper and he wanted to see what it was," Dave said.

"Your right," Walt said. "That was even dumber than I thought. So, what was on the paper?"

"The letter 'L' and four numbers," Dave said.

"Do you remember what the numbers were?" Pam interrupted.

"Yeah. It was easy to remember because they were all two-digit numbers. The first digit increased by one each time; and the second digits decreased by one each time: and the last number was forty-four."

"Seventeen, twenty-six, thirty-five, and forty-four, was that it?" Pam said.

"That was it," Dave said. "What does it mean?"

"I just wanted to see if I could push him to write what I told him to," Pam said.

"We will be having church here every Sunday," Rev. Zackery said smiling at Ash. "So, whenever you are in the vicinity, we would love to have you."

"Thank you, Rev. Zackery," Ash said. "I'll keep that in mind and I'm sorry about my involvement in all this mess."

"Don't be sorry," Rev. Zackery said. "You were sent by the Lord. He chose you to be His instrument of salvation."

"I'll keep that in mind, too," Ash said.

They loaded the casket into the hearse and watched as Ash drove away.

"Rev. Zackery?" Pam said softly as they entered the church. "Do we need to worry about my sister coming after us."

"I was praying before she left," Rev. Zackery said. "I asked the Lord that very question."

After waiting fifteen seconds for Rev. Zackery to continue, Pam spoke.

"Rev. Zackery!" Pam said loudly. "What did God tell you?"

"He told me, and He told me to tell you, to fear not. He said that He would take care of us."

"He said He would take care of me, too?" Jason asked.

"Especially you, son," Rev. Zackery said. "He gave me a special word for you. He told me to tell you, 'Vengeance is mine, I will repay.'" Then Rev. Zackery walked up to Jason and gave him a big hug.

Pam and Walt hugged each tenderly. Dave looked at the others hugging, then he looked up, hugged himself, and said, "Thank You, Jesus."

Pam and Walt separated slightly. "You are not planning on being a preacher, are you?" she asked.

"Why are you asking me that?" Walt said with a chuckle.

"I was just wondering if I would make a good preacher's wife," she said.

"Would you marry a preacher?" Walt asked.

"Only if that preacher were you," she said.

Walt dropped to one knee. He took her left hand and as everyone watched.

"Pamela Williamson," he said.

"Wait," she shouted.

Images appear in her mind. She remembers days earlier, when she and Walt were getting ready to leave the motel to go to the witch ceremony. Walt stops her at the door. He reached into his pocket and pulled out a brass compression sleeve which is used as a washer for plumbing fittings. Then he took her left hand.

"Will you officially be my girlfriend?" Walt said and tried to put the compression sleeve on her ring finger. It wouldn't fit. He tried her little finger, and it fit perfectly.

"It's official. We are boyfriend and girlfriend," Pam said as held her hand out in front of her, looking at her compression sleeve ring. She smiled at him, and they hugged tenderly.

The images in her mind disappeared and she came back in the present. She took from her finger, the compression sleeve ring he had given her at the motel, and she placed it in his hand.

"Pam, will you marry me," he said passionately as he slid the ring back on her little finger.

"Yes, Walt. I will marry you," she said as tears of joy rolled down her smiling face.

Everyone cheered as Pam and Walt kissed tenderly.

"Rev. Zackery," Dave said. "I guess you need to prepare for a wedding now."

"First things first," Rev. Zackery said. "We need to continue our Homegoing Celebration for Sister Mammie Scott. Jason, you and Dave can get a shower in the back."

"Your car is out front," Walt said, rubbing his ribs. "Did you bring extra clothes?"

"I brought everything that didn't get painted," Dave said.

"What?" Walt asked.

"It's a long story, but yeah, my suitcase is in the trunk."

"I'll get it," Walt said.

"Thank you for getting my car," Dave said.

"No problem," Walt said. "I like it. It looks like you."

"Thank you for taking care of Sibal," Jason said.

"My pleasure," Walt replied and then went to Dave's car.

"What is good for getting the smell of gasoline out of your hair," Jason said.

"A lot of soap," Dave said, "but I'm getting my shower first. I have more than just gasoline to get off me," Dave said to Jason.

"You didn't," Jason said.

"I wasn't going to let her burn my nuts off. Not today," Dave replied.

"Okay, but don't use up all the hot water," Jason replied. "I'm serious. I'm coming in after ten minutes. I don't care if you did cross over to the other side."

"Don't even play like that," Dave said frowning.

Walt came back in the church with the suitcase. He handed it to Dave and then he began to take off all his bulletproof padding. Both of his vests were damaged. He took off his fatigue shirt as well. Pam began to examine his ribs. There were several bruises on the front and the back, but there was no blood.

"Does this hurt?" Pam said lightly pressing one of the biggest bruises.

"Yeah," Walt said as he grimaced in pain.

Pam spat in her hand, rubbed them together until they were warm, and then pressed her warm hands against the largest bruises.

"Wow, babe, that feel much better," Walt moaned. "You have a healing touch."

"Shee-oot," Pam yelled cutting her eyes toward Rev. Zackery as she transformed a word from bad to good.

"What's wrong?" Walt asked anxiously.

"We forgot about the crystal," Pam said.

"Shee-oot," Rev. Zackery yelled.

"She probably put it back in the safe at Sibal's office," Pam said. "We need to get it and get rid of it." She looked at all the men. "While you good people are getting ready, Walt and I are going to back to Sibal's office and get that crystal."

"You said it was in Sibal's safe," Jason said. "Do you know the combination?"

"I do now," Pam said. "Left 17, right 26, left 35, and right 44."

"You made Howard write the combination to the safe on that paper," Jason said.

"Yes, I did," Pam said looking down at her bare feet. "I need some shoes."

"Here, take mine. I have some more in my suitcase," Dave said. He slid his feet out of his pointed toe Stacy Adams shoes and placed them at her feet.

"Come on Walt," Pam said putting on the shoes. "We'll be back in one hour."

Walt had put on his inner vest which only had three bullet punctures, and then he put on his ammo belt. Dave handed him a shirt from his suitcase. Walt put it on.

"Okay, let's plan to continue the service at five o'clock," Rev. Zackery said. "That gives you an hour and a half.

Pam and Walt walked toward the door. Walt picked up his M16 as he followed Pam.

Chapter 46
Closure

(Saturday 4:15 PM)

Howard opened the door and helped Tamera enter her house. Her coughing was less constant because she was taking very shallow quick breaths. However, her face was beginning to blister and sections of the hair on her head had been burned off wherever the communion table dust had landed.

"I'm going to kill that preacher, if it's the last thing I ever do," Tamera snarled softly as she looked at her reflection in a mirror in her living room. "He's going to suffer for what he has done to me. I'm going to kill him slowly."

"If I were you, I'd leave him alone," Howard advised. "He has beat you twice. If you try a third time you may end up dead yourself."

Tamera pushed away from Howard and faced him and raised her palms toward him.

"You dare to speak to me that way. I'll drop you where you stand," Tamera shouted and then coughed dark smoke.

Howard slowly pushed her hand down and looked into her eyes.

"You can kill me later. Right now, you need me. I'm all you got," Howard said tenderly.

"I can't let him get away with this," Tamera sobbed as angry tears rolled down her face.

"Okay, just have him killed," Howard said. "Don't take any more chances. He is too dangerous."

"Go and get that beaker on my nightstand and bring it in here and put it on the table," Tamera whispered as she sat down at the dining room table. Then she coughed with slightly less smoke coming from her lungs.

"Okay," Howard said. "Are you going to be all right?"

"Once I get the salve in that beaker," Tamera shouted and immediately started coughing.

"I'll get it right away," Howard said as he rushed to her bedroom.

"Bring me my blanket off my bed, too, and turn up the heat. I'm cold," Tamera said and coughed again. "The supply room door is not closed. Close it."

"Okay," Howard shouted as he picked up the beaker.

As Howard was leaving the room, he grabbed the end of the blanket on the unmade bed and pulled, dragging it on the floor behind him. He didn't notice that he had uncovered the sleeping Black Mamba that had been lying next to the bed, beside the wall, under the blanket. The snake coiled for a strike and opened its black mouth and hissed. Thinking that he had heard something, Howard stopped, turned his head back, and listened. He waited for a few seconds and then continued out the door. The Mamba raised its head above the bed. It saw the end of the blanket go out of the door, then it moved quickly over the bed and followed the blanket.

Howard put the beaker on the table I front of her. He put the blanket completely around Tamera and the chair she was sitting in, covering her head as well. Then he pushed her chair up to the table. She immediately began rubbing the salve from the beaker on the blisters on her face.

The snake went under a sofa as it made its way toward Howard and Tamera.

"Oh, that feels good," she said. Then she coughed and all the relief turned to severe pain. "Oh, oh, it hurts so bad. "Go and get me some jasmine incense. It's in the China cabinet draw." She pointed to the cabinet.

Howard, who was standing behind Tamera rubbing her shoulders, did not see the Mamba's head slide inside the dining room entrance. The Mamba opened its mouth, raised its head and was about to moved forward, when Howard moved around Tamera and went to the cabinet at the other end of the table. The Mamba saw Howard's feet as he got the incense. The snake moved quickly forward in between the chair and table legs. Howard turned around, went back to Tamera, and then put the incense on the table.

The Mamba turned as its view of Howard's feet went behind the blanket surrounding Tamera. The snake moved up to the blanket near Tamera's feet and stopped. It moved its head to the right side of the blanket. Not seeing Howard's feet move, it moved its head to the left side of the blanket. Then it went around the blanket slowly until it saw Howard's shoe and leg.

Tamera rubbed some of the salve on one side of the incense and lit it. She repeated the process three more times and then she began inhaling the smoke from the burning incense and salve. The burning in her chest began to subside. Then she felt a cold breeze.

"How many times do I need to tell you, to close," Tamera said angrily and then she stopped speaking and put her hand on her forehead. "I'm sorry. Howard, would you close the supply room door, please," Tamera asked meekly for the first time in her life.

The Mamba moved around Tamera's chair, raised its head, opened its mouth, and prepared to lunge toward Howard's ankle.

"Okay, boss. Sorry about that," Howard said as he walked quickly toward the supply room, moving his foot just before the fangs came down. The Mamba missed his ankle by an inch.

As Howard moved through the kitchen toward the supply room door, he remembered his Black Mamba encounter from the day before. He also remembered kicking the door shut before leaving the house that day. He stopped when he was two feet from the door and took a deep breath. That's when he saw something move out of the corner of his eye. He turned just in time to see the Black Mamba coming under the kitchen table toward him.

"Aaaa," Howard yelled as he pulled the supply room door open.

Howard moved as quickly as he could to get through the door and close it behind him, but he was not quick enough. When he pulled the door to close it, he closed the door on the Mamba. Around two feet of the snake was inside the supply room door. Its head was continuously trying to reach Howard with his fangs. Howard was holding the doorknob with one hand, pushing against the door frame with the other, and trying to keep his legs and body as far away from the snake's head as possible. He was fighting a losing battle, because with every second a little more of the snake was squeezing through the door. Howard looked back. The Mamba's cage was on the table.

"If she can do it, so can I," he said to himself, remembering how Tamera had slapped the back of the Mamba's head, caught it, and put it in the cage.

He watched the movement of the Mamba's head as it moved up toward the doorknob and then down and out toward his leg. He waited until the snake's head was moving down and out toward his leg, then removed his hand from the door molding and tried to hit the back of the snake's head. He missed, badly. The snake came up toward his hand on the doorknob. It still couldn't reach it, but it got a little closer. When the snake came down toward his leg again, Howard swung. He hit it but not hard enough. As the snake was raising its head again, Howard swung again. This time the Mamba moved its head to the side as Howard's hand went by, then followed Howard's hand and raked its fangs across the back of Howard's hand. The hand was not punctured, but there were two deep red scratches about an inch long. Howard stumbled backwards against a shelf full of cages as fear consumed his heart. He grabbed the shelf to his right as he slid against the shelf behind him down to the floor. The shelf and all of its cages fell on top of his legs, trapping him as he sat on the floor.

The Mamba, after being hit by a couple of cages, turned, and slithered back to the door and waited. It was watching Howard with its head raised a foot in the air.

"What in hell are you doing to my supply room," Tamera yelled and then coughed deeply, holding her chest in pain. There was no answer. "Howard! Howard! Are you okay?" she asked and listened for an answer. Then another coughing spell hit her.

Hearing Tamera's voice and her coughing, the Mamba's head turned toward the sound, then it moved slowly out of Howard's sight.

"The Mamba is out. It is coming for you." Howard had tried to yell. However, he could only get enough breath for a whisper. His lungs muscles were losing strength. All his muscles were losing strength. He was losing the ability to breathe. Howard closed his eyes and force himself to breathe short quick breaths for as long as he could. It wasn't very long. Howard took his last breath as the Mamba slithered across the kitchen floor and entered the living room. It stopped in the doorway, raised its head, and saw motion at the dining room table. It's tongue flickered out of its mouth as it sensed to the air.

CHAPTER 47
CRYSTAL LIES

(Saturday 4:15 PM)

The handle of the safe in Sibal's office was pulled open revealing several stacks of hundred-dollar bills in bundles of five thousand. Right next to them was the crystal ball.

"There it is," Pam sighed. "I never thought I'd be so glad to see that thing again."

"Get it and let's get back."

"You locked the door, didn't you?" Pam said slyly. "We have time for a little fun before we get back." Pam turned toward him and began unbuckling his ammo belt.

"What are you doing? We need to get out of here, now babe," Walt said sexily.

"I want you. You don't want me?"

"Premarital sex is a sin, babe," Walt said, stopping her from unbuckling his belt. "Let's wait until tonight. I want it to be very special when we make love as husband and wife."

"I like the sound of very special," she said. She turned around and pressed her buttock against his groins, bent over, and looked in the safe.

"I saw this money when we were locked in this safe," Pam said smiling, "and since I am Tamera's only living relative, that means that this is rightfully mine."

"The bible says 'Thou shalt not steal'" Walt said. "What if she is not dead?"

"Are you serious?" Pam asked dumbfoundedly. "She just threatened to kill you and everyone that's important to you and you want to leave this money caused she might not be dead yet."

"Well, I kinda promised the Lord, if He would let me save you, I would stop sinning."

"Okay, there is one way to find out," Pam said reaching into the safe, pulling out the crystal, rubbing it, and sitting it on the desk. The crystal began to glow. Then an image appeared on the desk and began to expand until it covered the entire desktop. Pam and Walt backed away from the desk. In the image, Pam and Walt could see a dining room and part of a living room.

They saw Tamera sitting at the dining room table with her hooded head about six inches from the table. She was inhaling the smoke from the incense she was holding under her blanket covered head. She was very still. Then they saw the snake when it came through the dining room entrance and stopped. It was about to turn around when the incense went out and Tamera raised her head and coughed. Since the incense had gone out, Tamera laid the stems on the table and then lowered her forehead down to the table. The Mamba went to the nearest chair which was two chairs from Tamera. It climbed up the leg, over the seat, and onto the table. Then it crawled up to the blanket covering Tamera's head and its tongue shot out as it sensed its surroundings. Then it laid its head on Tamera's and was about to crawl over it when Tamera slowly tilted her head back. As she did, the Mamba raised its head and slid its body forward for a strike. When Tamera's chin was a few inches off the table, she saw something on the table in front of her. She quickly pulled her head up and back as the Mamba's fangs shot forward toward Tamera's face. Just as the fangs were about to hit Tamera's lip, she opened her mouth as wide as she could and inhaled to screamed.

The image that Pam and Walt saw was a sideview of Tamera and the Mamba face to face. The snake's fang bearing head shot forward. It went toward the hood of the robe where only Tamera's nose and open mouth could be seen. The snakes head disappeared inside Tamera's mouth. Then they heard a loud cough followed by a foot-long flame coming from inside Tamera's mouth. Tamera released her grip on the blanket, and it fell to her shoulders. Then her head fell to the table, the hood of her robe covering her head as well as the Mamba's.

Suddenly the image disappeared, and the crystal reappeared on the desk. However, it was now black.

"I believe she is dead, now, and the money is mine," Pam said. "I guess I should feel sorrow or at least a little sadness, but I feel nothing but relief."

"I'm with you, babe," Walt said smiling. "Now we don't have to worry about her coming after our babies."

"Babies? How many children do you want?"

"I want a small family. Two boys and two girls," Walt said still smiling.

"Are you serious?" Pam shouted as she picked up the crystal from the desk.

"The bible says, 'Be fruitful and multiply,'" Walt said raising his palms up.

"Let's get this money and get out of here," she said shaking her head. "You and your bible verses."

They walked back to the safe. Pam picked up a stack of hundred-dollar bundles. Then they heard something behind them. They turned their heads back just in time to see the office door being kicked open. Three men dressed in matching flax jackets and helmets, walked just inside the door. The man in the middle was not holding a pistol. His pistol was in his holster on his side. However, the men beside him were holding pistols with attached silencers, and they were pointing them at Pam's and Walt's head.

Walt recognized them. They were the men who followed him to the grave site, the men he could have killed, but let go.

"You should have killed me when you had the chance, brother," the man in the middle said sternly.

"You promised me you would get you men and leave," Walt said as he glanced at his M16 lying on the desk in front and to the left of him. "I thought you were a man of your word. You're a ranger, right. I never thought you would turn out to be a liar."

"Brother, I didn't lie. We left, but when we saw what happened at the church, we followed you and your little honey back here. By the way, my name is Turk," the man said.

"So Turk, what now?" Walt asked.

"So, now we end this," Turk said. "I don't want to be constantly looking over my shoulder wondering when you are going to show up."

"Just take the money and go," Pam shouted, throwing the money in her hand at them. She dropped the crystal turned and grabbed the rest of the money with both hand and threw that to them, also. The stacks of hundred-dollar bills hit them and fell to the floor at their feet. "That's all of it. Just go and leave us alone. We promise we won't come after you."

"Kill em," Turk ordered.

Pam's arm went toward Walt, however, the two men beside Turk fired their weapons immediately. They saw their shots hit their targets. Walt was hit first. The men saw a hole appear in the middle of his forehead.

"No!" Pam screamed. The other man saw his bullet blow a hole in Pam's neck as she reached for Walt. They watched as she fell against Walt to the floor behind the desk.

"Pick up that money. We need to get out of here ASAP," Turk said bending down to pick up a stack of hundreds near him. "Tim, Raymond, we got them. Get in here and help us with the bodies."

The two men beside Turk holstered their weapons and began picking up the money. They didn't see Pam until she had jumped over the desk moving toward them. She moved so fast, that her blue dress was a blur. She kicked Turk under his chin, with the pointed toe of Dave's Stacy Adams, knocking him out the door to the floor. The pistol he had pulled from his holster fell from his hand as he fell on his back dazed from the force of the kick. Instead of defending themselves, the other two men reached for the pistols. That was a mistake. Pam dropped to one knee between them and raked her three sharp fingernails on each of her hands down their faces, simultaneously slicing their eyelids and the middle of their faces. The man on her left stood up and pulled his pistol from his holster. However, Pam grabbed his pistol with her left hand and then drove the bridge of his nose into his head with the palm of her right hand. Then, she looked over at the man to her right. He was still on one knee. He had pulled his pistol and was bringing it around toward her. She quickly raised her foot and kicked the side of his face, driving it hard against the door ceil. He was immediately knocked unconscious. Pam pulled the pistol from the man on her left and allowed his dead body to fall to the floor. She shot a hole in the head of the man she had kicked.

Turk was still unable to get up. He could only watch as Pam killed his men. Pam walked up to him with the pistol in her hand, and he raised his head and one hand as he laid there on the floor.

"Wait!" he pleaded.

Pam shot him in the head and Turk's head dropped to the floor.

"Turk, what's going on," Tim said as he turned into the hallway and saw Turk's body lying on the floor. "Turk is down. Get back!" Tim shouted as he moved back out of the hallway.

Raymond came up behind Tim.

"What's going on?" Raymond asked.

"They killed Turk and I guess Ricky and Percy, too," Tim said.

"If they kill them, we don't stand a chance. Let's get out of here," Raymond said.

"You boys aren't afraid of little old me, are you," Pam said in the headphone she had taken from the man she had kicked and shot in the head.

Tim looked at Raymond and pointed to the room on the other side of the hallway. Tim leaned out, pointing his M16 down the hallway as Raymond went across the hall into the room.

"You are not going anywhere, because I'm coming to get you right now," Pam said as she held the crystal in her hand. She could see their positions in the crystal.

"I'm getting outta here," Raymond yelled as he began running in place.

Pam rubbed the crystal and rolled it out into the hallway. Immediately an image of her appeared in the hall. Tim looked at Raymond and began a countdown with his fingers. When he got to one they moved. They leaned out into the hallway and seeing Pam, they started firing. As they fired, they began walking down the hallway. They saw Pam fall to the floor, but they continued firing until their weapons were empty. Then the image disappeared, leaving the crystal in the middle of the hall. Pam stepped out and shot Tim in his face. Raymond turned to run, but he didn't get far. Pam shot him in the back of his knee. He went down immediately. She shot him in the back of his head just below his helmet. Then, Pam wiped the pistol off and placed it in the hand of the man she had killed with the blow to the nose. She dropped three stacks of hundred-dollar bills next to him. Finally, she went to Walt who was lying face down, motionless, behind the desk.

Chapter 48
The Eulogy

(Saturday 5:00 PM)

Dave, and Jason had showered. They were wearing clothes which had spots and stripes of red on them. Since they were about the same size, Dave's clothes fit Jason well.

They were standing in front of the communion table talking when Rev. Zackery walked in.

"Did you see that huzzy sit on the communion table," Dave said.

"Yeah," Jason said. "I was sure we were going to see some flaming rump roast. This table must not be as holy as the old one," Jason said.

"Not yet," Rev. Zackery said. "It hasn't had the Lord's supper on it yet. That's what gives it power, the body, and the blood of Jesus. It's been an hour. Pam and Walt are not back jet?"

"No. If they are not back by five-thirty, we need to go after them," Jason said. "Rev. Zackery, do you know where Sibal's office is?"

"No, but if I ask around, I'm sure somebody will be able to tell me," Rev. Zackery replied.

"We should have killed her when we had the chance," Jason said angrily. "Now, we will never be safe."

"What do you think we should do Rev. Zackery," Dave asked.

"I think we should pray," Rev. Zackery said.

"You want us to sit here and do nothing but pray," Jason said disgustedly.

"No. I didn't say do nothing. We should ask God to guide us. We should ask Him to tell us what to do. Then we should do whatever He tells us."

"You mean, do whatever He tells you, don't you?" Jason said. "God is not going to speak to me or Dave. He is only going to speak to you. Isn't that right, Rev. Zackery?" "No, God speaks to everybody," Rev. Zackery. "Most people block Him out. They don't want to do what He says, so they act like they don't hear him."

"Are you saying that God will tell me what we should do?" Jason said.

"He will," Rev. Zackery said.

"If he tells me what we should do, will you help do it?" Jason asked.

"Yes, I will," Rev. Zackery said.

"Okay, go ahead and pray and ask God to reveal to me, what we should do," Jason said.

"Let's pray," Rev. Zackery bowed his head. "Lord God, we come to you in the name of Jesus, revealing to You that we don't know what happened to Pam and Walt, and we don't know what to do about it. We ask now that You would reveal to Jason, Your plan of action for us. Make it crystal clear to him, what we should do. In Jesus name we pray. Amen"

"What now?" Jason asked.

"God will speak to you," Rev. Zackery said. "Go over there and meditate for a minute. We still have a few minutes before five thirty."

Jason went and sat on a pew, closed his eyes, and thought about God. He thought about how he had escaped from the barn before it burned up. He thought about how Walt had saved his life when he was attacked when the barn was burning down. He thought about how Laverne had warned him before the men tried to assassinate him at his home, he thought about how Pam saved his life when Tamera was about to kill him in the crystal, and then he thought about how he had escaped out of the crystal. Then it finally hit him like a ton of bricks. It was God that got him out of all those situations. He asked himself the question, 'What is it going to take for me to trust God.'

Then he saw an image in his mind. He was standing at the alter of Rev. Zackery's church next to Walt and Rev. Zackery as Dave walked Pam down the aisle. She was wearing the same royal blue dress that she had on earlier only it was dirty, and it had blood stains on it.

Jason opened his eyes and walked over to Rev. Zackery and Dave.

"I know what we should do," Jason said. "The Lord gave me a vision."

"What did he tell you?" Dave asked suspiciously.

"We should get ready for Pam's and Walt's wedding. They are okay. God showed me a vision of their wedding and I was Walt's best man."

"What?" Dave shouted. "How did you get to be his best man?"

"Don't be jealous, Dave," Jason said. "You get to walk Pam down the aisle and give her away."

"Yeah," Dave said smiling. "I like that."

"Remember, we have to finish the Homegoing Celebration first," Rev. Zackery said.

They all went down to the first pew and waited. Five thirty came and went. Five forty-five came and went. When six o'clock came, even Rev. Zackery became anxious.

"Now, what did you actually see in this vision," Rev. Zackery asked.

"It was not really a vision," Jason said. "It was more like a very clear thought."

"You had a thought," Dave said.

"Yeah," Jason said. "I thought it was from God."

"Do you really believe in your heart that God gave you this thought." Rev. Zackery asked.

"I did when I first had it," Jason said. "Now, I'm not so sure."

"If you believe God gave it to you, don't doubt," Rev. Zackery said. "Hold on to your belief. God will come through."

"I know God gave me that thought because right before it happened it was thinking about all the dangerous situations He had brought me through. There was one miracle after another. So, I decided that from now on, I am going to trust Him," Jason explained.

"Well, praise the Lord," Rev. Zackery said. "That vision, strong thought, or whatever it was, had to be from the Lord."

"Amen, thank You Jesus," Dave said.

Dave and Rev. Zackery hugged Jason. Then they heard the door open. It was Pam. She pushed the door open, and they saw that she was carrying Walt over her shoulder. They ran to her, took Walt from her, took him down the aisle, and laid him on the front pew.

"What happened to him?" Rev. Zackery asked.

"I had to knock him out of the way, to keep him from getting shot. Some of Sibal's guards attacked us. I had to use the crystal to make them think they had killed us. Then I killed all of them." She rubbed Walt's head. "I may have hit him too hard, and I think he hit his head on Sibal's desk when he went down. I tried to revive him, but he won't come to. I think he's dying," she moaned as tears ran down her face."

"Just let him lay here for a few minutes," Rev. Zackery said. "I'm sure he will be fine. Jason had a vision from God."

Pam looked at Jason and he smiled at her.

"I saw you and Walt getting married, here in the church," Jason said.

They all looked down at Walt. As they watch him, suddenly Walt's entire body shook, and he let out a heavy breath.

"He stopped breathing," Pam screamed.

"Why don't we lay him on the communion table," Dave asked.

"Rev. Zackery said it doesn't have any power yet," Jason said.

"I don't care. Help me, I saw him in my mind awake on the communion table," Dave said as Jason helped him lift Walt's limp body.

Rev. Zackery quickly gathered everything on the communion table in his arms and laid them on the pew. Then as they stretched Walt out on the table, Rev. Zackery knelled down, placing both hands on the communion table, he began to pray.

"Father, in the name of Jesus, we come to you, asking that you would sanctify this, your holy communion table. Empower it right now Lord God. We have placed the body of Your child and servant on Your holy table. Just as You will change the bread and the grape juice that we will sit on this table, from a common use to a spiritual use, we ask that you will restore Walt's body, sanctify it for Your use and Your glory. Please, Father, restore his life and give him back to us. Please, Jesus, if it be Your will. Amen."

They all stood around the table for another minute, hoping for some sign of life. Then all the men sat down dejectedly on the first pew. Pam lowered her head to his chest and sobbed. Tears ran down the faces of each of the men as well.

Pam felt a hand on her head.

"Babe? What's wrong," Pam heard Walt whisper.

Pam raised her head and saw Walt's open concerned eyes.

"Walt, baby, are you okay? How do you feel?" she said holding his face.

"I have a headache, but other that, I'm good," Walt replied.

By now, everybody had gathered around him.

"It's another miracle," Rev. Zackery said joyfully. "Son, we though you were gone, but God brought you back to us."

"Thank you, Jesus," Dave said. "Thank You, thank You, thank You..." Dave said continuously with each 'thank You' louder than the other as skipped around in circles.

"Glory to God," Jason said, holding up both hands.

Pam showered Walt with kisses.

"I love you so much," Pam said passionately.

"I love you back, with all my heart," Walt said. "And I thank You, Jesus for giving her to me."

Pam helped Walt sit up, and he slid himself around so that his legs were now hanging off the table.

"Rev. Zackery?" Walt said. "I can't wait any longer to be married to my beautiful Pam. Have you ever had a double ceremony before?"

"A double ceremony?" Rev. Zackery.

"Yeah, a wedding and a funeral at the same time," Walt said.

No, but there is a first time for everything," Rev. Zackery said smiling. "Dave, would you escort Pam down the aisle, while me, Walt and his best man, Jason wait here at the altar?"

Within minutes, everyone is standing together again at the altar, and Rev. Zackery begins.

"Dearly beloved, we are gathered here together, in the sight of God, to join together this couple, Pam and Walt, in the holy state of matrimony. We are also here to cerebrate the homegoing of a great saint of God, sister Mammie Scott. We thank God, for the new life that Pam and Walt will share here on earth, and we also thank God for the new life in Jesus that Miss Mammie has found in heaven.

I now commit Miss Mammie's soul to sleep, awaiting the return of Jesus, and I now, with the power invested in me, pronounce Walt and Pam, to be husband and wife. Walt, you may now kiss your bride.

As the bridal party celebrated in the church, the black crystal ball, which was on the back seat of Walt's car, began to flicker with light. The blackness disappeared and an image appeared. It was an image of Tamera's dining room. The black hood of Tamera's robe still covered Tamera's head and the head of the Mamba. However, the head under the hood was smaller than before. The hood raised slightly, and a portion of the snake's body was pulled under the hood. Then it happened again. More of the snake was pulled under the hood. Then the robe shook as something underneath it began to wiggle.

The blanket fell back onto the chair. Seconds later the full head appeared from beneath the hood of the robe. It was the head of a large lizard. One of its legs crawled out of the hood. Then it crawled onto the table as the robe fell to the floor. It was a Komodo Dragon. It continued to devour the rest of the snake. Between bites it would cough smoke.

In addition to coughing smoke, there was something else that was very unusual about the lizard. One of the fingers on the right front paw of the lizard, was a that of a human female.

The End

Printed by Libri Plureos GmbH in Hamburg, Germany